A HEALTHY HOMICIDE

My route to work brought me down Main Street, and I slowed the car as I neared the Pampered Life. Three cop cars were parked at the curb, the only sign that anything out of the ordinary had happened. Still, three cars seemed like two too many, and I had to wonder how Carla had died.

According to Ashlee, Brittany had discovered Carla in one of the mud baths. Had she fallen asleep while taking a soak and somehow drowned? Slipped on the tile floor and hit her head before falling into the muck? Or had she been helped along by someone? While I knew nothing about Carla, I had a hard time envisioning anyone shoving that happy, smiling face into a trough full of mud and holding her down until she suffocated. I shuddered at the image and brought my attention back to the spa. . . .

Books by Staci McLaughlin

GOING ORGANIC CAN KILL YOU

ALL NATURAL MURDER

GREEN LIVING CAN BE DEADLY

A HEALTHY HOMICIDE

Published by Kensington Publishing Corporation

A Healthy Homicide

Staci McLaughlin

KENSINGTON PUBLISHING CORP.
http://www.kensingtonbooks.com

KENSINGTON BOOKS are published by

Kensington Publishing Corp.
119 West 40th Street
New York, NY 10018

All Kensington Titles, Imprints, and Distributed Lines are available at special quantity discounts for bulk purchases for sales promotions, premiums, fund-raising, and educational or institutional use.

Special book excerpts or customized printings can also be created to fit specific needs. For details, write or phone the office of the Kensington special sales manager: Kensington Publishing Corp., 119 West 40th Street, New York, NY 10018, attn: Special Sales Department, Phone: 1-800-221-2647.

Kensington and the K logo Reg. U.S. Pat & TM Off.

ISBN-13: 978-0-7582-9488-3
ISBN-10: 0-7582-9488-3
First Kensington Mass Market Edition: March 2015

eISBN-13: 978-0-7582-9489-0
eISBN-10: 0-7582-9489-1
First Kensington Electronic Edition: March 2015

10 9 8 7 6 5 4 3 2 1

Printed in the United States of America

Chapter 1

Esther O'Connell, owner of the O'Connell Organic Farm and Spa, burst through the kitchen door. Her gray curls were clinging to her forehead. Her plump cheeks were flushed. "We're ruined, Dana," she cried. She flopped into the nearest chair to catch her breath.

I felt a flutter of concern as I set the rooster-shaped mug I'd been hand drying on the counter. I hurried to where Esther sat, fanning herself. "What happened?"

"It's that new spa on Main Street. My friend Mary Beth stopped in the other day to see what all the fuss was about. She said it's fancier than beaded lace." Esther let her hand droop. "Who'll want to visit my ordinary old spa now?"

As the designated Jill-of-all-trades here at the farm, I knew it was time for some damage control. I pulled out the chair next to her and sat down. "People rave about your place. I know for a fact we've been booked all week."

The worry lines in her face only deepened. Esther was a fairly recent widow who had plowed her life savings into the place, and she constantly fussed about the financial status of the farm and spa. I couldn't say I blamed her. "They come here because we're the only spa in town," she said. "At least we were. Who's to say they won't switch to this new place?"

I rested a hand on her knee. "I say."

"Say what?" asked Zennia, the spa's creative and health-minded cook, as she walked in from the hall.

I hadn't heard Zennia approach in her Birkenstocks, but I immediately roped her into the conversation, knowing her serene demeanor would help. "Esther's worried about that new spa on Main Street."

Zennia didn't pause on her way to the refrigerator. She swung open the door and pulled out the lemonade pitcher. "People are always curious about a new business, but their loyalty will win out. Everyone loves Gretchen."

Twenty-four-year-old Gretchen Levitt, our newest employee, had started a few months back. Between her knot-melting massages and wrinkle-reducing facials, she'd quickly cemented her place at the spa.

"I hope you two are right," Esther said. "Seems like there's always something to worry about with this place." She rose from her chair and glanced down at her faded plaid shirt. "I'd better change. I have bunco in a bit." She trudged out of the kitchen, leaving Zennia and me alone.

I returned to the counter and picked up the dish towel before grabbing another mug from the rack. "Have you heard anything about the new place? It's called the Pampered Life, right?"

Zennia flicked her long black braid over her shoulder. The gray streaks were becoming more noticeable, but no way would Zennia dye her hair. Too many chemicals. "Right. I heard a woman from San Francisco moved up here to open it."

I set the dried mug on a cupboard shelf. "Well, I'm sure once the newness wears off, it won't impact Esther's place." *Much,* I added silently and mentally crossed my fingers. While customers seemed happy with our modest offerings, a full-scale spa that provided all the services we couldn't might draw people away. But I kept that thought to myself.

I finished drying the dishes and hung the towel on the oven door handle. "I'm going to run into town for my lunch break."

"We have plenty of leftover chickpea and seaweed salad, if you'd like some," Zennia offered. "It's chock-full of iron and magnesium."

"And the guests didn't gobble it all up?" I said in mock surprise. "I'm stunned."

Zennia gave me a knowing smile. "You'll come around one day."

"Today's not that day, I'm afraid. I have my mind set on a BLT." I licked my lips. "With extra mayonnaise."

Zennia clapped her hands over her ears. "Stop. Don't say such things."

Laughing, I headed down the hall to grab my purse from the desk drawer in the office. I spent most of my working hours here in the office, promoting the spa, although Esther occasionally asked me to serve meals, catch loose animals, and help with pretty much anything else that needed doing around the place.

I crossed the unoccupied lobby and pushed open the front door. A breeze tickled my skin, and the chatter of birds greeted me on the cool spring day. A flock of ducks drifted on the surface of the small pond near the front.

I walked to my aging Civic in the corner of the lot, climbed inside, and started it up. The engine had begun to make a funny squealing sound on colder days, but I'd decided to ignore it. Having just moved from my mom's house into a barely furnished apartment with my younger sister, Ashlee, I couldn't afford any additional expenses right now.

The drive down the highway was quick, and within five minutes, I was cruising the three blocks of businesses and restaurants that made up Blossom Valley's main strip. With the slumping economy the past few years, the downtown had experienced a considerable number of turnovers and vacancies, but I'd noticed a recent uptick in new businesses, and those that had managed to stay afloat during the downturn didn't look like they were closing their doors anytime soon.

Now I eyed the front of the Pampered Life as I passed by. If I hadn't known it used to be a hardware store, I'd have never guessed. The new owner had darkened all the windows, etching the words *The Pampered Life* in cursive script across the glass. A green-and-white-striped awning stretched across the front, and a redwood and wrought-iron park bench sat to one side of the door. A sandwich board on the sidewalk announced a Botox party next week, only ten dollars per filler. I reached up and felt the skin next to my mouth, wondering if twenty-nine was too young to worry about wrinkles. Still, even at ten dollars a pop, I wouldn't be getting Botox anytime soon. Or ever.

I drove to the next block and pulled into the Breaking Bread Diner lot. I parked between a dusty pickup truck and a motorcycle and walked inside. The stools that lined the counter were empty, and I settled on the closest one.

Betty, the waitress who normally took my order, was helping a customer at a nearby booth. She nodded in my direction. "Be with you in a minute, hon."

I nodded back and pulled my phone from my pocket to check for messages. I sent a quick text to Ashlee to see if she'd had a chance to pick up any toilet cleaner, and then I stuffed the phone back in my pocket. We were still working out chore duties, even resorting to a chart on the fridge. Ashlee's plan seemed to be to ignore the dirty dishes and grime-covered counters until I broke down and cleaned them myself. Sometimes her plan worked, much to my self-loathing.

Betty finished with the customer and made her way over to where I sat. "What can I get you today?" she asked.

"BLT and iced tea, please."

"Extra mayo?"

"Absolutely." An idea popped into my mind. "Say, make that to go. I have to run an errand right now."

"Sure thing. Give me ten minutes." She finished scribbling on her pad and stuck it in an apron pocket.

"I'll be back by then," I told her and slid off the stool. I pushed through the door and walked out onto the street, taking quick strides toward my intended target: the Pampered Life.

Now that Esther had told me how fabulous her friend thought the place was, I wanted to see it for myself. Surely it couldn't be that much better than ours. And if this spa was the greatest thing since laser-hair removal, then maybe I could collect ideas for Esther's place. While I loved our little spa, there was always room for improvement.

As I neared the building, I slowed to peer through the windows, but the tinted glass made it impossible to see inside. I pushed open the door and stepped in. Soothing piano music flowed from speakers mounted in the corners of the dimly lit space. The scent of jasmine reached my nose. In the corner, a small tranquility fountain burbled, the large marble ball in the middle spinning merrily. Three overstuffed recliners filled the small lobby area, along with several potted ferns. Photos of woods and meadows lined the walls. I was about to take my phone from my pocket to sneak some pictures when an ultrathin girl stepped through the archway at the back of the lobby and moved behind the counter.

"Welcome to the Pampered Life," she said. Her rose-red lips shone brightly against her pale skin. "Do you have an appointment?"

"No," I said, my voice sounding unnaturally loud compared to her soft lilt. "I noticed you opened recently, and wanted to stop by." I approached the counter, noting all the lotions and bath salts for sale on the shelves behind her, then looked down at the counter. "Oh, good. A brochure." I picked one up from the stack and flipped it open, eager to see what they offered.

The prices next to the list of services immediately drew my attention, and I stifled a gasp. They were charging twice what Esther charged for the thirty-minute massages, and even more for their facials. This place would make a killing if they could line up enough clients. My mind churned as I thought up promotional deals to keep our own customers from straying. We already offered a lunch and spa treatment package, but we might need to implement a loyalty rewards program or a bring-a-friend discount until the excitement over this new place waned.

I was only halfway through the list of offerings when the girl started talking again. "We have a wide range of services here," she said. "We do all types of massage, including Swedish and deep tissue, plus facials."

Everything we offered at Esther's place. I felt myself relax a notch.

The girl picked up a pencil and tapped it in time with her words. "Then, we've got the extras, like mud baths, Brazilian waxes, Botox injections . . ."

My muscles tensed again. So this place wasn't exactly like Esther's. At least the farm had animals, a unique plus. The guests always commented on how much they enjoyed our ducks, pigs, and chickens. "Sounds like you've got everything I could ever need," I interrupted as she rattled off more items.

The pencil tapping stopped, and she nodded excitedly. "Yes, and we offer payment plans. The last thing you want to stress about is how to pay to relax."

"An excellent point," I said. Could we afford to institute payment plans at Esther's? I might have to run the idea past her.

"Hey, let me tell you about our wrap treatment. You start with an all-over body exfoliation—"

The girl broke off her explanation as a woman in her midforties entered from the back. With her perfect posture and tall, willowy frame, she was the type who could make yoga pants and a T-shirt look like formal business attire.

She appraised me for a moment and then turned toward the girl. "Jessica, do you know what we have here?"

Jessica shook her head, her eyes wide in anticipation.

The woman raised her hand and pointed her index finger at me. "A spy. She's a spy."

How did she know? I gulped as a wave of heat washed over me. I was in some deep seaweed.

Chapter 2

I crossed my arms and tried to appear fierce under the woman's watchful gaze. "I'm no spy."

She pointed at my shirt. "Sure you are. It says so right there."

I looked down and sighed. Gordon, the spa's business-minded manager, had recently insisted on adding O'CONNELL ORGANIC FARM AND SPA to our work shirts, figuring it would be free advertising when we went into town for lunch or to run errands. I kept forgetting that everyone now knew where I worked simply by looking at my clothes. I offered a sheepish smile. "I forgot about that."

She grinned back, her smile instantly putting me at ease. "Don't worry. I'm only giving you a hard time." She crossed the room and held out her hand. "I'm Carla Fitzpatrick, the owner."

I shook her hand. "Dana Lewis. I was grabbing lunch down the street and couldn't resist stopping by. How long have you been open?"

"About two weeks. Long enough to work out most

of the new business kinks, although I'm still learning." She checked her watch. "Would you like a tour? I'm so excited my place is finally open that every time someone new comes in, I drag them around to look at everything."

I thought about my BLT, but the diner was notoriously slow with take-out orders. I had time. Still, I put a finger to my lips and tapped them while pretending to consider her offer. "Hmm, I don't know. Wouldn't I be fraternizing with the enemy?"

"We'll call a truce for today." She hooked her arm with mine, and together, we walked toward the archway like two pals on an afternoon stroll.

Jessica held out a slip of paper as we went by. "Erin called a while ago. She sounded upset."

"I'll deal with her later." Carla took the slip of paper and folded it in half without reading it. "My niece," she said to me.

On the other side of the arch, a long hallway stretched before us, with a door at the other end marked EXIT. A series of additional doors, some open, lined each side. Carla stopped partway down the hall, at the first open door. "Our nail station," she announced quietly.

I surveyed the room. Three chairs and three small tables with manicure and pedicure equipment and stools occupied the space. An older woman with a gray perm sat at one table while a young woman in a smock worked on her nails. The room smelled like chocolate, and I glanced around for the source of the aroma. If it was some type of air freshener plug-in, I wanted one for my apartment.

After a moment, Carla and I crossed the hall, where she showed me the waxing room. The room was tastefully furnished and pleasant enough, with a blanket draped over the table and a soft-looking pillow on top, but I still viewed it as some kind of torture chamber. I knew what went on in here. I hustled down the hall as Carla entered the last room on the right.

"This is my favorite room," she said over her shoulder. She switched on the light.

I blinked against the glare and looked around. The entire room was tiled, except for two large troughs in the back. What I assumed was mud filled both, the dark brown goo shimmering under the lights. With the extra warmth of the room and the soft saxophone music in the background, I could easily see myself sinking into that glop for a relaxing soak.

Carla watched me, her face full of pride. "Everyone who calls for an appointment wants to know about the mud baths. I use a secret blend of volcanic ash, mineral water, and peat moss. I think this room will be very popular."

I felt a tendril of worry worm its way through my gut. After seeing Carla's spa, with all its modern services and its comfortable atmosphere, the tent that we'd erected at the back of Esther's farm seemed downright amateurish in comparison. We didn't even have solid walls, for crying out loud. Maybe Esther was right to feel threatened.

"Well, now you've seen my place," Carla said.

"It's fantastic. You'll be a huge hit." But I wouldn't be telling Esther that. I stepped out of the room, and Carla turned off the light. I led the way down the hall, Carla following behind. When we got to the front of the spa, I turned around. "We should have lunch sometime. We could compare notes on the spa business." Even though we were direct competitors, Carla seemed like someone I'd like to hang out with.

"Great idea. Let me give you my card." She stepped behind the counter and extracted a business card from a shelf underneath. I tore a blank page off a pad of paper that sat near the phone and jotted down my number.

We traded, and I stuck the business card in the back pocket of my khakis, along with the brochure I still carried. I nodded to both Carla and Jessica, who gave me a wave and a smile, and stepped out onto the sidewalk. The air outside the spa felt especially cool on my skin compared to the warmth of the mud room. I hurried back to the diner, worried that my BLT would be ice cold after all this time, but Betty was only now wrapping up my sandwich. She stuffed it into a paper bag with a napkin and set it on the counter with my drink before ringing me up at the nearby register. I paid for the food and trotted to my car, eager to eat my lunch before the hour was up.

Back at the farm, I followed the path along the vegetable garden, turned at the row of guest cabins, and crossed the patio area to the back door. The kitchen was empty, and I sat down at the oak table, pulling my sandwich out of the bag. The bacon was still warm, and I was savoring the salty crunch of the first bite when Gretchen walked in. She must have been in between spa clients.

As I watched, she went straight to the sink and turned on the tap. Her shoulders drooped noticeably as she scrubbed her hands and dried them roughly with the hand towel. When she turned around, her gaze dropped to the floor. Her mouth was set in a grim line.

Alarmed, I swallowed hastily. The half-chewed bacon scraped its way down my throat. "Is everything all right, Gretchen?"

She threw the towel on the counter. "No. I ran into Esther this morning, and she told me how amazing the new spa is. Then I called one of my friends to see what she knew, and she said her mom couldn't even get an appointment, it's so busy. What will happen to my job when everyone stops coming here and goes there?"

I drank some iced tea to encourage the bacon the rest of the way down. Between Esther and Gretchen, I was starting to feel like a therapist. "You're great with the customers. They won't abandon you."

Gretchen sank into a chair on the other side of the table and ran a hand through her short dark hair. "I hope you're right. I drive past the place all the time, but I haven't worked up the courage to go inside yet. What if we can't compete?"

"We'll be fine. In fact, I stopped there while getting lunch, and you have nothing to worry about." I thought of the Brazilian waxes and manicure stations and then banished the images from my mind.

Gretchen reached across the table and gripped my

free hand. Her icy fingers sent a shiver up my back. "What's it like? Is it as nice as everyone says?"

I removed my fingers from her grasp. "Well, it is trendy. Massages, mud baths—"

She gasped. "So it's true. They have mud baths."

I set down my sandwich, then stuffed an errant tomato slice back into place. "The Pampered Life will attract a different clientele. Our regulars won't desert us."

Gretchen's eyes, accented by heavy black eyeliner, never left mine. "I've already noticed a drop-off in bookings." Concern was etched on her face.

"For now, because it's new," I said firmly, holding her gaze. "But then they'll come back."

"This job is too important for me to lose. I've worked too hard."

"No one's losing their job. Esther wouldn't allow it."

Shaking her head, she slapped her hands on the table and rose. "You better be right." She strode out of the kitchen.

I stared at the empty doorway for a moment, wondering about her change in behavior. She'd sounded so angry. I returned to my sandwich, though my appetite had shrunk considerably. The bacon tasted too salty; the mayonnaise seemed less creamy. Would people sour on Esther's place, like I'd soured on my sandwich?

After I'd swallowed the last bite, I crumpled up the paper before dropping it in the trash with my drink cup. I walked down the hall and settled into the office chair, glancing around at Esther's photos of the farm and of her deceased husband. He'd passed away before he and

Esther could realize their dream of turning their former farm into a bed-and-breakfast, but Esther had assured me that he was watching from heaven and nodding his approval. I'd never met her husband, but she'd worked hard to get this place running, and I suspected she was right.

I took a few minutes to answer blog comments from today's post. Then I focused on the new marketing materials I was developing. I soon found myself immersed in work, forgetting all about the Pampered Life as the afternoon sped by. When five o'clock rolled around, I powered down the computer, pulled on my sweatshirt, and gathered my belongings.

On my way out the door, I ran into Gretchen in the hall. She barely raised her eyes to acknowledge me, and I automatically placed a hand on her shoulder. "Everything will work itself out, Gretchen. Don't worry."

She sighed. "I hope so, but I'm not leaving it up to fate. I have a plan." Before I could ask what she meant, she slipped past me and into the kitchen.

I gave her retreating back a long look. She and Esther were both convinced that the Pampered Life would put an end to the spa here. Were they right?

And what exactly was Gretchen's plan?

Chapter 3

After dealing with Blossom Valley's rush-hour traffic, such as it was, I pulled into my designated parking spot at the Orchard Village Apartments and shut off the engine. A salsa-red Camaro sat in the space next to me, which meant Ashlee had beaten me home again. I looked up at our apartment for signs of activity, but the front door was closed and the curtains in the nearby window were drawn. Knowing Ashlee, she was happily ensconced on the couch, watching a reality show.

I locked my car and headed up the outside stairs to the apartment. When I opened the door, the sounds of shouting and breaking furniture greeted me. Ashlee turned from her place on the couch, looking comfy in pink-and-white-striped pajama shorts and a pink T-shirt. She pointed at the TV. "Check it out. Catfight!"

I dropped my purse on a kitchen chair and shrugged out of my sweatshirt. "I'd rather watch the real cats that hang out by the Dumpster downstairs. It'd be more interesting."

Ashlee waved the remote at me. "You don't know what good TV is."

"I know bad TV when I see it."

"Whatever." She concentrated on the screen as the two women continued sparring. After one ended up with her skirt bunched around her hips, a couple of guys from the sidelines stepped in and pulled the women apart. I shook my head and went to my bedroom to change, stepping over Ashlee's jacket where it lay on the floor. Her flip-flops blocked my doorway, and I gave one a good kick, sending it bouncing off the nearby wall.

I switched into a long-sleeved T-shirt and lounge pants, washed my face, and brushed my shoulder-length dishwater-blond hair, then wandered into the kitchen to see what was for dinner. Up until a couple of months ago, Ashlee and I had been living with our mom, who had insisted on serving a healthy meal every night after our dad died of a heart attack almost two years ago. Between her dinners and Zennia's dishes at the farm, which were both healthy *and* organic, I thought I'd never get to eat lip-smacking, mouthwatering foods again.

Now that I was in charge of my own meals, I tended to gravitate toward processed snacks and frozen entrées. Every now and again when I was leafing through a magazine, I'd eye a picture of a green salad with longing, but the feeling went away as soon as I ate a doughnut.

I inspected the handful of items in the refrigerator and pantry before grabbing a package of Top Ramen and tossing it on the counter. While I waited for my pot of water to boil, I glanced over the counter into the living room and saw that Ashlee's show was on a commercial break.

"Hey, Ashlee," I called to her, "have any of your friends tried that new spa in town, the Pampered Life?"

Ashlee muted the volume and twisted around to face me. "You remember my friend Brittany? She got a job there. Which is super awesome, 'cause she can get a huge discount for all her friends, and that means me. Julia already went there for a manicure. The manicurist put a little skull and crossbones on every nail."

"So everyone's pretty excited about it?"

Ashlee tucked a strand of hair behind her ear. "Sure. It's the hot new place in town."

Great. Just what I didn't want to hear. The water started to boil, and I yanked open the pack of Top Ramen, sending little curls of noodles skittering across the counter. I dumped the rectangle of glued-together pasta into the pot, then tore the top off the seasoning packet and watched the roiling water suck up the powder. "Think it'll affect Esther's place?" I called over my shoulder.

"Naw. All the cool chicks will hit up the new spa, but where you work gets all those fuddy-duddies with the giant purses and support hose. They wouldn't set foot in a place so hip."

No one matching Ashlee's description had ever come to our spa, but at least she was confirming my earlier comment to Gretchen that the two spas would simply attract different types of people.

That settled, I poured my ramen into a bowl, grabbed a spoon from the silverware drawer, and sat down at the kitchen table to read a cooking magazine. I couldn't live on instant soup and frozen meals of fried chicken and mashed potatoes forever. I marked a page for an easy macaroni and cheese with bacon recipe while I slurped up my noodles.

Dinner done, I dashed off a text to Jason to see if he wanted to hang out tonight. Before I had time to finish wiping down the table, he replied that he was tied up with a traffic accident on Main Street. As the lead reporter for Blossom Valley's only newspaper, he covered everything from fender benders to burglaries to serial jaywalkers.

I set my phone on the counter and joined Ashlee on the couch, where she'd switched the channel from the battling women to a man trying to pawn a Revolutionary War–era musket. When the shop owner lowballed an offer, I thought the man might test out the musket right then and there, but he grabbed his gun and stalked out instead.

I slumped down in the cushions and put my feet on the coffee table. "No date tonight?"

Ashlee tore her gaze from the TV. "Chip had to go see his grandma, poor guy."

"Why poor guy?"

"She's ninety-six and thinks he's George Clooney. It can get awkward when your grandma keeps hitting on you every time you visit."

Yeesh. "You've been seeing Chip awhile now. You guys getting serious?"

Ashlee snorted. "God, no. The last thing I want is to end up like you and Jason, watching TV every night like an old married couple."

I put my feet down. "Old married couples are usually pretty happy, like Jason and me. You could learn a lot from us."

"How to die of boredom, maybe."

"Or how to enjoy a stable, long-term, fulfilling relationship." Jason and I had been dating for less than a year, but that was a lifetime commitment by Ashlee's definition.

I hopped off the couch to retrieve a bag of chocolate chip cookies and end the argument, then flopped back down and munched a cookie. While Ashlee flipped through the channels, I picked up a farming magazine I'd borrowed from Esther, and started reading. Within minutes, I was absorbed in an article about the local food movement. The next time I looked at the clock, it was time for bed.

I marked my page and said good night to Ashlee before going to my room, feeling one last nagging worry about the new spa as I closed the bedroom door.

The next morning, I felt someone shaking my shoulder. Still half asleep, I squeezed my eyes shut and tried to roll over, but a hand grabbed me and halted my movement. Then Ashlee spoke right in my ear, her grip on my shoulder firm. "Dana, get up. Hurry."

I slapped her hand off me and inched over to my nightstand to check the clock. Not even six yet. Ashlee was never up this early. A jolt of panic brought me to a sitting position. "What's wrong? Is Mom okay?"

"Mom's fine, but Brittany called."

I rubbed my eyes, trying to get my brain working. "Why is she calling so early? Did she get fired for giving out discounts to too many friends?"

"No, smarty, but she did call about the Pampered Life." Ashlee grabbed my shoulder again. "That boss of hers there? She's dead."

Chapter 4

At Ashlee's words, all remnants of sleep vanished. "What? Are you talking about Carla?"

Ashlee settled onto the edge of the bed. "I guess that's her name. It's whoever runs the place."

"How? When?" I couldn't quite grasp what Ashlee was saying. I'd met Carla only yesterday. She'd looked ridiculously healthy and seemed so happy. How could she be dead now?

"Brittany found her in one of the mud baths, her feet sticking straight up. She swears there were all sorts of weird symbols painted in mud on her feet, like maybe someone killed her as a gang ritual or something."

I shook my head. "Don't be silly. Blossom Valley doesn't have any gangs. Sure Brittany's not looking for a little drama?" I shoved Ashlee off my bed, and she squawked in protest. "Never mind. I'll find out myself." I threw back the covers and rushed into the kitchen to retrieve my phone. If anyone knew the details of what had happened, Jason would. I called his number and got voice mail. Without leaving a message, I texted him to see if he'd heard anything from the police about Carla dying last night.

I waited to see if he'd reply right away, but gave up after a minute and grabbed the bag of ground coffee out of the cabinet, frowning at how light the bag felt. Now was not the time to run out of coffee. The way this day had started, I might need more than one pot.

While I listened to the machine gurgle, I heard the sound of a train horn, which meant I had a text. I snatched up my phone and read the display. Jason's reply confirmed my fears. Carla *was* dead. I looked away from the words on the screen, caught off guard by the incredible pressure that had settled in my chest. I'd barely known the woman, so why did I feel like crying?

I absentmindedly scanned the rest of the text. Jason promised to call when he had a break, but I knew not to wait around. Major crimes didn't happen often here, and he'd be busy hunting down every witness to interview and every extra detail to write about.

My hand trembling, I set the phone on the counter. The coffee machine beeped, and I automatically went over and poured myself a cup. I took a sip and winced as the hot liquid scalded my tongue. I needed to shake off this gloom. What had happened to Carla was terrible, but Esther still expected me at work this morning.

With the coffee cup feeling unnaturally heavy in my hand, I went into the bathroom to get ready. On my way out of the apartment, I grabbed a packet of Pop-Tarts for breakfast, vowing to toast the things one of these days. My car started with only minor grumbling, and I backed out of my parking space.

My route to work brought me down Main Street, and I slowed the car as I neared the Pampered Life. Three cop cars were parked at the curb, the only sign that anything out of the ordinary had happened. Still, three cars seemed like two too many, and I had to wonder how Carla had died.

According to Ashlee, Brittany had discovered Carla in one of the mud baths. Had she fallen asleep while taking a soak and somehow drowned? Slipped on the tile floor and hit her head before falling into the muck? Or had she been helped along by someone? While I knew nothing about Carla, I had a hard time envisioning anyone shoving that happy, smiling face into a trough full of mud and holding her down until she suffocated. I shuddered at the image and brought my attention back to the spa.

Several people stood at the back corner of the building, Jason included. At over six feet tall, he was easy to notice. I debated pulling over and talking to him, then thought better of it. The cops must be in the middle of their investigation, and I really had no reason to talk to him, other than pure nosiness. I kept driving.

At the farm I parked in my usual spot and followed the path toward the house. Heavy gray clouds hung low in the sky, suppressing the usually vibrant reds and yellows of the flowers lining the walk and silencing the warbles of the songbirds I knew were perched in the nearby trees. I spotted a guest in the distance jogging toward the Henhouse Trail, which cut through the trees and brush toward the back of the property, providing solitude for early risers. I was tempted to take a walk back there myself after everything that had happened this morning, but work beckoned, and I turned toward the main house.

When I reached the kitchen, I found Zennia breaking eggs into a ceramic bowl. On one hand, a large red mark glowed brightly against the soft, pale flesh near her thumb.

"Berta mad at you again?" I asked as I snagged a bunch of grapes out of the fruit bowl. *The perfect complement to my strawberry Pop-Tarts,* I reasoned.

"That hen is so cantankerous," she said.

"I don't know why. She has plenty of room to run around in. We feed her that all-natural grain. She should be the happiest chicken on earth."

"No kidding. I've tried singing to her when I collect the eggs, reciting poetry, anything to improve her mood, but nothing works."

I popped a grape in my mouth. "We could always stop stealing her eggs."

Zennia rubbed the spot on her hand. "Trust me, I've considered it."

I thought about telling Zennia that Carla had died, but I didn't feel much like sharing the news yet, especially since I knew so little. Instead, I cradled the grapes in one hand and took a napkin off the stack on the table. "I'll be writing my blog, if you need any help serving breakfast."

"I should be able to handle it, but I'll let you know if anything changes."

Once in the office, I set my grapes and the napkin on the desk and slipped off my jacket. I was placing my

purse in the bottom desk drawer when the door opened
and Gordon entered.

With his three-piece suits and greased-back hair, he
always reminded me of a pit boss in a Las Vegas casino,
rather than Esther's right-hand man. He'd once owned
his own bed-and-breakfast over in Mendocino, but it
had folded a few years ago. I suspected he saw the farm
and spa as his chance for redemption, and I had to
admit that his business experience and tight control of
the budget were the reasons this place was still afloat.

We'd butted heads the first several months after I'd
started working here, but now we'd reached a tentative
understanding in our working relationship. Plus, we
didn't see each other too often, which helped.

I slid the drawer shut and pulled the chair closer to
the computer. Gordon set the clipboard he always
carried next to the keyboard and perched on the edge
of the desk. He placed his hands on one knee, clearly
planning to stay awhile.

"Good morning, Gordon," I said, wondering what
had prompted this unexpected visit. "Did you need to
use the computer this morning?"

"No thank you, Dana. I'll complete my inventory
tracking this afternoon. The reason I'm here is that it's
come to my attention that we may have a problem."

Not what I wanted to hear. "What kind of problem?"

"This new spa downtown."

I raised my eyebrows. He'd heard about Carla's death
already? Gordon was usually the last to learn what
happened in town. "How did you find out?"

"It's right on Main Street. I couldn't possibly miss it."

I leaned back in the chair and crossed my arms. "You must have seen the police cars. I figured everyone would notice those."

Gordon twisted one of his pinkie rings. "Police cars? I have no idea what you're talking about. I'm worried that this new spa will cut into our profits. Our bottom line cannot withstand any decrease in customers."

Was Gordon just now finding out about the Pampered Life's opening? "I wouldn't worry right now, not after what's happened."

Before I could explain further, Gordon slid off the edge of the desk and pointed a finger at me. "That's why I'm in charge of running this place. Of course I need to worry. We have to make sure we don't lose our clients."

I straightened up in the chair, the rough fabric scraping against my back. "We won't. Who knows if the spa will even stay open now?"

He looked at me as if I'd told him we were giving away free towels. "It's brand new. It's not going anywhere."

I could tell he was winding up for a long lecture, so I held up my hand. "Gordon, stop. The owner died last night. For all I know, the Pampered Life will never open for business again."

Gordon settled back down on the desk and adjusted the knot in his tie. "Died, you say? How?"

"I'm not sure. I heard she drowned."

His face took on a calculating expression. "Her death certainly changes things."

If I didn't know any better, I'd think he was almost

pleased. Actually, maybe I did know better. I wouldn't put it past Gordon to place business above all else, even someone's life. "Carla was a good person. You shouldn't be happy about what happened to her."

"I'm not, of course. But let's not lose sight of what this means for the spa."

"And let's not lose sight of the fact that a woman has died, well before her time."

Gordon nodded as if he agreed, but I could tell his mind was elsewhere. He stood and tapped the desk once with two fingers. "Back to work, then. Good job on the blogs lately." And with that, he walked out.

I grumbled to myself at his insensitive attitude, then booted up the computer and answered half a dozen e-mails. That done, I tried to think up a topic for the day's blog, but all I could focus on was Carla. I hadn't heard much gossip about the Pampered Life before it opened. Had she known anyone in town? Surely she had family or friends around here who would miss her.

My train horn ring tone sounded, and I grabbed my phone, thankful for the distraction. My mood instantly lifted when I saw a text from Jason. Wrapping up story. Coffee at ten?

I sent back my assent, knowing he wanted to meet at the Daily Grind. Maybe by the time I got there, Jason would have answers to all my questions, or at least some of them. With that in mind, I refocused on work and blogged about all-natural cold remedies. I posted the finished write-up to the spa's Web site and then busied myself with a marketing document, one eye on the clock. At a quarter to ten, I headed out, eager to learn what Jason had uncovered.

* * *

The Daily Grind coffee shop was an interesting mix of urban meets rural. Behind the counter, stainless-steel espresso machines hissed and steamed as baristas prepared cup after cup of nonfat, no-whip triple concoctions of caffeinated delight. On the customer side of the counter, farm-fresh jams, jellies, and olive oils crowded the shelves. I grabbed a jar of blackberry preserves and placed my coffee order. The coffee shop wasn't busy, and I easily spotted Jason sitting at a corner table.

I threaded my way past the mostly empty tables, noticing the hint of gold in Jason's reddish-brown hair as I approached. When he turned toward me, he flashed a smile that emphasized his dimples and made my heart flutter. I slid into the chair across from him and set my preserves on the table.

He held up his coffee cup. "Sorry I ordered without you. I got here early to make a few calls."

"No worries. I know you're busy."

"Between last night's car accident and this murder, I've been swamped."

My stomach lurched at his words, and I gripped the preserves with both hands. "Did you say *murder?*" My voice squeaked, and I cleared my throat. Earlier this morning I'd briefly considered the possibility that someone had pushed Carla into the mud bath, but I'd chalked that idea up to watching too many episodes of TV crime shows. "Carla was murdered?" I asked again.

Jason eyed my death grip on the blackberries. "I'm afraid so. Did you know her?"

"We'd only just met, but still, how terrible. Are the police sure it wasn't an accident?"

"They're waiting on the test results, but they suspect someone struck her from behind and then pushed her in the mud bath."

I remembered the pride in Carla's voice when she declared the mud baths were her favorite part of the spa. And now they were her grave. "No chance she slipped and fell in?"

"Her head wound doesn't match up with that scenario."

"Ashlee's friend said there were drawings on Carla's feet, like gang markings. Is that true?"

He smirked. "Is Ashlee's friend named Brittany?" When I nodded, he said, "She's an odd one. I've never met anyone who giggled through an entire interview before, especially one that involved a murder." He sipped his coffee. "She told me the same thing about the mud symbols, but the police denied it. Said some mud splatter had dried on the foot that was sticking out. Nothing more."

I stared out the window, and Jason took one of my hands, his fingers warm and comforting. I turned back to find his green eyes filled with concern. "Are you all right? You seem pretty upset."

"She was so excited about her new business. And she seemed genuinely nice. Her death is such a shame."

Jason squeezed my hand in reply as the barista called my name. I started to rise, but Jason waved me back down. "I'll get it." He returned a moment later and handed me my white mocha.

"Thanks." I took a sip, feeling the hot beverage course its way down my throat. "I know Brittany found her only this morning, but do the police suspect anyone yet?"

"Not that I know of. They're still investigating how the killer gained entry to the spa."

I picked at the hole in the plastic lid on my coffee cup. "Do they think someone broke in to rob the place and Carla interrupted them?"

"That's one theory. If Carla let her killer in, that changes things. It means it wasn't a random killing."

I trembled at the thought and looked at my cup. Was it worse to be killed by a stranger or by someone you knew and trusted? Definitely the latter, knowing in your final seconds that you'd been betrayed. I hoped Carla hadn't suffered. But death by mud? It sounded awful.

Jason drained his cup and tossed it in the nearby trash can. "Let's pick a more cheerful topic. I'd love to get together tonight, if I'm caught up at work."

"Sure. Come on over. I'll make you my famous chili dogs."

"Wow. You're making chili from scratch? I didn't know you cooked."

I'd been planning to open a can that I had sitting in my cupboard, but still, I didn't appreciate Jason's incredulous tone. "I might," I hedged. "And I'll add extra cheese and jalapeños."

Jason laughed. "How could I refuse such a tempting offer?"

I leaned toward him. "You'll be so fired up that you'll need an extinguisher to put out the flames."

Jason's gaze drifted from my eyes to my lips. "Are we still talking about the chili dogs?"

"Maybe." I winked at him.

"I'll be there at seven."

We stood at the same time. Jason followed me out of the coffee shop, the barista nodding at us on our way by. When we reached my car, Jason pulled me into a hug, and I rested my head on his chest for a moment. I caught the spicy scent of his cologne as we broke apart.

"See you tonight," he said before stepping over to his car.

With a wave, I got in my own car and drove through town. Whenever thoughts of Carla crept into my mind, I chased them away. The police would find her killer. Jason would keep me updated. I had no reason to obsess over her death. Except I couldn't help it. One minute, she was laughing and showing me around her treasured spa, and the next, she was buried in a mud bath. I still couldn't quite accept that fate.

I took the exit for the farm and bounced and jolted down the potholed lane. When I reached the lot, I noticed a dark blue Ford Taurus parked in one of the spaces and slammed on my brakes, craning my head to study the car. I could be wrong, but I was almost positive that car belonged to Detective Palmer, one of Blossom Valley's finest. What was he doing here?

Chapter 5

I hit the gas pedal and shot into the first available parking spot, then stomped on the brakes. The car jerked to a stop. I jumped out and trotted to the lobby door, my heart beating faster with each step. Inside, Gordon stood behind the counter, jotting notes on his clipboard. My step faltered as I noted his calm behavior. Maybe I'd been wrong about the car.

He glanced up when I entered and slapped his ballpoint pen on his clipboard. "Did you know the police are here?" he demanded.

Then again, maybe I'd been right. I crossed the room and stopped before the counter, bending over slightly to catch my breath. "I thought that was Detective Palmer's car outside. What does he want?"

"He didn't say, other than to ask if Gretchen was working today."

I straightened up. "Gretchen? Why would he want to talk to her?" With such a small police force, every detective, including Palmer, would be working on Carla's murder, but I failed to see how Gretchen was involved.

"Again, the detective did not share that information with me." Gordon checked his watch. "They've been in the dining room for the past fifteen minutes. They'll need to leave soon so we can set up for lunch service."

"Forget lunch. I want to know why he's interested in Gretchen." I moved down the hall toward the dining room.

"Tell him he has five minutes," Gordon called after me.

Right. I was going to kick out a police officer while he was investigating a murder just so guests wouldn't have to eat on the patio. *Not likely.*

I stopped at the open door of the dining room and peeked in. Detective Palmer sat at one of the tables, facing the door. Gretchen sat across from him with her back to me, but her stiff posture and the way she clenched the chair seat told me she wasn't enjoying the conversation.

Detective Palmer raised his eyes to me, and I'd swear he fought the urge to roll them. His buzz cut was longer than the last time we'd spoken, but his face was as stern as ever. "We'll be done in a minute."

I stepped fully into the room. "What's going on?"

Gretchen lifted her head but didn't turn around.

"Official police business," Detective Palmer said. "Please wait outside."

I didn't budge. "Anything I can do to help?"

"No."

I'd dealt with Detective Palmer a few times before, and we'd established a reserved yet mutually respectful relationship. Sometimes he even joked with me. I had a feeling today wasn't one of those days.

When he didn't say anything else, I gave Gretchen one last look, then crossed the hall to the office. I didn't even attempt to get any work done, knowing it would be a waste of time. Instead, I sat in the swivel chair and swung back and forth while keeping an eye on the dining room door. When Gretchen and Detective Palmer didn't emerge after three or four minutes, I went down the hall to see if Zennia knew anything.

She was sitting at the kitchen table, shelling peas. As I entered, she tossed an empty pod into an already full bowl. The pod teetered on the pile but didn't fall. Without my asking, she said, "I'm making my pea and mint salad. I thought it would balance well with my seasoned tofu, rather than the lamb people often serve it with."

I cringed as an image of a tofu lamb running across a field popped into my head, but I managed to say, "Sounds delicious. I'll have to try some."

Zennia gave me a questioning look.

"Well, the pea salad, anyway." I gestured toward the hall. "Any idea why the cops are talking to Gretchen?"

She sucked in her breath. "The police? No. I didn't realize they were here."

"Detective Palmer is in the dining room with her now. I'm sure it's related to Carla's murder, but I don't know why."

Zennia dropped the peas in her hand. Two rolled across the table and fell onto the floor. "The new spa owner? Gordon mentioned something about her dying.

Seemed almost happy about it. But you say she was murdered?"

I rubbed my arms and shivered, though the kitchen wasn't drafty. "Yes, but how is Gretchen involved?"

Zennia wiped her hands on a dish towel. "That dear girl? She can't be. Her spirit is pure."

"Maybe Detective Palmer wanted to ask her some questions about spa procedures, since Gretchen has so much experience." It was a ridiculous theory but the only one I could come up with. I thought back to my talk with Gretchen the previous evening. She'd said she had a plan to keep the new spa from impacting our business. Was her plan somehow tied to Carla's death?

Zennia interrupted my musings. "I'm glad Esther went into town to run errands. She'd be so frazzled to find the police here."

"I'm not exactly thrilled myself," I said. I heard the sound of voices in the hall, and I stuck my head out. I saw Detective Palmer standing outside the dining room. He said a few words, presumably to Gretchen, then walked toward the lobby. I waited a moment, but Gretchen didn't come out. "I'll be back," I told Zennia.

She lifted a hand in acknowledgment and resumed shelling peas. I entered the dining room and saw Gretchen still at the table, her shoulders shaking. I could hear her sobs as I approached, and I placed a hand on her back.

She flinched at the touch and looked up. "Oh, hi, Dana." She swiped at the tears and sniffed. "Sorry for the waterworks."

I eased into the chair next to her and clasped my

hands between my knees as I leaned toward her. "What's wrong, Gretchen?"

"Someone killed the owner of the Pampered Life last night."

"I heard. But why was Detective Palmer talking to you?"

Tears filled Gretchen's eyes again. I went to the sideboard against the back wall and grabbed a beige cloth napkin, then returned to my seat and handed it to her. She dabbed at the tears.

"Someone saw me there," she whispered.

I felt my eyes widen. "At the Pampered Life? You went there?"

Gretchen gulped. "After work. From the way the detective was talking, it must have been around the time of the murder. I bet he thinks I killed that woman." Gretchen broke into fresh sobs.

I leaned my elbows on the table and studied Gretchen's face. "But why were you there? Is this related to the plan you mentioned last night?"

Gretchen wiped her eyes again. "I wanted to see what everyone was talking about. You told me how stylish it was, and I thought I could steal a few of their ideas, beef up our place if it didn't cost too much."

"I had the exact same thought. Surely Detective Palmer understood that."

She lurched up from her seat and began pacing between the tables. "But I got there after closing. People saw me peeping in the windows. Probably thought I was planning a robbery. I even tried the back door. It was unlocked." She stopped next to the chair in which she'd been seated and turned toward me, her eyes pleading. "But I didn't go in. You have to believe me."

I held up my hands, afraid she'd start crying again. "Of course I believe you."

"But the detective didn't. I bet he thought I broke in to steal equipment and killed that lady when she caught me."

Jason had said that a botched robbery was one theory the police were investigating, but Gretchen didn't need to hear that. I shook my head. "I've dealt with Detective Palmer before. He isn't the type to jump to conclusions."

Gretchen gripped the back of her chair. "I hope you're right. This is the first job I've had where I can see myself staying for a while. I've been working my butt off to earn everyone's respect."

"And you've got it. Esther knows you'd never kill anyone. No one will fire you."

She straightened up and rubbed her hands over her short dark hair, every muscle in her arms tense. "Gordon might try. You know how uptight he is about any bad publicity for this place."

I could definitely attest to that, considering Gordon had tried to get me fired once upon a time. "Esther won't listen to him."

"Esther won't listen to whom?" Gordon demanded from the doorway.

I hadn't seen him approach and could only hope he hadn't heard much. "One of Gretchen's clients keeps insisting that he needs a massage without the towel," I lied. "Claims it chafes him. He said he'd complain to

Esther next time." I kept my eyes trained on Gordon, not trusting myself to look at Gretchen.

"Preposterous," Gordon said. "The towel stays on."

"Exactly what I said." I rose. "I'll get back to work now."

Gordon lingered in the doorway, as if he didn't quite believe my tale, but he moved aside as I walked toward him. "See that you do." As I headed for the office, I heard him say, "Gretchen, I want to talk to you about this visit from the police."

I shook my head. I knew what it was like to be on the receiving end of Gordon's wrath. It wasn't pretty.

Even with thoughts of Carla's murder lingering in the back of my mind, I was able to finish the marketing document. At noon I helped Zennia serve the tofu to the guests before I sampled the pea and mint salad. It was the first vegetable I'd eaten all week, and it didn't taste half bad.

After lunch I wandered out to the pigpen to visit Wilbur and his pink and black buddies. When he saw me, he plodded over to the fence, nose working overtime as he sniffed the air for any hint of food. I pulled my hand from behind my back and offered him a handful of grapes I'd taken from the kitchen. With a snort and some gulps, he gobbled them up.

"Did you hear the news? Someone killed a spa owner last night."

Wilbur sniffed in my direction, but he was probably searching for more grapes.

"Detective Palmer came by a while ago to talk to Gretchen."

Wilbur snorted.

"She said she visited the place last night, and the back door was unlocked. That must be how the killer got in, but did Carla normally not lock her doors? Or was it bad timing that she picked this one night to get lax with her security?"

Wilbur sighed, as if this whole conversation was boring him. He lowered himself to the ground and rolled on his side.

"Fine. Be that way," I said. I walked down the path to the chicken coop. Several chickens wandered about the yard, pecking the dirt, but none paid any attention to me. I passed the guest cabins, where all the doors were closed, and spent a few minutes straightening the lounge chairs near the pool. The weather was too cool for swimming, but the guests still enjoyed the Jacuzzi. I gathered two bunched-up towels from the pavement and dropped them off at the laundry room before returning to the office.

I toiled away at the computer for the rest of the afternoon. When quitting time arrived, I grabbed my purse and jacket, anxious to get moving. I needed to stop by the store for hot dog buns and then clean the apartment before Jason got there.

Traffic on the highway was nothing compared to commuter traffic in the Bay Area, where I'd been living until a few months after my father's death. Still, I found myself tapping my fingers on the steering wheel as we puttered along well below the speed limit. Finally, I reached my exit and zipped off the highway and into downtown.

On my way past the Pampered Life, I noticed a

grouping of candles and flowers on the bench outside the door. *How nice.* Most people probably hadn't even known Carla, but they still felt the need to acknowledge her passing.

At the Meat and Potatoes grocery store, I walked straight to the bread aisle for a bag of buns. On the way to the checkout, I passed a stand full of flower bouquets and paused. I'd felt so touched when I saw the memorial for Carla, maybe I should add to the offerings. I could spare a few minutes.

I selected a bouquet of carnations and daisies and took it to the counter with my hot dog buns. The cashier slid the flowers in their plastic wrapper over the scanner. "These are awful pretty. Buying them for someone special?"

"That spa owner who was killed last night." I felt myself blush as I spoke, though I wasn't sure why I should feel embarrassed. "They've set up a memorial outside her business."

"That's real thoughtful." She rang up the buns, then announced my total. "I couldn't believe when I heard what happened. I mean, a killer loose here in Blossom Valley? I have to work till closing most nights, and you can bet I'll have my husband come pick me up from now on. No way I'm walking to my car by myself anymore."

I handed her a twenty. "I'm sure it was an isolated incident." At least I hoped so.

She counted out my change. "Well, she was new in town, so maybe she brought the trouble with her. You know how different the city is."

"Maybe." I pocketed the money and hurried out of

the store. In the car I drove the few blocks back to Carla's spa and parked along the curb. Three women milled around the bench, and I recognized one of them as Jessica, the receptionist who'd been working at the spa when I visited the day before. She and another girl, who looked to be a few years younger than me, maybe around Ashlee's age, stood close together, talking. The third woman, wearing a jogging suit and brilliant-white athletic shoes, stood to the side, clutching a lit candle.

I approached the group and laid my bouquet with the others on the bench. I closed my eyes and said a quick prayer for Carla. The two girls temporarily halted their conversation and then resumed talking.

"I hate to look for another job. I mean, I just got this one," Jessica said.

"Yeah, but what can you do?" the other girl said. The tips of her shoulder-length bright red hair looked like they'd been dipped in a tar pit. "I mean, I gotta work if I want to pay my phone bill. My folks are, like, so uptight that way." She giggled.

I took the opportunity to wedge myself into the discussion. "You guys think the spa will close down permanently?"

They both looked at me, then at each other. The red-haired girl laughed again. "What else could happen? Carla's dead. Who's going to pay us?"

The woman in the jogging suit frowned at the girl but didn't speak.

"Knock it off, Brittany," Jessica said. "Who cares about the money now?"

Wait, Brittany? Was this Ashlee's friend Brittany?

Ashlee talked about her all the time, but I'd never actually met the girl. I was sure I would have remembered the red hair. And the inappropriate laughing. Hadn't Jason mentioned that?

"I do." Brittany flipped up a chunk of hair and studied the black tips. "Don't get me wrong. I'm totally bummed about losing this cush job, too. And about what happened to Carla, of course."

"Good place to work?" I asked.

Jessica nodded. "The best. Carla was super flexible with my hours. I can work only certain days because I go to school, and she fixed the schedule for me."

"Yeah, and the work was easy," Brittany said. "Answering phones and making appointments, stuff like that."

For a second, I thought she'd finish speaking without giggling, but she threw one in at the end. I gritted my teeth. When Brittany didn't say anything else, I turned to the woman with the candle. "Did you work for Carla, too?"

She set the candle under the bench, where the flame reflected off the cellophane wrappers of the various bouquets, creating a semicircle of fire. "No, I never met the woman, but her death is so tragic. I felt I should pay my respects. How about you?"

"I met her only briefly, but she seemed like a nice person. She certainly didn't deserve to die the way she did."

Jessica snapped her fingers. "That's where I know you from. You came in the shop yesterday."

"That was me." My phone vibrated, and I pulled it

from my pocket. Beside me, both Brittany and Jessica glanced at their phones, too, as if the movement was as contagious as a yawn.

On the tiny screen, I saw a text from Jason that he was on his way. *Criminy.* Where had the time gone? At this rate, he'd probably beat me to my apartment, and I hadn't even cleaned the bathroom yet.

I stuffed the phone in my pocket and pulled out my keys. "Good luck with the job hunt," I told Jessica and Brittany. "I hope the cops figure out who killed Carla."

Jessica straightened a group of flowers on the bench and turned with an air of importance. "I already told them who did it."

"What?" Brittany and I said in unison. Why hadn't she said anything before?

Jessica looked all around, as if eavesdroppers were lurking behind the buildings, but the only activity outside of our group was the occasional car driving past. For all I knew, one of them might even be Jason's.

"She was so mad at her niece the other day." She elbowed Brittany's side. "You remember, don't you? We were straightening up the front office, and she kept ragging on us about every little thing. It's the only time she was ever mad about anything."

Brittany shrugged. "I thought she was mad because I kept texting my friends during work. It's not like we had any customers right then. Well, except the ones in the back rooms. And the ones waiting in the lobby. I don't know why my texting would bug her so much."

I choked down a laugh while Jessica rolled her eyes. "That wasn't it. It was something Erin did."

"What did she do?" I was torn between waiting to see what Jessica had to say and hightailing it back to my apartment, where I knew a sink full of dirty dishes likely waited for me, along with Ashlee's clothes strewn all over the place. I'd give her thirty more seconds to get to the point.

"I don't know. But one thing I do remember. When she called Erin later on the phone, I heard Carla say not to threaten her. She wouldn't stand for it." Jessica took a step toward me, the glee clear on her face. "And that's why I told the cops that Erin must have killed her."

Chapter 6

"That's what you're basing your theory on?" I asked. "One snippet of a conversation you overheard?" Jessica had sounded so confident that she knew who killed Carla, but obviously she was guessing. I couldn't resist peeking at the time on my phone. I needed to get going. My kitchen wouldn't clean itself.

Anger flashed across Jessica's face at my obvious doubt, replacing the brashness from a moment ago. "You got anything better?"

"No," I admitted. "But that threat Carla was talking about could have referred to anything from blabbing a family secret to borrowing her car for a destruction derby. I doubt it's connected to her murder."

"Well, the cops were pretty interested in what I told them. I bet it's the big break that'll get Erin arrested."

Brittany grabbed Jessica's wrist. "If that happens, a bunch of news channels will want to interview you. You might even be on a talk show." She giggled. "I'd totally watch that."

"You think so?" Jessica asked.

The woman in the jogging suit made a disgusted snort and turned away. I felt like doing the same.

"Okay, well, good night," I said to no one in particular. I walked off as the two girls started discussing what Jessica should wear for her debut TV appearance. Once in the car, I overcranked the engine and then scraped the curb as I sped toward home.

At the complex, I surveyed the guest parking spots and let out a breath. Jason's Volvo was nowhere in sight. I grabbed the hot dog buns and my purse off the passenger seat and trotted up the stairs. In my haste, I dropped my keys as I tried to unlock the door. I mumbled under my breath as I bent to retrieve the keys, and then I let myself in. The apartment was dark. My foot struck an object on the carpet as I headed for the kitchen.

I switched on a light and turned back to find a pair of Ashlee's sandals on the floor. I was starting to think she had no idea what a closet was for. I snatched up the shoes, grabbed her jacket and socks off the couch, and tossed everything into her room before slamming the door shut, shaking my head at the mess. The weatherman hadn't reported any tornado activity in Blossom Valley, but maybe Ashlee's room had suffered an isolated incident.

I hesitated in the hall, torn between cleaning the kitchen and wiping down the bathroom. Jason would definitely see the kitchen, since he usually helped me with dinner, but he might not need to use the facilities. I quickly transferred the dirty dishes from the sink to the dishwasher and grabbed the bottle of cleaner and a rag from the cabinet. I was scrubbing off the last smears of chocolate ice cream that had dried on the counter when the doorbell rang.

The sound gave me a burst of energy, and I hurriedly stowed the cleaning supplies back under the sink before I rinsed my hands and took down a can of chili from the cupboard. I cranked open the can and dumped the contents into a pot as the doorbell rang again.

"Coming!" I tossed the empty can in the recycling bag under the sink, where Jason wouldn't see it, put the pot on the burner, turned the burner on, and then ran my hands over my hair to smooth any errant strands. After a last look around the kitchen, I trotted over and opened the door.

Jason stood on the porch, a six-pack of amber ale in his hand. His hair looked damp, the ends curling along his collar. He must have run home to shower before coming over, which was more than I could say for myself. I looked down at my work khakis and polo shirt and winced.

"I'm running behind schedule. I haven't had a chance to change."

Jason pulled me close for a kiss. "You always look like a knockout to me." He stepped into the apartment.

"Thanks, but I'm sure you'd prefer I not smell like pig."

He smiled. "I thought we were having bacon with our chili dogs."

He set the beer bottles on the counter, and I rummaged through the silverware drawer for a bottle opener. I popped the top off a beer and handed it to him. "Enjoy. I'll be right back."

I dashed into the bedroom, tore off my work clothes, and donned a pair of dark red jeans and a long-sleeved white top. I ran a brush through my hair and tossed the brush behind me onto the bed on my way out of the room. Jason waited in the kitchen.

"I would have started dinner, but I didn't know if you wanted me snooping around your kitchen," he said. "My mom used to hate when guests did that."

I ran my hand along his back as I walked over to the counter. "You're not just any old guest, but I admire your restraint. That's impressive for a reporter." I dug a red onion out of the back of a cabinet, praying it wasn't moldy, and peeled off the outer layer. "That reminds me. How are your stories on the murder going? Any new leads?"

"Only bits and pieces." He took a pull on his beer. "The police didn't have an update when I called this afternoon, at least none they're willing to share this early in the investigation. I'm also having trouble finding anyone who knew her."

I grabbed a knife from the drawer and began dicing the onion. "I ran into a couple of the employees at the spa, Jessica and Brittany, on my way home." I felt my eyes well up as the strong fumes of the onion hit me, and I swiped at the tears with the back of my hand. "I know you already talked to Brittany, but what about Jessica? She has this ridiculous theory that Carla's niece, Erin, is responsible for her murder."

"I talked to her," Jason said. "Her reasoning for why Erin is the killer is flimsy, but I'd sure like to know more about Erin threatening Carla."

I finished with the onion, then opened the fridge

and removed a package of hot dogs and a bag of shredded cheese. "Have you met Erin yet? Does she live around here?"

"She lived with Carla. I stopped by the house, but no one answered the door. A car was in the driveway, so she might have been hiding out."

I kissed his cheek. "No offense, but I'd hide, too, if a reporter came knocking on my door after my aunt was killed, even one as good looking as you." I pulled open the hot dog package.

"You never know. Some people are eager to talk. They see me as the best way to tell their story." Jason set his beer on the counter. "I can't let you do all the work." He grabbed the bag of cheese, tore the top off, and then worked to pry the zippered pieces apart.

I got the hot dogs started, then stirred the chili and turned down the heat. "Who else did you talk to?"

"The neighbors, although that was a dead end. Seems Carla moved in four months ago but kept to herself. Her niece showed up a month later."

"They didn't move in at the same time?" I asked.

Jason retrieved two dinner plates from the cupboard. "Not according to the neighbors. One of them thinks Erin's mom lives in Santa Rosa, but she's not sure."

I was surprised that Carla's neighbors knew so little about her, but then again, I didn't often talk to my neighbors, either. When I was younger, people sat on their porches, chatting with anyone who happened to walk by. Now most everyone came home from work, went inside, and watched movies online or clips on YouTube.

"Did you learn anything else from the neighbors?" I asked.

"Not much. The one across the street said Carla occasionally had guests. One guy in particular was a repeat visitor, but she didn't know any names."

I used a fork to spear the hot dogs in the boiling water and placed them on the buns. "Let's hope the police have more luck. Their job sounds impossible right now."

I spooned the chili over the hot dogs and sprinkled everything with a healthy dose of cheese and red onion, while Jason found the forks and napkins. I took a plate in each hand, along with a bag of chips, while Jason carried the beers in one hand and the napkins, forks, and jar of sliced jalapeños in the other. Together, we walked into the living room and settled on the couch. I set our plates on the coffee table and picked up the remote.

"What's on tonight?" I asked.

"No idea." Jason picked up his plate and took a bite of his chili dog. "Wow. This is good. You should cook more often."

I looked down at my meal of a processed hot dog, canned chili, and pre-shredded cheese. Well, at least I'd diced the onion myself. "Thanks." I switched the television to a news channel, and we watched the latest headlines while we ate our chili dogs.

I was almost finished with mine when I heard a key in the lock and Ashlee burst into the apartment.

"Hi, guys!" she sang.

"Hey, how was work?" I asked.

She kicked off her mules and shoved them under the coffee table. I gave her points for sticking them somewhere where I wouldn't trip over them. "Awesome. Somebody left a box full of puppies at the vet office, so I got to spend the day playing with them." She glanced around the room. "We should keep one. We could put his bed by the TV."

"No pets allowed, remember?"

Ashlee stuck out her lower lip. "Couldn't we lie and say it was a therapy dog?"

"Then I'd need actual therapy from the guilt of lying."

She flopped down on the couch next to me, and I gripped my plate to keep from dropping it. "You're no fun."

"So you've been telling me all my life." I scraped the last of the chili off my plate and set the plate on the coffee table. "I met your friend Brittany today."

"Really? Where?"

"Outside Carla's spa. She and one of her coworkers were hanging around." I dropped my crumpled napkin on the dinner plate. "Does she always giggle like that?"

Ashlee gave me a questioning look. "Like what? I've never heard her giggle."

I stared at her. Maybe the sound was the type you could tune out after a while, like a leaf blower or background music. "She giggles after every sentence."

"Bullpucky."

Jason leaned forward so he could see around me. "It's true. I interviewed her for the paper, and she laughed the whole time."

"She must have been nervous," Ashlee said. "She's totally worn out from the murder. She swears she was talking to the cops all day. They kept asking her when she left work last night, if the back door was locked when she left, if she saw anyone hanging out where they shouldn't have been."

"And what did she say?" I asked. Beside me, I felt Jason tense up, no doubt wondering if he'd find out anything useful for his next article.

"She left at five, when her shift ended. Said Carla was busy typing in her office."

I hadn't seen an office during my earlier visit, but it had to be one of the rooms Carla didn't show me. I turned to Jason. "What time was she killed?"

"They're waiting for the report, but probably not more than an hour or so after that."

I returned my attention to Ashlee. "Was the door locked?"

She didn't answer, as she was too busy staring at the television. I looked at the screen, where a glammed-up couple was heading down a red carpet, flashbulbs from dozens of cameras blinding them.

"Ashlee," I said more loudly. "Was the door locked?"

She dragged her gaze from the screen. "What? Oh, sure. Brittany locked the front door on her way out."

"What about the back door?" Jason asked. He leaned toward her to hear the answer. I muted the volume on the TV.

She frowned at me and then looked at Jason. "How should I know if she locked it?"

"Maybe Brittany said something," he said.

"I think the cops asked her that, but she couldn't remember. She almost never used that door." Ashlee grabbed the remote from my hand and turned the volume back up.

I ignored the show and turned to Jason. "Do the police think the killer got in through the back door?" Gretchen had told me the door was unlocked when she stopped by, but I was looking for confirmation.

"They don't know, but it's the obvious choice if Brittany is sure that she locked the front door. If someone knew Carla kept the back door unlocked, they could take advantage of that information."

"So you think the murder was planned?" The chili dog in my stomach ran around in circles, chasing its tail.

"Too soon to tell." Jason stood and stretched, then grabbed both plates and carried them to the kitchen. I heard him running water and then two clinks as he set the plates in the dishwasher.

When he returned to the living room and sat back down, I patted his leg. "Thanks."

"Thanks for dinner."

Ashlee made a gagging noise.

"Don't you have a date tonight?" I asked her sweetly.

"Chip's having dinner with his cousin. He's visiting from out of town."

I put a finger to my lips. "Hmm . . . first a visit to his grandmother, now dinner with a cousin. I think you're losing your touch."

"I am not," Ashlee snapped. She touched her blond

hair, three shades lighter than mine, like it was a magic talisman. "Am I?"

She sounded so worried that I couldn't keep torturing her. "No. I'm sure he'd rather be with you tonight."

Ashlee flipped her hair back. "You're right. But I think I'll text him, anyway." She disappeared into her bedroom and closed the door.

Jason pulled out his phone. "That late already? I'd love to hang out, but I've got an early day tomorrow."

I sighed. "Me too."

I rose from the couch, and Jason followed, placing an arm around my waist. At the door, we engaged in some heavy lip locking until I heard Ashlee come out of her room, muttering to herself.

I broke free from our embrace. "Good night."

Jason ran a finger along my cheek. "I'll call you tomorrow."

I watched him go down the stairs and to his car before I closed the door.

I drifted into my bedroom, savoring the warmth that lingered on my lips, and stretched out on the bed. As I lay there, dark thoughts about Carla's death crept in from the corners of my mind and smothered the contented feeling from my evening with Jason.

Carla was alive and well when Brittany had left work at five. She was dead by the time Brittany returned the next morning. What had happened during the hours in between?

Chapter 7

Light rain pattered against the window when I awoke the next morning. After a quick shower, I donned my long-sleeved work polo and khaki pants and went into the kitchen to zap a frozen breakfast burrito in the microwave. I watched the news while I ate, keeping the volume low so I wouldn't wake Ashlee. By the time I finished eating, it was time to get to work.

Thanks to the steady drizzle, traffic was slower than usual through downtown. As I passed the Pampered Life, I saw that the memorial for Carla had grown. I watched a middle-aged woman in a poncho move the bouquets and stuffed animals around, placing some under the redwood bench and others against the building, beneath the green-and-white-striped awning, where they were somewhat protected from the rain.

A car horn blared, and I whipped my head forward, my eyes back on the road. I'd hate to get in an accident on my way to work. Jason might write an article about me.

At the farm I parked near the entrance. The rainfall

had increased, and I dashed across the parking lot, purse held over my head. As I sprinted up the walk, I caught a glimpse of the ducks splashing in the nearby pond. A few quacked hello.

When I reached the office, I hung my jacket on the back of the chair to dry and settled into my seat, thinking about the workday ahead of me. With no pressing deadlines, I had time to focus on new material. A few days ago Gretchen had mentioned an advanced waxing method she was considering for the spa. Now might be a good time to ask her for more details. If we were adding new services, I definitely wanted to update our marketing materials.

On my way to the kitchen, I could hear the clatter of silverware and murmurs of conversation coming from the dining room. I retrieved the spare umbrella we kept in an old milk can near the back door, nodded to Zennia, who was up to her elbows in a sink full of dishes, and stepped out into the rain. The drops drummed a steady beat as I sidestepped puddles and worms. I followed the path past the cabins and wiped my feet on the welcome mat before entering the spa tent.

When Esther had first agreed to add a spa to the farm's property, she'd envisioned a sprawling redwood building with plate-glass windows to let in the natural light and hardwood floors to complete the look. After she and Gordon had studied the contracting quotes and permit requirements, they'd settled on something that was more akin to a large tent. The exterior was comprised of large vinyl panels set in metal frames, complete with exterior windows and doors.

The inside included a heating and cooling system and was partitioned into several areas with those cloth cubicle walls you'd find in an office building. Not quite as elaborate as Esther had originally planned, but still functional and a whole lot cheaper.

The lobby area, with its brown rattan chairs and small mosaic-tiled table, was empty, so I continued on to the back. Gretchen was lying on the massage table in the last cubicle. Her hands were crossed over her stomach as she stared at the ceiling.

"Gretchen?"

She jerked her head around. When she saw me, she sat up and swung her legs over the side of the table. "Dana, I didn't hear you come in."

"No customers this morning?" I asked, although clearly we were alone in the tent.

Gretchen jumped down from the table and brushed her hands on her tan pants. "I have a client in half an hour."

"Perfect. I wanted to know more about this waxing service you told me about. Have you decided if you'll add it to our services?"

Gretchen let her gaze wander to the floor. "I don't know. Seems kind of pointless now, but I guess I could tell you about it, if you want me to." As glum as she looked, she might prefer getting a tooth extracted at the moment.

"Is this a bad time?"

Gretchen looked up and offered a weak smile. "No, sorry. I'm just distracted."

"Is Gordon still on your case about Detective Palmer's visit?"

She pressed her lips together. I waited.

"Worse," she finally said. "The detective called again. He had more questions about my visit to Carla's spa."

That didn't bode well. "What kind of questions?"

"He wanted to nail down exactly what time I'd been there, and asked me again about anyone walking by or hanging around. I already answered all those questions."

I knew from watching TV that the detective wanted to see if Gretchen gave different answers to repeated questions so he could catch her in a lie. For a fleeting second, I wondered if he had.

Gretchen moved to a table full of lotions and oils and started shuffling them around for no apparent reason other than to give herself something to do. "I think he wanted an excuse to talk to me again."

I hoisted myself onto the massage table where Gretchen had been lying a moment ago and swung my legs back and forth. "If he wanted to talk to you, he wouldn't need an excuse."

Gretchen's voice was low. "He would if he was here for another reason."

My legs slowed. "Such as?"

She didn't answer, instead moving the jars and bottles back to their original positions.

"Gretchen, what aren't you telling me?"

She turned around slowly, her hands twisting a terry-cloth washrag. "I had it rough as a kid."

The sudden change in topic threw me. What did this

have to do with Carla's death? I said, "Okay," in what I hoped was an encouraging tone.

"My mom died when I was twelve, and my dad had to work three jobs to support us. I pretty much took care of myself."

I thought about how lost I'd been when my own dad died a while back, and I'd been a full-fledged adult then. I couldn't imagine losing my mom at such a young age, right before those teen years. "That must have been tough," I said, feeling as if my words were completely inadequate.

She wound the washrag around one hand. "With my dad at work all the time, I started hanging out with other kids who had nowhere to go. Some of them were troublemakers, but I was so happy to be part of the group that I didn't care. We started shoplifting, pick-pocketing a little. I even helped rob a place or two." She focused on the washrag. "We never planned anything out and didn't even try to hide what we were doing, so the cops had no trouble catching us. I was arrested five times before I even turned sixteen."

I cringed. While I was growing up, I was never even suspended from school. Being arrested that many times seemed incomprehensible to me. "I had no idea."

Gretchen threw the washrag in the nearby wicker basket, which we used for soiled linens. "No one does. A teacher helped me get my act together. I finally concentrated on school, and the judge agreed to seal my juvie records."

I hopped down from the table and moved next to

Gretchen. "Look, you've obviously changed. You have a great job now. You have nothing to be ashamed of."

"But that detective must have looked into my background and seen my records. He probably thinks I had a relapse and decided to rob the spa. Killed Carla when she caught me." She started moving bottles and jars around again, knocking one over in the process. The plastic bottle full of peach blossom lotion tumbled to the floor.

I grabbed the bottle and placed it back with the others. "You're assuming too much. Did he make a reference to your record when you guys talked?"

She shook her head. "No, but maybe he was waiting for me to bring it up."

"I'm not sure how sealed records work, but maybe even the police can't see them without special permission. Don't read more into his visit than there is. Plenty of people could have killed Carla."

"Were they spotted at the murder scene, too?" she asked bitterly. She stepped away from the table. "If I were that detective, I would have already arrested me." She turned on her heel and strode from the room.

I exhaled loudly through my nose, then grabbed a towel and a bottle of homemade cleaner and wiped down the massage table. Too bad Gretchen couldn't erase her troubled past as easily as I was cleaning the table. She must be in a constant state of dread that someone would find out about her record, someone like Gordon. The man couldn't stand to hear even a whisper of a scandal and would have never hired her if he'd known about her past. Even now he might try to force Esther to fire her if he got wind of it. If Detective Palmer knew about the record, he was too much of a professional to release the information, but these kinds of secrets had a way of slipping out, anyway.

I left the spa tent without seeing Gretchen again and made my way past the cabins and pool area. I used the French doors to enter the dining room. With breakfast over, the room was silent. Zennia had already removed the silverware and linens from the tables. I cut across the hall and went into the office. I'd been so distracted by Gretchen's story that I'd forgotten all about the waxing, but I had other projects to work on.

For the next hour, I tried to concentrate but failed miserably. I felt too restless sitting at the desk. With lunchtime approaching, I called it quits and went into the kitchen to help Zennia, whether she needed it or not.

She stood at the stove, stirring the contents of a large pot. Her tie-dyed dress reached to the floor, and her usual braid looped around her head like a crown.

"What's for lunch?" I asked as I went to the sink to wash my hands. "A plateful of vitamins and minerals?"

She turned from the pot, still holding the wooden spoon. "More like a bowlful. It's curried lentil soup with seven-seed bread baked fresh this morning."

Not exactly my cup of tea, or, rather, soup, but others might enjoy it. I removed a stack of white ceramic bowls from the cupboard and set them on the counter. "I'd love to help you serve. How many are we expecting?"

"Twelve or so, depending on whether or not we get

anyone from the spa. I heard a couple of the guests discussing whether to drive to Mendocino for the day, but they were worried about the weather, so they may have changed their minds."

I thought of the narrow highway that twisted through the towering redwoods, the sun shut out completely by the mammoth trees, the road slick with water. "I know I don't like driving over there in the rain, even when it's only a shower."

"I agree. No sense tempting fate. Their auras already looked a bit unsettled when I saw them at breakfast, so I hope they stayed here. My soup will soothe their souls."

"How's my aura today?" I joked, though a tiny part of me worried about her answer.

Zennia stared at my forehead long enough that I found myself shifting my feet. "Same as most days," she said. "If you improved your eating habits, it would be brighter."

"Maybe I could try a spoonful of your soup." I heard voices in the hall as people moved into the dining room. "But for now, I'll serve it."

I ladled soup into two bowls and carried them out of the kitchen and next door to the dining room. An older couple sat at a table near the French doors. They nodded their thanks as I placed the steaming bowls before them, and then they resumed talking. I returned to the kitchen for a basket of the multi-seeded bread and dropped that off, as well. More people drifted in, and I shuttled between the kitchen and the dining room until I'd served everyone.

While people savored their soup, I filled a pitcher with ice water and slowly wandered the outer circuit of the dining room, keeping an eye out for anyone who needed a refill. In one corner two women in their mid-thirties were deep in conversation, the subject apparently more tantalizing than their untouched soup.

The blonde removed a slice of bread from the basket. Her nails looked freshly polished, and I recognized Gretchen's handiwork in the fleur-de-lis design on each finger. At least Gretchen's worries weren't affecting her work. As the woman talked, she tore the bread into smaller and smaller pieces. I edged closer to find out what had her so worked up.

"To think she was killed right in her own business," the woman was saying. "So scary." She shuddered and tore another piece off the bread slice.

I realized with a start that she was talking about Carla. I froze next to their table, praying the women wouldn't notice me.

The other woman ran her hand through her short brown hair and dusted off the shoulder of her red cardigan. "I know. It makes me nervous to even be out at night now." She looked up at me expectantly. I guessed my statue impersonation wasn't as convincing as I'd hoped.

I held the water pitcher aloft and raised my eyebrows. She studied her already full glass of water for a second and looked back to me. I shrugged and moved to the next table as slowly as possible, waiting for their conversation to resume. I didn't have to wait long.

Behind me, one of them cleared her throat. I snuck a peek over my shoulder.

"I wouldn't worry about it," the blonde said. "I don't think you're the type that gets murdered."

"What type is that?" her companion asked.

I hastily refilled the water glasses at the next table and then shifted back over to hear the answer.

"I heard she had a boyfriend." Again, she cleared her throat. Maybe she should drink some of the water I was offering. I dared a glance in her direction, noting a smirk on her heavily made-up face. She tossed the remains of her bread slice on her plate. "And guess what? He's married."

Chapter 8

I almost dropped my water pitcher. Carla not only had a boyfriend, but a married one?

The brunette gasped. "No. You don't say."

The blonde with the painted nails leaned back, looking pleased with herself. "That's just what I heard. Don't quote me on it."

"Do you know his name?" the other woman asked. She shoved her bowl away, causing a few drops of the lentil soup to slosh over the side. She ignored it. "Is he from here in town?"

"I have no idea. All I heard is he's some older guy and a total knockout. On a scale of one to ten, we're talking an eleven. I know if I was going to deal with all the hassle of sneaking around with a married man, he'd have to be worth it."

The brunette ran her hands through her hair, exposing her gray roots. "I agree. Otherwise, why bother?"

The two women fell silent. I weaved among the rest of the tables, filling water glasses here, checking bread baskets there, my mind far away from the dining room, busy concentrating on Carla and her love life. Jason had mentioned that one of the neighbors had spotted the same guy visiting Carla multiple times. Was that the boyfriend in question? If so, was he actually married, or was the Blossom Valley gossip factory working overtime in the fabrication department?

I went back into the kitchen and set the half-full water pitcher on the table. I flexed my fingers to work out the cramps from clutching the handle so tightly.

"How's the lunch crowd?" Zennia asked as she layered mango slices atop dishes of yogurt lined up on the counter.

"Good. Everyone seems to be enjoying your soup."

"Wait until they try my mango parfait."

I went back to the dining room to clear the tables and see which diners wanted dessert. In the corner, the brunette had pulled her soup bowl back and was spooning up the soup, while her companion nibbled on a chunk of bread and looked out the window. By the time I'd cleared the dishes from the other tables and delivered the desserts, they'd finished eating, but they weren't talking. I guessed they didn't have anything new to say about Carla and her boyfriend. Just as well. They'd given me enough to chew on for now.

After the guests had vacated the dining room, I helped Zennia with the dishes, my mind still on Carla. When I'd dried the last glass, I went into the dining room and pulled the tablecloths and napkins from the tables, then dumped them into the industrial-size washer in the laundry room. I started the cycle and went to the office to call Jason, hitting three wrong keys in my haste to dial the number. I finally hit the right buttons and pressed the phone to my ear.

He answered on the first ring. "Hey, babe. How's it going?"

I skipped the usual niceties, too absorbed in my news. "I used my vast connections of underworld spies and informers to uncover top secret information about Carla." That sounded more impressive than admitting I'd been eavesdropping while serving lunch.

"Seriously?" His voice took on an urgent tone. "I know you wouldn't tease me about info for a news story."

"Of course not." I paced around the office, the excitement in Jason's voice compelling me to move. "There's a rumor that Carla was dating a married man."

I heard typing on the other end of the line. "Did you get a name?"

"Afraid not. But I thought you could ask around. I heard he's older and really good-looking. Maybe it's that guy the neighbor kept seeing over at Carla's house."

Jason murmured agreement. "Makes sense. I'll ask the neighbor again, but maybe this connection of yours already knows. I could use any other information they have, too."

I had figured Jason would be so distracted by Carla's boyfriend that he wouldn't even consider my imaginary informant. I tried to think up a name for her, but all I came up with was Jane Doe, which was not the best choice. "Oh, all right, I don't have any connections. I overheard a couple of women in the dining room."

Jason laughed. "Hey, I'll take the information any way you can get it. Continue to keep your ears open."

"You bet."

"Let me get on this, and I'll give you a call later."

We said our good-byes and hung up. I stuck my phone in my pocket and turned to the computer.

The rest of the day flew by as I contacted local publications about ad pricing, struggled with a formatting issue in one of my documents, and thought up new promotional ideas. I considered all the extra services Carla's place had offered, and wondered how much it would cost to train Gretchen to administer Botox injections. Then I shook my head. Carla hadn't been dead two days, and I was already trying to profit from her. *Shame on me.* That was more Gordon's style.

Around five, I wrapped up my work. After a quick good-bye to Zennia and Esther, and a wave to Gordon, I stepped outside. Ahead of me, Gretchen was walking to her car, an older-model Nissan with a missing hubcap. With her head down and her back hunched, she looked as if the weight of a thousand massage stones rested on her shoulders.

Did the police know about Carla's possible married boyfriend? That might ease some of Gretchen's worries that the police were targeting her. The boyfriend or his jilted wife was a more likely suspect than a masseuse at a competing spa.

Gretchen pulled out of the lot, and I got into my own car, started it, then cranked up the heat. The light rain that had followed me around all day had dissipated, but clouds still cast a blanket over the sky. The weatherman had hinted at a warm front moving in, which I would be happy to see.

As I exited the highway and made my way down Main Street, I noticed that the same woman who'd been moving the flowers and stuffed animals out of the rain at the Pampered Life this morning was now taping a flyer to the spa's window. I squinted as I slowed, but I couldn't read the flyer's words from the street.

Curiosity got the better of me, as usual, and I pulled to the curb. The woman set the stack of flyers on the bench and looked up as I stepped onto the sidewalk. In her forties, she was fairly attractive in a plain way, with a friendly smile and large blue eyes. My mom would have described her figure as pleasantly plump, whereas Ashlee would have handed her a card for Weight Watchers.

As I got closer, she took a flyer from the stack, marched over, and thrust the paper at me. It advertised a Celebration of Life for Carla tomorrow evening at an address here in town. According to the flyer, everyone was welcome, and all attendees were encouraged to "bring a dish to share."

I looked up to find the woman staring at me. "I'm glad someone is arranging a service," I said. "I'm Dana, by the way."

"Patricia Porter. She has cousins in Colorado who are preparing a funeral, but I thought the locals might like to pay their respects. Did you know her?" she asked, sounding borderline suspicious. "I don't remember ever seeing you before."

"I met her only a few days ago. Did you know her long?"

Patricia nodded. "I probably knew her better than anyone. We grew up together in Denver. After I got married, I came out here, while she finished college and settled in San Francisco, but we stayed in touch. When she started talking a few months ago about getting out of the rat race in the city, I talked her into moving up here. She'd been working on opening the spa ever since."

"I'm surprised I didn't hear more about the spa before it opened. I'm sure you know how excited people get around here when a new business is in the works." Some locals had even been known to start a betting pool to see who could guess what would open in a vacant spot.

"Well, of course, I knew all about it," Patricia said, "but I'd never breathe a word until everything was absolutely ready. She and I both knew this spa would be a huge success." Tears welled in her eyes. "I only wish she'd had a chance to prove it. To be killed so soon after opening the place seems wrong." She started to cry.

I struggled for something to say and was relieved when a man in his midfifties joined us. He wore brown slacks, a white dress shirt, and a jacket that almost hid a modest paunch. The way he carried himself implied he'd been an athlete in his younger days. In his hands were two take-out coffee cups from the Breaking Bread Diner.

He set the cups on the bench and pulled a handkerchief from his pants pocket. "There, there, Patricia.

Don't let yourself get upset." He dabbed ineffectually at Patricia's cheeks until she took the handkerchief and dried her own tears. He retrieved the coffee and handed one cup to her.

"Thank you, Stan." She wadded up the handkerchief and gave it back to him.

He used the square of cloth to mop his neck before stuffing it in his pocket. "I added two sugars just like you like it, dear."

"You know everything about me." Her mouth turned up in a smile, but her tone implied that wasn't necessarily a compliment. Stan glanced at her nervously.

I eyed him. Here was a married, older guy who fit the description the woman at lunch had provided when talking about Carla's boyfriend. I wouldn't exactly call him a knockout, but maybe the woman had different tastes than me. Either way, it couldn't hurt to talk to him. I stuck out my hand. "Hi. I'm Dana."

He switched his coffee to his other hand, and we shook. "Stan. Pleased to meet you."

"We were talking about Carla's memorial service," I said. "Are you helping Patricia organize it?"

Stan opened his mouth to answer, but Patricia jumped in. "Oh, no, my husband is much too busy with work. I'm doing everything myself, from the decorations to drinks to these flyers." She tapped the one in my hand for emphasis.

"Now, honey," Stan said, "if you need my help, all you have to do is ask. I know how much Carla meant to you." He turned to me. "I'm an accountant. Tax season is our busy time. I've been working late every night the past couple of weeks."

Patricia laid a hand on my arm. "Please tell me you'll come to the service. I'd appreciate it so much."

I'd been waffling about attending ever since I'd read the flyer. Tomorrow was my day off, and I didn't have much planned. "I'll be there," I decided.

"Wonderful," Patricia said. "I'm hoping for a nice turnout for Carla."

Stan reached into his inside jacket pocket and pulled out a business card. "Now that that's settled . . ."

Patricia tried to put up a hand to block him. "Stan, now's not the time."

"Nonsense, honey. It's always a good time to talk about taxes." He handed me his card. "If you don't already have an accountant, I'd like to offer my services. My rates are reasonable."

I studied the card, plain white with his name and CERTIFIED PUBLIC ACCOUNTANT written in black across the middle. The typical info was listed at the bottom. Considering I had no property, no stock portfolio, and no deductions, my taxes took me all of ten minutes to complete. "I've got it covered, but I'll be sure to keep you in mind if I have any problems," I told him.

A loud rumble came from behind me on the street, and I turned around. An older-model muscle car, polished to a high sheen and with flames painted on the side, pulled to the curb behind my Honda. The engine continued to thrum as the passenger door opened and a girl in her late teens or early twenties got out, her long brown hair swishing around her shoulders. She looked

over at our little group before speaking to the driver of
the car, a young-looking guy with an angel tattoo on his
right forearm.

She shut the car door and walked to the entrance of
the spa. Without acknowledging us, she pulled a key
ring from her pocket, selected a key, and stuck it in
the lock.

"Erin!" The shrillness in Patricia's voice made me
wince. "Did the police say you could go in there?"

This must be the niece who, Jessica was convinced,
had murdered Carla. I took a closer look at Erin. With
her petite stature and wispy frame, she looked more
like a potential victim than a cold-blooded killer.

Erin turned toward us and rolled her eyes, drawing
attention to her glittery eyelids and blue eyeliner. "Of
course, Patricia. I'm not an idiot."

Patricia pursed her lips but softened her tone. "I
didn't say you were. Only, I'd hate for you to mess anything up while the police are looking for your aunt's
killer."

Erin's gaze traveled to the flyer on the window. Her
face darkened as she read the words. "Nice of you to
invite me to my own aunt's memorial service."

Patricia blushed. "I called, but you never answer
your phone."

"You could have left a voice mail."

At the curb, the driver of the muscle car honked.
Erin gave him a little wave while Patricia glared at him.

"I see Ricky drove you over," Patricia said. She

reached for Erin, but Erin shifted away. "What would Carla say?"

Erin's head whipped up. "Nothing. She's dead. Now, let me get my stuff." She twisted the key in the lock, pushed the door open, and disappeared inside.

Patricia sighed, and Stan started rubbing her back. "After all Carla's done for that girl," she said, shaking her head.

I couldn't help asking, "Like what?"

"Gave her a place to live, for starters, after her no-good drunk of a mother—"

"Patricia, please," Stan said. He removed his hand from his wife's back and drummed his fingers on his coffee cup, the sound inaudible over the noise from the car still idling at the curb.

I expected Patricia to chastise Stan for interrupting her, but she gave him a little smile. "You're right. I shouldn't say bad things about Carla's sister." She addressed me. "Carla had such high expectations for Erin, and I'm afraid it will be all for nothing now that Carla's gone."

Erin came back out the door and frowned when she saw us still standing there. She clutched a small bag in her hand, but there was no way to tell what was inside through the opaque plastic. She pulled the spa door shut and locked it.

"I hope you'll remember how Carla felt about Ricky," Patricia said as Erin walked past.

Erin paused in midstride before continuing on. At the curb she turned back. "He's the only one I can count on now." With that, she yanked open the car door and slid onto the passenger seat, slamming the door behind her. The engine revved, and the car roared away from the curb.

I felt like I'd been caught in the middle of an after-school special in which the young, naive girl was drawn to the bad boy from the wrong side of the tracks, and her family was trying to keep the two lovers apart. I half expected a cheesy sound track to start playing over an invisible sound system.

Patricia handed her coffee cup to Stan and grabbed the stack of remaining flyers. "I hope those two don't show up at my house tomorrow night. I put a lot of effort into planning this memorial, and I won't have it ruined by any of their shenanigans." She retrieved her tape dispenser, head held high. "Let's go, Stan."

"Yes, dear," he replied, but she'd already walked away. He trailed after her, carrying her coffee, along with his own.

I got back in my car and drove home. I couldn't wait to change out of my grungy work clothes, thaw a meal in the microwave, and call Jason and tell him about what I'd witnessed. Between telling him about Carla's married boyfriend at lunch and now this information about her niece, he might include me in the byline of one of his articles. Or take me out for a romantic dinner. Considering I'd uncovered at least two solid suspects in Carla's murder, we might even need to order some champagne.

Chapter 9

At home I parked in my designated spot next to Ashlee's Camaro, climbed the stairs, and opened the door to a dark apartment. I stopped. Ashlee's car was here, but where was Ashlee? At the on-site gym? Visiting a friend? I heard slurping noises coming from the direction of the couch and hit the light switch on the wall.

Ashlee and Chip were sitting on the couch. Well, Chip was sitting on the couch. Ashlee was propped in his lap, with their limbs intertwined and their faces mashed together. The sudden burst of light must have penetrated their consciousness, because they pulled apart. Ashlee then turned and gave me a big grin, while Chip tried to wipe the lip gloss off his face.

"Hey, sis. Home so soon?"

"Same time as every day." I tossed my keys on the kitchen table and slipped off my jacket. "Don't let me interrupt anything."

"Naw, we gotta get going, anyway," Chip said, still

wiping his cheek. "My roommate's having a party tonight. Hey, you wanna come?"

I'd been to one of Chip's roommate's parties shortly after we'd moved to the complex, hoping to meet some of my new neighbors. The party had involved beer bongs, Ping-Pong shots, and random girls running around looking for their underwear. Thank goodness Ashlee hadn't been one of them.

"Maybe next time."

"You got it."

Ashlee slid off Chip's lap, her fingers still interlaced with his. "Guess I'll get ready."

Before she could walk away, Chip gave her hand a tug and pulled her back down. "Maybe we got a little more time, after all."

Ashlee giggled and leaned in for a kiss. I made a dash for my room, the slurping sounds following me. I'd been planning to eat dinner before calling Jason, but after that little display, I wasn't hungry anymore. I'd call Jason first. Talking to him always got my appetite revving.

I shut the door to my room, changed into a T-shirt and pajama pants, and lay across my bed, on my belly, to dial. Jason answered right away.

"I was about to call you," he said warmly. "How was the rest of work?" I could hear traffic in the background.

"Nice and boring. It was the ride home that was interesting."

"What happened?"

I flipped over on my back and leaned against the pillows, shifting from side to side until I'd made a comfortable hollow. "I stopped by Carla's spa. A friend of hers was posting flyers about a Celebration of Life for Carla tomorrow."

"You must mean Patricia. She brought a flyer by the *Herald*'s office as I was leaving just now. I'll be covering the event for the paper."

"Great. Guess I'll see you there. I'm planning to stop by."

"An even better reason to go," Jason said softly.

I felt my insides heat up and started mentally sifting through my closet for what I'd wear tomorrow night, forgetting for a moment that I'd be attending a memorial service, not going on a date.

"You still there?" Jason asked.

"Yep, sorry. Anyway, while I was chatting with Patricia, Carla's niece showed up."

Jason whistled. "This isn't the elusive Erin I've heard so much about, is it? I can't find her anywhere."

"The same. And she brought along her boyfriend, who Carla didn't approve of, according to Patricia."

"Did you catch his name?"

"Ricky's his first name, but that's all I know." I rested my head on the headboard and studied the water stains in the corner of the ceiling. The stains had first appeared after a good rain last week, and the landlord had promised to find and patch the leak. So far, I hadn't seen any signs of repair. I guessed I needed to remind him.

Jason brought me back to the present conversation. "I talked to Patricia briefly when she dropped off the flyer. I tried to dig for info about Erin, and she mentioned that she and Carla had butted heads the past few weeks. Carla had even said something about Erin moving out."

"Interesting. Maybe Carla asked Erin to move out, and Erin didn't take the news too well." I sat up and opened my nightstand drawer. I rummaged around for a pen to write myself a note about the landlord. "Did Patricia know anything about Carla having a boyfriend?"

"I asked, but she made some excuse about hanging more flyers and rushed off without answering."

I gave up on the pen search and flopped back down on the bed. "Patricia's husband was with her tonight. I wondered if maybe he was the boyfriend, but he seems the type who would ask his wife's permission before cheating on her. More likely, Patricia is embarrassed that her friend was dating a married man, and didn't want to admit it to you."

"I plan to ask her again tomorrow." I heard rustling sounds over the phone, and then Jason spoke again. "I've got to get to this city council meeting. Any chance you'd like to join me?"

I considered the offer. As much as I liked hanging out with Jason, I'd had a long week, and my pajama pants were awfully comfy. "Will there be any chairs thrown this time? Any nude protestors?"

Jason chuckled. "Not twice in a row. That last meeting was a rarity. Tonight's topics are replacing the stoplight at the edge of town and the contract for the new trash collector. Not exactly nude-worthy stuff."

"Forget it, then. No offense, but even with you there, it's not worth getting dressed for."

Jason gave an entirely different type of whistle this

time. "You're not dressed? I can always skip the city council meeting. I could be at your place in five minutes."

I felt myself blush and was glad he couldn't see it. "Oh, stop. I'm wearing pajamas."

"Don't tell me what kind. I'd rather imagine it." The murmur of voices came over the line. "Looks like the meeting's about to start. I'll see you at the service tomorrow."

"See you then," I said and hung up, my face still radiating heat. Before leaving my bedroom, I poked my head out first to make sure I wouldn't be interrupting any R-rated activity. The couch was empty, the slightly flattened cushion the only evidence of its recent occupants.

I padded over to the kitchen and rummaged around for dinner, pulling a tray of macaroni and cheese from the freezer. While I watched the package of pasta rotate inside the microwave, I wondered about Carla's service. I certainly didn't expect any nude protestors there, but if Ricky and Erin showed up, I might just see someone throw a chair. No way was I missing that.

The next morning my eyes flew open at 6:00 a.m. I reminded myself that it was my day off, but my mind was already racing through my to-do list for the day. After five minutes of trying to relax, I admitted defeat and threw back the covers. A short while later I emerged from the bathroom with my hair still damp from my shower and went into the kitchen for breakfast.

I grabbed the box of Pop-Tarts out of the cupboard.

I shook the box, then turned it upside down. Empty. Ashlee must have eaten the last packet. I grabbed a box of cereal from the same shelf and dumped a pile of flakes into a bowl. I retrieved the half-gallon carton of milk from the fridge and tipped it over the cereal. Three drops fell out. Not a good start to the day.

Ashlee emerged from her room at that moment, her blond hair flat on one side and sticking straight out on the other. I was still trying to shake loose an extra drop or two of milk, and a look of guilt flashed across her face.

"I meant to go to the store last night," she said. "I'll run by this morning."

"Pick up some Pop-Tarts while you're there, would you? Get two boxes if they're on sale."

Ashlee dropped into a kitchen chair and put a hand on her head. "I have to remember to get some aspirin, too. These late nights are killing me."

I got a spoon from the silverware drawer and carried that and the bowl of cereal to the table. I sat down across from Ashlee. "Good party?"

Ashlee scowled at her fingernails. "Crap, I chipped my manicure already. Must have been from bowling."

"There was bowling at the party?" I ate a spoonful of dry cereal, dreaming of milk all the while.

"No, the party started to get rowdy, so Chip and I went to the bowling alley. That place was more packed than Chip's. We hooked up with Brittany and some guy she's been dating. I should have stayed at the party."

"Why? What happened at the bowling alley?"

Ashlee reached over and snagged the box of cereal.

"This girl Brittany knows showed up and kept crying. She totally ruined the mood."

Only Ashlee could make a trip to the bowling alley sound like a soap opera. "What was she so upset about?"

"Brittany said her aunt died. She should have stayed home if she was that bummed out, but she guilted Brittany into attending some memorial service today." Ashlee scooped out a handful of cereal and shoveled it into her mouth, crumbs and flakes falling all around her.

I pulled my bowl closer so she wouldn't drop her drool-covered cereal in it. *Dead aunt? Memorial service?* "Was this girl named Erin?"

"Yeah, that sounds right." Ashlee rose to her feet with a groan. "Guess I'll get ready for work. We've got a lizard coming in that needs its stitches removed."

"You're making that up," I said.

"Am not. Poor guy fell off the roof and got scratched by a nail. It happens more than you'd think." Ashlee disappeared into her room.

I finished my cereal, my thoughts on Ashlee's comments, not about the lizard but about Erin. So she was going to the memorial service, after all. Between that and Brittany the giggler attending, Patricia was sure to be in a foul mood. This evening might turn out to be even more interesting than I'd originally suspected.

Now I needed to figure out what dish to bring. What went with a side of drama?

Chapter 10

I owned so few cookbooks that I hesitated to even call them a collection. Every book was a hand-me-down from my mom and offered small meals with few ingredients that took less than twenty minutes to make. Perfect for a single girl in an apartment, but not so great for a Celebration of Life. An event like that called for warm, comforting casseroles and plates of gooey chocolate brownies.

After glancing through a few recipes in one of the newer cookbooks, I slammed the book shut, cleared my breakfast dishes, and grabbed my jacket. Time to call in reinforcements. I went down to my car.

Ten minutes later I pulled up in front of Mom's house. It was a one-story ranch-style house, painted light blue with white trim. Up until a few weeks ago I'd called this place home. Now I stood on the doorstep and wondered if I should knock or use my key. Before I could decide, the door swung open.

"I thought I heard a car," Mom said. She ushered me

inside and shut the door. "I'm so happy to see you. Come on in and sit for a while."

I headed toward the living room, Mom bustling along behind me. On the TV a group of women sat around a table, chatting. Mom muted the volume and smoothed down the front of her twin sweater set before taking a seat in the tattered brown corduroy recliner, which used to be my dad's favorite spot. Her salt-and-pepper hair looked freshly permed, and I noticed she was careful not to lean her head against the chair's thinly padded headrest.

"What brings you by this morning?"

I perched on the edge of the couch. "I need a super-easy casserole recipe for a party tonight. With all your cookbooks, I thought you might know of a dish like that."

"Nothing comes to mind, but I'm sure one of my books will have what you're looking for. You'll need to drag them out of the garage. Now that we're eating healthier, I packed most of them up. They all use pounds of butter and too much cheese."

I stood and rubbed my hands together. "Yum. That's exactly the kind of recipe I'm looking for."

"Why doesn't that surprise me?" Mom picked up the remote control. "The boxes are in the corner by the water heater."

I went out to the garage and eased around her sedan to reach the far corner. A tall stack of boxes waited for me. I pulled the top one toward me, fell back against Mom's car from the weight, and dumped the box on the cement floor. A girl could get a workout looking up recipes. Fortunately, when I opened the top, an array of covers featuring housewives wearing aprons smiled up at me. I closed the top, shoved my fingers under the bottom of the box, and lugged it into the house. Mom had returned to watching television but muted the volume once more when I came in.

"That was fast," she said.

"First one I opened looks promising." I dropped the box on the floor with a thump and sat down cross-legged in front of it. Before I took out the first book, I paused. "Do you have to work this morning? I can take this with me."

"No, I go in after lunch." Mom had recently gotten a part-time job at Going Back for Seconds, a women's clothing consignment store downtown. Ever since my father died, I'd worried that his pension wouldn't cover the bills. Now that Mom had gone to work, I could breathe a little easier and stop trying to sneak money into her purse.

Mom rose from the recliner and crouched down on the floor near me. She pulled a cookbook out of the box and ran her hands over the cover. "I bought this the first year your father and I were married." She glanced at the picture of Dad on the mantel and smiled wistfully. She set the book back in the box. "What kind of party is it? A potluck dinner?"

Did people still have those? "There's a Celebration of Life for that spa owner who died. Everyone's supposed to bring a dish."

"In that case, I know just the book you need." She began rummaging through the box. "You know,

Sue Ellen called me all in a tizzy yesterday about the woman who was killed."

If Blossom Valley ever had a gossip club, Sue Ellen would be president. Nothing happened in town without her knowing it. Sometimes she even gossiped about things that hadn't actually happened, which was probably why everyone was always so nice to her. No one dared get on her bad side, in case they became her next target.

"What was she upset about?" I asked. "Did she find some dirt on Carla?" As soon as I asked, I knew that couldn't be right. Uncovering other people's secrets was what made Sue Ellen happy.

"Aha." Mom pulled a book from the box and handed it to me. I read the cover: *Hearty Dishes for Any Occasion.* Perfect. "No, the opposite," Mom said. "Apparently, everyone liked Carla. No one's had a bad word to say about her."

"Sue Ellen must hate that." I paged through the book, looking for the casserole with the least amount of ingredients and prep time. "So she hasn't found out anything?"

"Nothing exciting. She's got a friend at the bank who provided Carla with her business loan. She had perfect credit and put up her own house for collateral."

While Mom talked, I ran my finger down the list of ingredients for a recipe: ground beef, cream of mushroom soup, a can of corn, and Tater Tots. This one definitely had possibilities. It even had a vegetable. I studied the instructions. "So you're saying a loan shark didn't sneak up to Blossom Valley and kill Carla when she couldn't repay a loan?"

"I'm afraid not."

I used the back flap of the cover jacket as a bookmark and held up the cookbook. "Mind if I take this one?"

"You can take them all. I don't use them anymore."

A vision of our modest-size apartment full of boxes of cookbooks I'd probably never use filled my mind. "I'll start with the one book." I began repacking the others. "What about Carla's personal life? I heard she was dating a married guy."

"Sue Ellen said something along those lines, but no one seems to agree on whether it's true."

"That she had a boyfriend or that he's married?"

"Married. But you know how people in this town love to talk."

Boy, did I ever. I thought back to when a nosy parent had spotted me with my prom date at the local make-out spot years ago. We were only talking, well, mostly talking, but by the time the story got back to Mom, I was five months pregnant and we were plotting to run away together. It had taken me an hour to calm her down.

I brought myself back to the present. "Even if he is married, maybe he's separated from his wife. I've heard some divorce proceedings last longer than the actual marriage." I put the final cookbook in the box, refolded the top, and rose to my feet. "Let me put this back." I hefted the box and carried it back to the stack in the garage.

When I returned to the living room, Mom was brushing lint off of her gray slacks. "I just remembered that I wanted to fill a prescription before work. Of course, you're welcome to stay as long as you like, but if you don't mind, I need to get going."

I picked up my jacket and the cookbook. "That's all right. I'll leave now, too. I need to stop by the store and then go home and make this casserole. After that, I think it's my turn to vacuum."

"How are you and your sister getting along? I'm guessing the new arrangement is working, since Ashlee hasn't called me even once to complain."

What did she have to complain about? I did most of the cleaning and grocery shopping. If anyone should be whining about her roommate, it was me. I clutched the cookbook tighter. "We're still working out the kinks, especially when it comes to who cleans what, but I think we'll manage." At least we'd gotten a place with two bathrooms. I couldn't imagine how much we'd argue over counter space and cleaning duties otherwise.

Mom kissed me on the cheek. "That's what I like to hear."

"Okay, well, thanks for the cookbook." I pulled my keys from my pocket and let myself out of the house. Back in the car, I tossed the cookbook on the seat and drove to Meat and Potatoes. A quick trip down the aisles netted me all the ingredients I needed, including a disposable foil casserole dish. Ashlee and I owned very few dishes, and none of them were large enough to accommodate the recipe.

Back at the apartment I stood in my kitchen, torn

between making the dish right away, in case I totally messed up and needed to try again, or daring to make it shortly before I had to leave. Surely I could wait. How hard could it be to make a casserole with a Tater Tot topping? And I could always grab a rotisserie chicken at the market if the dish was a total flop.

I decided to tackle my bathroom instead. While I had the supplies out, I went ahead and scrubbed the kitchen after that, then figured I might as well vacuum the carpet while I was in a cleaning mood. By the time I finished, the place was almost as clean as when we first moved in. The only messy spot was Ashlee's room, but that place needed a hazmat suit and one of those super vacs the car wash used.

A quick glance at the clock on the microwave showed me the afternoon was quickly disappearing. Where had my day gone?

I pulled the skillet I'd picked up at a garage sale out of the cabinet and dusted the insides off with a dish towel. Fifteen minutes later my ground beef casserole was simmering in the oven, and I was watching a game show on TV while snacking on cheese puffs. Now that was my kind of cooking.

Ashlee came home as the contestant won the top prize and collapsed onstage, in shock. "What the heck happened?" she asked as soon as she walked in the door.

"That lady won a hundred thousand dollars. I'd probably pass out, too."

She dropped her purse on the floor. "No, I mean this place. Why is it so shiny?" She sniffed the air. "Have you been cooking?"

I licked the cheese puff powder off my fingers.

"Contrary to what you might believe, I do know how to follow a recipe. And this place needed a good scrubbing."

"Thanks, sis. Guess I don't need to do the kitchen this week, after all."

I rubbed the rest of the gunk off my fingers with a napkin. "You can take over the job for me next week."

"Uh-uh, that's not what the chart says." She marched into the kitchen. I twisted around on the couch to watch as she jabbed at the calendar that was held to the fridge door with a magnet. "See? I'm on kitchen duty this week. Just because you cleaned when it was my turn doesn't mean I have to do it next week. That's when I'll be doing the rest of the apartment."

"I'll remember that when you're down with the flu and can't even move your little pinkie finger."

Ashlee shrugged one shoulder. "You're the one who insisted on this schedule, so that's what we follow. But enough about boring old chores. I need to change my clothes." She slipped off her shoes and left them in the middle of the floor before going to her room.

The kitchen timer dinged. I kicked Ashlee's shoes into the corner by the sink and removed the casserole from the oven. The Tater Tots were a toasty brown. Liquid bubbled up from underneath. The dish even smelled pretty good. I wrapped the casserole in foil and went into the bedroom to get ready.

I'd never attended a Celebration of Life before, and I wasn't sure how it differed from a funeral. Should I wear black as a sign of mourning? Or were bright colors more appropriate since we were celebrating Carla before her death? I perused the contents of my closet before settling on black slacks and a red top. Either way, I'd be half right.

By the time I'd brushed my hair and touched up my makeup, it was time to go. I used hot pads to carry the casserole to the car and place it on the floor on the passenger side, then got in on my side and started the engine.

I'd never been to Patricia's house before, but based on the street name, I assumed it was over in the newer subdivision in town. Sure enough, after cruising down Merlot Avenue and past Chardonnay Lane, I reached the turnoff for Vine Street.

I checked the street numbers until I located Patricia's address. Her house was a two-story stucco affair with a well-tended yard and two brightly painted birdhouses hanging from a pair of trees. Cars lined both sides of the street, so I drove past and parked on the next block. As I walked back to the house, several more cars slowed down near Patricia's house. For someone who no one seemed to know, Carla was certainly drawing a crowd. Maybe people liked potlucks. Or more likely, the allure of murder.

The front door was partly ajar, and I could hear voices drifting down the walk. I stepped inside and was immediately greeted by Patricia, who had been lurking off to one side of the door.

"Hello again. Dana, right?" Patricia lifted a corner of the foil covering my casserole. "Are those Tater Tots? How cute. I haven't eaten those since grade school, when my mom made me eat the cafeteria lunches." She started to walk away and waved me along. "Come on. We'll put it by my fruit salad."

Fruit salad wasn't exactly haute cuisine. Who was she to mock my Tater Tots? I followed her through clumps of people until we reached a spacious kitchen. A long wood table, already laden with bowls and platters of food, sat against the wall. Patricia took my dish and set it beside a carved-out watermelon full of star-shaped kiwi slices, peeled grapes, and plump, juicy strawberries. Where had she found such ripe strawberries this early in the season?

Patricia leaned in close. "It took me four hours to make this," she whispered, "but I wanted to create a dish worthy of Carla's memory."

I considered the fifteen minutes it had taken me to assemble my Tater Tot and hamburger mess. Well, it was the thought that counted. Right?

"It's lovely." I looked around the kitchen, at the dark hardwood floor and marble countertops. "Your home, as well."

Patricia beamed. "Thank you. I personally decorated every room in this house."

A woman came up to the table, grabbed a thick paper plate, and began loading it with everything in sight.

"You certainly have an eye for design," I told Patricia as I watched the woman try to squeeze half a dozen prawns onto her already full plate.

"I planned to be an interior decorator, but you know how it goes. Met Stan in college, when I was a student and he was a TA. I always did go for the older man. Anyway, I got pregnant my junior year, and life got in the way. I couldn't finish my degree and take care of a new family at the same time."

The woman moved away, and I grabbed a plate from the stack. I took a scoop of Patricia's fruit salad and saw her nod of approval. "Did you ever consider going back to school?" I asked.

Stan walked up to the table right then, and Patricia gave him a loving look. "I already had my hands full with the house and one child, and then the second came along. School seemed like the last thing I had time for." Patricia put her arm around Stan's thick waist. "Besides, someone has to take care of this big lug."

Stan kissed the top of his wife's head. "Another couple of months and both kids will be done with college. You should come up with a project for yourself now, honey. You have such a good head for business. It's too bad that plan with Carla didn't pan out."

Patricia pressed her lips together as her face noticeably reddened. A man at the buffet table bumped into me, then muttered, "Excuse me." I stepped to the side and grabbed a large strawberry before it could roll off my plate.

When I looked at Patricia again, her face was returning to its original color. "Don't forget I've got big plans of my own." She patted Stan's arm. "I need to check the ice." She walked toward the living room.

Stan gave me a little smile and muttered something about the other guests before moving away, leaving me to wonder about his comment.

What plan did Patricia have with Carla? Why had she gotten so upset when Stan brought it up? I'd have to try to talk to either Patricia or Stan again before I left.

I spooned up a few more items, including a helping

of my own casserole. My hand trembled as I rolled a Tater Tot around with my fork. What if it stank?

I scooped up a pile of corn kernels and hamburger and then speared the Tater Tot before raising the forkful to my mouth. I closed my eyes in anticipation. The slightly salty, soupy filling spread across my tongue. *Not bad. Not bad at all.*

After I'd finished my helping, I nibbled some noodles while I observed the dozen or so people who now stood around the kitchen. I spotted Brittany in the corner, dressed in a short black dress and four-inch heels, talking with another girl her age. A moment later Erin joined the group, wearing faded jeans and a hoodie. I wiped my mouth with a napkin, tossed my paper plate in the trash can at the end of the table, and walked over.

"No way was I letting her keep me away from Aunt Carla's memorial. Who does she think she is?" Erin was saying to Brittany and her friend.

Brittany nodded rapidly, reminding me of a bobble head. "You're totally right. She's such a witch." She giggled.

The girls watched me approach and stopped talking, as if by some secret signal. They all looked at me, waiting.

"Hi, Erin. I don't think I offered my condolences to you yesterday. I'm so sorry about Carla's passing."

Erin looked at her shoes, while Brittany and the other girl shuffled away. I guessed the talk had turned too serious for them. "Thanks. She was pretty cool."

"I've heard only wonderful things about her from everyone." No need to mention the rumors about the married boyfriend, but the thought made me glance around the room, as if he might be standing nearby this very minute. No luck. I saw only women. Even Stan hadn't returned.

"I owe her a lot," Erin said. "Without her help, I would have quit nursing school ages ago."

Her eyes kept flitting to where Brittany and the other girl huddled nearby, so I shifted a bit to block her view. "Where do you go to school?"

"Santa Rosa. I was in one of my night classes when Aunt Carla died."

So she'd been dozens of miles away when Carla was murdered. Or had she? Back in college I'd taken more than one class that contained well over a hundred students, and the professors never bothered to record attendance. Were these nursing classes held in small classrooms or large lecture halls? Would anyone remember if Erin had been there?

I saw her attention stray to her friends again. "That's quite a drive to attend class every day," I said.

She focused back on me. "Yeah, but the rent's free. School costs too much already. Thank God I have only one more semester. Who knows what'll happen now that Aunt Carla is gone." She flipped her hair back, and some strands got caught in a gold chain around her neck. As she worked to untangle her hair, she pulled the chain up and revealed a gold locket with delicate roses etched on the front.

"Beautiful necklace."

"Aunt Carla gave it to me when I moved in with her."

She unclasped the necklace, pulled the final strands out, and handed it to me.

I cracked the locket open to find a younger version of Carla staring up at me on one side and a picture of Erin when she must have been six or seven years old on the other.

"Carla remembered the pictures were in an old album, and thought I might like them," Erin said. "The locket's my favorite thing she ever gave me." Erin's eyes misted up, and she passed a hand over them. "I wish we hadn't been fighting so much the last couple of weeks."

"What were you fighting about?" I didn't expect Erin to actually answer, but she surprised me.

"My boyfriend. Aunt Carla decided she didn't like him, but she never even gave him a chance. It got so bad, I told her I'd move out if she didn't at least try to like him. He's an awesome guy, and I wasn't going to have her nagging me all day about the two of us."

Was that the threat Jessica had overheard that day, when Carla was talking on the phone to Erin? Was Erin simply choosing her boyfriend over her aunt?

"Oh, crap," Erin said from beside me.

I looked over and saw Patricia come into the kitchen. When she caught sight of Erin, she frowned, then re-arranged her face into a smile. She made a beeline for where we stood. Out of the corner of my eye, I saw Stan heading our way from the other direction, as if hoping to intercept Patricia, but he was too slow.

I tensed as I recalled the ugly scene between Patricia and Erin outside the spa last night. Was I about to witness an encore performance?

Chapter 11

"Erin, so glad you could make it," Patricia oozed, clasping her hands in front of her.

"Thank you for planning a memorial for Aunt Carla," Erin replied, a frosty edge to her tone.

"And thank you for not bringing Ricky."

"He's waiting for me outside."

Patricia managed to squeak out an "Oh" before Stan joined us. He put his arm around Erin's shoulders and gave her a squeeze. "Hiya. It's good to see you."

"You too."

There was an awkward silence. I could feel people around us watching our little group like we were stage actors putting on an impromptu performance.

"Erin was telling me about nursing school," I said.

Patricia gave Erin a concerned look. "Oh, dear, will you be able to continue school? I assume you'll be moving out of Carla's house now."

Erin stiffened. "I can take care of myself, thank you."

A young man in loose jeans and a black T-shirt appeared in the doorway. A thin patch of dark hair sprouted from his chin, making me wonder if he was trying to grow a beard. When he shifted around, I spotted an angel tattoo on his forearm and realized this was Erin's boyfriend. Judging by the look of distaste on Patricia's face, she'd spotted Ricky, too.

Erin caught the look and smiled. "I've gotta go."

"Please," Patricia said, laying a hand on Erin's arm. "Carla would be so upset to know you were throwing your life away on that boy."

Erin shoved Patricia's hand away, and Patricia jerked it back with a gasp. In a flash, Stan took the hand and clasped it between both of his.

"Ricky is amazing," Erin said. "Aunt Carla would have realized that eventually, if she hadn't been killed." She hurried past Patricia and over to Ricky. She gave him a hearty kiss on the lips and then cast a backward glance at Patricia for good measure. The two walked hand in hand out of the kitchen.

Patricia sniffed, as if Ricky had left a bad smell in the room. "She'll ruin her life. Carla was her only hope."

"She must be doing something right if she's almost finished with her degree," I said. "That takes commitment."

Patricia didn't acknowledge my comment as she continued to stare at the doorway through which Erin and Ricky had disappeared.

Stan patted the hand still trapped between his. "I think she'll be fine, honey."

She whirled on him. "How can you say that? You know what she's done. Why, she's just lucky that her mom's boyfriend didn't call the police. If her mom hadn't talked him out of it, that girl would be in jail right now."

Now, that was interesting. "For what?" I asked.

Patricia placed a hand over her mouth, but it seemed like a practiced gesture. "Oh my, I shouldn't say." She paused with dramatic flair. "Erin stabbed one of her mom's boyfriends."

"What?" I blurted. "And she wasn't arrested?"

Patricia shook her head. "Can you believe it? Her mom patched the guy up and convinced him to keep his mouth shut. That's when Erin moved in with Carla. I told Carla not to allow it—you can see how unstable Erin is—but Carla always had such a big heart."

"She sure did," Stan added. "One of her many attributes."

Erin hadn't struck me as the violent type, but then again, I barely knew her. As I considered the implications of what Patricia had said, I became aware that I was gripping a small object in my hand. I looked down to find Erin's locket dangling from my closed fist. In all the excitement, I'd forgotten to return it.

"Excuse me," I told Patricia and Stan as I pushed my way through the throng of people, who seemed intent on blocking my way. Maybe I'd luck out and Erin and Ricky were slow walkers. Maybe they were making out in front of Patricia's house just to spite the woman.

I threw open the front door to rush after them but stopped short when I almost ran into Jason on the other side.

He stepped back in surprise. "Leaving already?"

I moved past him to the walkway. "Hang on a sec. I'll be right back." But even as I spoke, I heard the rumble of an engine on the next block. I jogged out to the sidewalk in time to see Ricky's muscle car pull out and drive away, heading in the opposite direction. *Shoot.*

Jason joined me on the sidewalk. "What was that about?"

I pointed toward Ricky's car, the taillights barely visible from down the street. "You missed all the excitement."

He groaned. "Never tell a reporter that."

"It was quite the show." I swung my arms around. "Fireworks, dancing bears, guys on stilts."

Jason crossed his arms. "What really happened?"

"Patricia and Erin had another fight about Ricky. But get this. Patricia told me that the reason Erin moved out of her mom's house was that she stabbed her mom's boyfriend."

Jason dug his notebook out of his back pocket and flipped through the pages. "That never showed up in my background check."

I lowered my voice as a couple came out of the house and walked to their car. "That's because the boyfriend didn't call the cops. Erin's mom convinced him not to."

"So we have no way of knowing if this story is even true," Jason said.

"Unless you ask Erin, but she could easily deny it. I also discovered that she was in class when Carla was murdered, or at least that was her claim." I held up the necklace. "Maybe I'll work both of those topics into the conversation when I return her locket."

Jason reached out and opened it. "Why do you have her locket?"

"I was looking at it when she and Patricia started talking. She flew out of here before I could give it back. No way can I trust Patricia to return it, the way those two ended things a minute ago."

"I can take the locket back for you."

I removed the necklace from his grasp. "Right, sure you can. Then you can ask Erin all those reporter questions you're dying to know the answers to." I dropped it in my pants pocket. "She commented on how important the locket is to her. I'm the one who had it last, so I'm the one who should return it."

"Let me know if you change your mind." More people came outside, and Jason watched them. "It's not ending already, is it?"

"Not that I know of." I took his arm. "Come on. I'll go back in with you. I never had dessert."

I led him through the living room, where I noticed a blown-up photo of Carla on a side table, which I'd somehow missed the first time through, and on into the kitchen. Jason headed straight for Patricia, and I stepped over to the buffet table to let him work. While I snacked on a brownie, I watched as he infiltrated the group with an easy smile and a handshake.

Brittany wandered past the table, eyeing all the dessert platters. "I wish I wasn't on a diet," she whined.

She didn't have an extra inch to pinch as far as I could see, but maybe she was like Ashlee, who always seemed to be on one diet or another. She saw the brownie in my hand. "Bikini season is coming up, you know."

I smiled at her. "But brownie season is here now."

"Huh?" She surveyed the table again. "I guess this mini chocolate chip cookie would be okay." She nibbled the tiniest bite off one edge. "Say, you work at that spa outside of town, right? That place with all the pigs and stuff?"

"Right."

"Someone told me that a girl from your place killed Carla because our spa was so much cooler. A bunch of people saw her sneak in the back door, and then *bam!* Carla's dead."

Oh God, is that what people are saying? "No one from Esther's place killed anyone."

"That's not what I heard." Brittany giggled. I hoped she choked on that ridiculously small cookie.

While I stood fuming, I became aware of a handsome Hispanic man in his early fifties standing alone by a curio cabinet. He sipped a cup of punch, his eyes constantly shifting around the room. The only other men I'd seen so far tonight had been accompanied by a wife or girlfriend, but this guy appeared to be alone.

I nudged Brittany and nodded in his direction. "Do you know who that is?"

Brittany peered at him. "I saw him drop by the spa once or twice around closing, but Carla never told us his name. He sure is hot."

Interesting. Was this the mystery boyfriend? I'd considered Stan as a likely option, but this guy was way better looking. Definitely an eleven out of ten, like the woman at lunch had said.

I finished eating my brownie and dusted off my hands. I left Brittany hovering over the cookies and muttering, "I guess a couple more would be okay," and made my way over to the man in the corner.

He watched my approach with a small smile playing on his lips.

"Nice turnout," I said, failing to come up with a more original icebreaker.

"Yes, Carla would be pleased."

I stuck out my hand, hoping I'd gotten all the brownie crumbs off. "I'm Dana."

He brought his own hand up. "Miguel."

"Did you know Carla well?" I asked.

He gave me that indulgent smile again, and I realized he thought I was one of those gossipmongers who liked to meddle in other people's business. Actually, he wasn't too far off the mark in this case.

"Well enough." He took another sip of punch, and I looked at his ring finger as he raised the cup to his lips. Was that a faint tan line I detected or merely a shadow? "Were you and Carla friends?" he asked.

I shook my head. "No, I met her only that day . . . the day she, uh, died. Terrible what happened to her."

"Yes. I still can't believe it. But the police will catch her killer."

"I hope so." And I did, for Gretchen's sake as much as Carla's. "Any idea who would want to harm Carla?"

Miguel inspected his punch. "You'd know the scuttlebutt more than I."

I found myself slightly offended by the accusatory tone in his voice. "I'm afraid I'm out of the loop these days."

He seemed to relax with that answer. "Me too. Sorry if I offended you. I feel like everyone in the room is staring at me. Guess it's making me paranoid."

"Oh, they're staring at you, all right, but it's because you're the only guy here."

He looked around and laughed. "You're right. I hadn't noticed that."

Patricia materialized at my elbow and laid a hand on Miguel's arm. "Oh, Miguel, I was hoping you'd come tonight. How have you been dealing with everything?"

From the way she spoke, it sounded like Miguel had known Carla quite well. Looked like my assumption that he was the boyfriend was correct.

He shifted uncomfortably under Patricia's questioning gaze. "I'm coping. Thank you for asking."

"Is there anything I can do?" she asked.

"Kind of you to offer, but I'll be fine."

Patricia would not be deterred. "Still, come with me. Talk to Stan. He lost his mother last year, so I'm sure he can offer some insight into dealing with your grief."

Miguel held up a hand. "I really don't think—"

"Nonsense," Patricia said. "I insist."

Miguel turned his head so that only I could see him roll his eyes and allowed himself to be dragged away.

A moment later Jason took the place recently vacated by Miguel. The light from the curio cabinet lit up the gold highlights in his reddish-brown hair. "Who was that?"

I looked around to make sure we were fairly isolated in our corner. "I'm almost positive that's Carla's boyfriend."

"Mind waiting here a minute?" Jason asked. Without staying to hear my answer, he went in the direction Miguel and Patricia had gone.

I walked over to the buffet table and helped myself to another brownie. I hadn't even finished it before Jason returned. "That was fast," I said.

"He didn't feel like talking. Shut down like the lights when the power goes out. I'll try again another time." He grabbed a cookie off the table. "I did talk to Stan, but he wasn't much help. He mentioned working late with his assistant, Alonzo, the night Carla died, but he didn't know anything about Miguel."

So Erin was in class, and Stan was working late. I wondered who else had an alibi for that night. I glanced around the room. The crowd was thinning out. Even Brittany had disappeared, taking her giggles with her. "Get what you need for your next article?"

"Enough. Patricia gave me more personal background, such as what Carla was like growing up, how they dreamed of rooming together in college, that sort of thing. It'll make a nice personal angle for a story."

"Good for you. I think newspaper articles should center more on the victims and less on the killers."

"Unfortunately, that's not what sells copy." Jason

picked up a plate from the end of the buffet line. "What's good here?"

I pretended to survey the spread. "The Tater Tot casserole is pretty terrific."

Jason picked up the serving spoon and poked at the contents of the casserole. "Are you sure?" he asked uncertainly. He studied Patricia's watermelon basket. "That fruit bowl looks good."

I picked up a fork and speared a chunk of cantaloupe to hold up. "It's fruit. Plain, boring fruit. The casserole is a compilation of sweet and savory, with a warm, gooey filling that's perfect for such a somber event."

"You made the casserole, didn't you?" He scooped up a large mouthful and took a bite. As he chewed, he gave me an appraising look. "Between the chili dogs and this dish, you're becoming quite the cook."

I stepped closer to Jason until our toes were practically touching. "Keep sweet-talking me, and you may get dessert."

Jason glanced back at the table. "You brought dessert, too?"

"Nope, it's a special dessert. Just for you." I winked at him. "When we're alone."

Jason laughed a deep, throaty laugh. "Can't wait."

We chatted while he ate his plate of food. By the time he was finished, few people remained in the kitchen, and I didn't know any of them.

"Ready to go?" I asked.

We left the kitchen together, Jason's hand on the small of my back. As I walked, I could feel the locket in my pants pocket, a reminder that I needed to return it to Erin.

I wanted to spend more time with that girl. If she'd stab her mother's boyfriend, who was to say she wouldn't kill her aunt?

Chapter 12

My trip to see Erin and return her locket would have to wait until my lunch break. Before Jason and I could slip out the front door the previous evening, Patricia had roped us into gathering with the few remaining attendees in the living room to reminisce about Carla, not that I had much to offer. By the time we left, it had been too late to stop by Erin's place. Instead, I had gone home to bed, questions about Miguel, Erin, and Carla whirling around in my head.

Now, as I drove out to the farm the next morning, I thought about the coming workday. I'd seen Zennia in the garden recently, practically rubbing her hands in anticipation of the peppers, tomatoes, and zucchini that would soon be flourishing. Plenty of other people liked to garden, so I'd focus today's blog on growing summer vegetables.

I pulled into the mostly empty parking lot and drove past the lobby. The flock of ducks basked in the early morning sunshine, while a trio waddled across the grass. I parked in my usual corner spot and took the long way past the cabins and along the back trail, stopping to say good morning to Wilbur and his pals. They snorted in reply.

In the kitchen Zennia was removing a container of her homemade yogurt from the refrigerator. She had an apron tied around her loose pants and dashiki top, and her long braid swished back and forth as she moved.

"Morning, Zennia. Need any help?" I grabbed a tangerine slice from the fruit tray and popped it in my mouth before she could stop me. I really needed to buy some fruit to eat at the apartment. Those Pop-Tarts had only so much filling, and I wasn't even sure the goo was real fruit.

She set the container on the counter. "I think I've got it covered, but thanks." She removed the lid from the yogurt and grabbed a spoon.

I sneaked another piece of tangerine as Esther bustled into the kitchen, her red-and-white-checkered blouse reminding me of the fabric that often covered the contents of a picnic basket. Her brown slacks, the same color as a basket, only enhanced the effect.

"Oh, good. You're both here," she said when she saw Zennia and me. "Gretchen called, and she won't be coming to work."

"Is she sick?" I asked.

"Sick with worry, maybe." Esther fiddled with the hem of her shirt. "You were out yesterday, so you missed it, but she was acting strange the whole day. Forgetting appointments, mixing the wrong ingredients for the facials. One of the clients even complained Gretchen was too rough during her massage."

I swallowed the tangerine slice. "That's not like Gretchen."

"Don't I know it," Esther agreed. "Gretchen is so dedicated to her work, but this spa owner's murder has got her all worked up."

"I suggested she try meditating," Zennia said, "but I don't know if she listened to me."

I knew the questions from the police had rattled Gretchen, but I had never expected the interview to impact her work like this. Was there more to the story that I wasn't aware of?

Esther turned to me, breaking into my thoughts. "Dana, would you be a dear and call all of Gretchen's appointments for the day and reschedule?"

"Absolutely." I glanced at the rooster clock on the wall. "Any idea when her first client is due?"

"She said someone has a facial at ten."

"That gives me plenty of time to notify everyone. I'll wait a bit to call so I don't wake anyone up. Will she be back tomorrow, or should I reschedule for later in the week?"

"She seemed to think she'd be all right by the morning." Esther tugged on her shirt. "I knew you'd take care of things. Heaven knows how I'd get anything done without all of you." She smiled at Zennia and me.

I followed her out of the kitchen and turned into the office while she continued on toward the lobby. After booting up the computer, I drafted a blog about successful methods for growing tomatoes. By addressing a different vegetable each day, I'd have enough blogs for the next week or two. If those topics grew tiresome, I could move on to flowers.

By the time I finished editing and posting the blog, it was time to start calling Gretchen's clients. I left the house and passed the pool area, nodding to an older couple playing backgammon at one of the picnic tables. I walked past the row of cabins and entered the spa tent.

Gretchen's appointment book sat on the little shelf built into the hostess stand. I pulled it out and flipped it open, running my finger down the list of today's clients. Thank goodness Gretchen was organized. She'd included everyone's phone number next to their name. I picked up the cordless handset and the appointment book and carried them over to the waiting area to settle into one of the rattan chairs.

I spent the next twenty minutes leaving messages and rescheduling appointments. By the time I was finished, the muscles in my jaw were tight from the unexpected tension. Two of Gretchen's regulars had asked if she was absent from work because she'd been arrested for Carla's murder. Another had said, "Made a run for it, has she?" I had had to literally bite my tongue to keep from telling these people to take their business elsewhere. Who wanted them here at the farm with that kind of attitude?

Their thoughtless comments proved that the situation was far more serious than I'd realized. Brittany had mentioned last night that people were wondering about Gretchen's involvement in Carla's death, but I figured it was confined to her circle of gossipy, immature friends. I had never imagined others in town shared this belief.

I set the phone back in the cradle, returned the appointment book to the hostess stand, and walked out of the tent, rubbing my forehead. If people were willing to say these things to me, were other clients voicing their concerns directly to Gretchen? No wonder she'd called in sick. I would have, too.

Back at the office, Gordon sat in the desk chair, his head bent over his ever-present clipboard. I suppressed a groan and prayed he'd somehow missed all the chitchat about Gretchen over the past few days.

Just as I considered slipping out the door without speaking to him, he raised his head. "I'll be done in a minute." He returned to his clipboard and jotted down more notes.

I took a step backward toward the hall. "I can come back."

"No, all finished." He capped his pen and stood, straightening the lapels of his suit jacket. He gave me a long look. "What's this I hear about Gretchen calling in sick?"

My stomach dropped. "Well, there is that bug going around. She must have caught it from one of her clients."

He snorted, almost sounding like Wilbur. "Nonsense. She's hiding out because everyone in town thinks she killed the other spa owner."

"That's another possibility," I said.

He jammed his pen in the breast pocket of his jacket and twisted his pinkie ring. "This is bad for business. People won't book sessions at the spa if they believe our masseuse is a killer. Our profits will be severely impacted."

"Look, I rescheduled all of Gretchen's appointments, and everyone I talked to agreed to come back another day. No one canceled." Even the women who'd asked if Gretchen had been arrested couldn't possibly think she'd killed anyone. No way would they let her put her hands so close to their necks during a massage otherwise.

"Mark my words," Gordon said, "if the police don't catch the killer soon, our spa is sunk. Perhaps we should take the initiative and think about hiring another masseuse."

"What? You can't get rid of Gretchen."

"I don't want to. Gretchen has been a real asset, but I have to think of the farm." He held up his phone and touched the screen. "Look, I'd love to discuss this, but I have a meeting in town. A friend and I are setting up a business club for some of the high school students. I figure that not only will I be molding the minds of future businessmen, but it's also a good way to get the farm's name out there."

While I liked the idea, I couldn't allow myself to be distracted. "At least give Gretchen more time. She hasn't done anything wrong," I said.

"I'll think about it. That's all I can promise." He brushed past me and walked out of the office.

I watched him go. Gordon often worried unnecessarily about the state of Esther's place, but a tiny part of me, that part in the dark recesses of my mind that kept me awake at odd hours of the night, wondered if he was right this time. Would people stop coming to the spa if the police didn't catch Carla's killer?

All of a sudden, I was looking forward to my lunchtime errand. Maybe Erin knew more about her aunt's death than she was letting on. Maybe a tidbit or two would slip out while we talked, information I could pass along to the police or at least to Jason.

Then we could get this whole thing wrapped up.

And Gretchen could stop looking over her shoulder.

Chapter 13

I drove toward town, Erin's locket on the passenger seat. Jason had given me Erin's address the previous night, after only a little begging on my part. I recognized the street name and found Erin's, or rather Carla's, house in minutes. Painted white, with dark green eaves, it was a modest single-story house not unlike my mom's place. The yard sported a small lawn and three rosebushes planted close to the house.

After parking at the curb, I locked the car door and stepped onto the sidewalk. A chain-link fence surrounded the yard, but I didn't see any signs of a dog. I let myself in the gate and walked up the cement path to the front of the house. After a quick knock, I tried to peek through the diamond-shaped beveled glass set into the door while I waited for someone to answer. Behind me, birds chirped in the nearby trees, and I could hear the drone of a far-off lawn mower. After a minute I knocked again. There was no car in the driveway. Maybe she wasn't home. I was about to give up when I saw a shadowy figure approaching through the glass.

The door flew open, and Erin squinted out at me. She wore a T-shirt and shorts. Her hair was hanging loose, and her face was bare of makeup. She rubbed her upper arms in the cool air.

"I'm Dana—," I began, but she cut me off.

"Right. I remember you from last night. Come on back."

"I'm just returning . . . ," I said, trailing off when she disappeared down the hall. I hesitated before reminding myself I was on a fact-finding mission while I was here.

I went in the direction Erin had gone, noting the single nature print on the wall in the dimly lit hallway. At the end, I stepped into a large but sparsely furnished kitchen. A small wooden table sat in a breakfast nook, four chairs parked around it. The shelves of a hutch against one wall were empty, and a stack of boxes waited in the nearby corner. Jason had said that Carla bought the house about four months ago. Maybe she'd been so engrossed in opening her new spa that she hadn't taken the time to unpack. Seeing this bit of unfinished business was another reminder that Carla would never complete a project again.

Erin stood at the island, in front of the sink. I sucked in my breath when I saw the large chef's knife she held in her hand. Light from an overhead bulb bounced off the blade as she moved around, and I felt myself swallow convulsively as I thought about Erin stabbing her mother's boyfriend. What had possessed me to stop by alone after Patricia told me that story? Why hadn't I taken up Jason's offer to return the locket?

"Come over here," Erin said, gesturing for me to join her. "We can't talk with you standing all the way over by the door."

I crossed the room slowly and stepped up to the island, making sure to stay on the opposite side of the tiled countertop. That would give me precious seconds to run if things turned ugly.

Erin grabbed a large red and green mango from the hanging fruit basket and set it on the cutting board. She used the knife to cut through the mango as easily as if she were cutting through melting ice cream. I jumped as the blade made a loud thwack against the wood.

"So what are you doing here?" Erin asked as she brought the knife down again. She seemed entirely too comfortable holding that thing.

I held up the locket. "You forgot this last night. I wanted to make sure you got it back."

She stretched across the counter and snatched it out of my hand after I hurriedly uncurled my fingers so she didn't break the delicate chain. "Thanks. I didn't even notice I'd lost it."

"Well, you left in a bit of a hurry."

She began cutting up the mango with swift, powerful strokes. That poor mango didn't stand a chance. "No thanks to that busybody Patricia." She glared at me, and I felt a surge of panic in my chest. "I was nice to that lady because Aunt Carla liked her. Now that Aunt Carla is dead, don't think I'm spending another minute with Patricia."

"Why are you so angry with her?"

"She's so phony-baloney, acting like she's your best friend so she can try to run your life. And I know she talks about me behind my back."

I tried to keep a neutral expression on my face, but something must have slipped through, because Erin noticed.

"I knew it." She pointed the knife at me, and I took a half step back. "What did she say about me?"

"Nothing big. I'm sure she didn't mean anything by it," I said. "She seems to want only what's best for you."

"You saw the way she tried to boss me around. Just because she and Carla were such good friends, Patricia acts like she owes it to Carla to make sure I become this poster kid for Middle America, Ms. Upstanding Citizen herself. Well, I know what she really thinks of me, and I won't stand for it." She grabbed a papaya from the basket.

I thought back to Stan's remark about Carla and Patricia almost being partners. Maybe Erin knew about the situation and could fill me in. "It's probably a good thing she didn't go into business with Carla. Then she would have been around all the time," I said, taking a wild guess that this was the deal Stan had been alluding to.

She gave me a smug smile, proving I'd hit the mark. "Heard about that, did you? Man, was Patricia steamed when it didn't happen. It was all her idea, and Aunt Carla wanted nothing to do with it."

"Patricia made it sound like they were both in favor

of a partnership," I said. I dared to lean on the counter, like we were two girlfriends sharing a little gossip.

Erin paused in her slicing. "That's what Patricia wants to believe, but it's not true. She gave Aunt Carla some decorating tips for the spa and somehow got it in her head that she needed to help run the place. She doesn't have a business degree. She has no experience. She's just some bored housewife with nothing better to do."

"How did Carla get out of it?"

"Gave her some line about not wanting to risk all of Patricia's money on a new business. Told Patricia that if the place went under, she'd never be able to forgive herself."

While the answer sounded legitimate, it was still a pretty weak reason to turn down her best friend. I wondered if Patricia had recognized the excuse as the brush-off that it was. Had she gotten mad enough to kill Carla?

"How did Patricia take the news?"

"Pretended like everything was fine, but she was always making little comments under her breath like she wanted to run the show. And now she's set her sights on me. Well, she can forget it." Erin brought the knife down in a series of quick strokes until the papaya collapsed into a pile of mush, her breath coming out in short puffs. "Say, what are you asking for, anyway?" she demanded, eyeing me. "You spying for Patricia?"

Definitely my signal to leave.

"No, of course not. Stan talked about a possible deal last night, and Patricia seemed upset about it. I was only wondering." I made a show of looking at my wrist, even though I wasn't wearing a watch. "I should be getting back to work. My lunch break's almost over." I backed toward the door. "Maybe I'll see you around sometime."

"If I even stay in this stupid town." Erin rammed the knife tip into the cutting board, leaving the blade quivering upright, like an exclamation point to her statement. "You can pass that along to Patricia."

I didn't respond as I hastened down the hall to the front door before she could pull the knife back out and hurl it at me. Once outside, I hurried down the walk but stopped at the gate when I saw a familiar muscle car parked across the street. Erin's boyfriend, Ricky, sat behind the wheel. I winced at the ugly dent that marred the back panel of the driver's side. As clean and waxed as he kept that car, that dent had to irritate him every time he looked at it. I didn't remember the dent being there before, but then again, I wasn't positive that I'd seen the driver's side on previous occasions. Who knew how long it had been there?

As I opened the gate, Ricky climbed out of the car and walked across the street, his expression hard to read with his plastic-framed sunglasses covering his eyes. I tensed as I felt him studying me. He wasn't a big guy, but sometimes the little ones were scrappy. I could only hope he was more even-tempered than Erin.

"You a friend of Erin's?" he asked as he reached the gate.

"More like an acquaintance. I knew her aunt." *Barely,* I added silently.

He removed his sunglasses. "Rough stuff. Carla was a nice lady."

My nose twitched as I caught a whiff of cigarette smoke. "Did you know her well?"

"No, but she took good care of Erin."

"That's what I heard."

He hooked the sunglasses onto his T-shirt. "'Course, I was hoping we could be friends. I felt bad about the way things ended between us." I'd swear he sounded hurt. Had Carla's approval meant that much to him? He cleared his throat and jerked his head toward the door. "I should get up there."

He stepped to the side so that I could move past him. As I unlocked my car door, I glanced back at the house and saw Erin open the door. When she saw Ricky, she threw her arms around him, and I felt a tug at my heart at her obvious adoration. Smiling in spite of myself, I got in my car and pulled away.

My smile drooped as I headed to the nearest fast-food restaurant with a drive-through. Erin obviously cared about Ricky, but at what cost? Had Carla insisted that Erin stop seeing Ricky, and had Erin killed her aunt rather than give up her true love, or had I been watching too many made-for-TV movies? I'd heard of cases in the news where a teenager killed her parents over a boyfriend, but Erin was a grown woman and Carla was her aunt, not her mom.

And what about Patricia's assertion that Erin had stabbed her mom's boyfriend? I'd learned nothing about that, other than Erin was handy with a knife. Had Carla been using that knowledge as leverage against Erin?

On the flip side, Erin had exposed a possible motive for Patricia. If she'd set her sights on owning half the spa or at least helping to manage it, she might have re-acted badly when Carla turned her down. Erin had mentioned she was a control freak. Maybe she'd snapped.

And what of Ricky? Erin was clearly smitten, but Carla and Patricia both seemed to think he was nothing but trouble. I hadn't gotten that vibe, but I'd spoken to him for only a few minutes.

I felt a headache coming on, no doubt from all this convoluted thinking. Nothing a chocolate milk shake couldn't cure. I added one to my cheeseburger order, retrieved my lunch at the take-out window, and headed for the highway.

Back at Esther's place, I pulled into my parking spot. The day had warmed considerably, and I decided to eat at one of the picnic tables, provided the guests weren't already dining there. I grabbed my bag and followed the path that wound by the vegetable garden. I was about to turn past the cabins when movement over by the spa tent caught my attention.

I watched Gretchen enter the tent and frowned. Wasn't she supposed to be sick? Why was she here, skulking around the farm? For one wild moment, I thought she might be robbing the place, cracking under the pressure from the police, but I immediately admonished myself. Entering the place where you worked could hardly be considered skulking. Gretchen was an employee at the farm and could come and go as she pleased. She'd probably recovered from whatever illness had kept her home this morning, and decided to come in.

While I stood there, waiting to see if Gretchen would emerge, I sucked on my straw and noticed the shake was already beginning to soften, even in this mild spring weather. I took one last drag on the straw and walked toward the spa tent, pausing at the doorway.

Gretchen was slouched in the same rattan chair I'd occupied that morning, when I'd called to shuffle her appointments around. Her legs were stretched out in front of her; one arm was draped over her eyes.

I coughed to announce my presence, and she lowered her arm, squinting against the light. *Hmm . . . pale skin, sensitivity to light.* I'd seen Ashlee with these exact symptoms last week, when she'd come home from an all-night party. Perhaps Gretchen's mystery illness was a hangover.

"Feeling better?" I asked in a hushed tone, in case she *had* tied one on last night.

"Not really," she said. She pushed against the armrests to raise herself in the chair. The wood creaked in protest. "But all I was doing at home was staring at the wall, feeling sorry for myself. I thought if I came here, I'd at least get some work done."

I sat down in the other chair and set my lunch on the small table in between. "I'm afraid I canceled all your afternoon appointments. Esther didn't think you'd be back today."

"That's okay. I'm not ready to face any clients yet." She rubbed at her eyes. "I need to make sure we have enough supplies, put in some orders, and give the massage tables a good cleaning."

Cleaning seemed to be an activity a lot of people did when they were upset, myself included. After my father passed away, my apartment down in the Bay Area had never been so clean. I'd spent hours scrubbing every square inch, as if I could wipe away my grief, or at least forget about it for a little while.

Gretchen groaned, dragging me from my memories. "What am I going to do? I'm in such a mess."

She sounded even more morose than the last time we'd talked. Between the rumors from the townspeople and the questions from the police, I didn't know how much more she could handle.

I leaned forward and laid my forearms on my thighs, my hands dangling between my knees. "Look, keep your head up. As soon as the police find the killer, people will stop gossiping about you. Try not to let the rumors get to you so much. These people don't know you like I do."

Gretchen sat up even straighter, her brow wrinkled in confusion. "People are talking about me? What are they saying?"

Now it was my turn to be perplexed. "Isn't that what you're upset about?"

"No, I'm worried about getting in trouble with the police."

I let out an exasperated sigh. "Gretchen, we've been over this. The police are not focusing solely on you. They have other suspects."

Gretchen shook her head. "But you don't know what I've done."

That stopped me. What was she confessing to? I almost didn't want her to continue, afraid of what she might admit to. "What did you do?" I finally asked.

She pressed a hand to her temple. "I can't say."

I threw myself back against the chair, trying to hide my annoyance. "Look, Gretchen, I want to help, but I can't if you don't tell me what's going on. Nothing you've done can possibly be as bad as you think." At least I hoped not.

"But it is." She rubbed her forehead and then let her hand drop. "I lied to the police. If they find out, I know they'll arrest me." She reached out for me. "Oh, Dana, what's going to happen?"

I could only stare at her. Did the local jail allow visitors? I might need to find out.

Chapter 14

Gretchen slapped a hand over her mouth and grimaced, like she was trying not to throw up, but I was too worried about her admission to pay attention to any stomach troubles.

"Gretchen, what did you lie to the police about?" I asked.

She squeezed her eyes shut. "What happened at the Pampered Life the night of the murder."

"Did Carla catch you snooping in the spa, after all?"

Her eyes flew open. "No, I swear, she never saw me there."

I wanted to believe her, but she'd already lied once. My face burned as I thought about how I'd defended her reputation against those gossipers. She might have been playing me for a fool the whole time. "So what happened?"

"I told you. I checked the back door to see if it was locked." Gretchen paused. "But instead of walking away, I went inside."

A chill ran through me. Gretchen had been at the murder scene. "What did you see?"

"Nothing," she insisted. "No one was in the hallway, but I did hear voices. It sounded like they were arguing."

"Who're *they*?"

"I don't know, but I think it was a man and a woman."

Had Miguel visited Carla that night? Had Gretchen almost overheard Carla's murder? She might have been in danger and not even realized it. "Did you hear what they were saying?"

"Only a little. The woman kept telling the guy not to worry, but he kept repeating that everyone would know."

"Know what?" Maybe Miguel was worried that people would find out he and Carla were dating. But then, why had he been at her Celebration of Life if he didn't want people to know about their relationship?

Gretchen plucked at the chair cushion. "I didn't hear the rest. I panicked that they'd catch me in the spa, so I took off. I don't know what possessed me to go inside in the first place."

I felt frustration well up. "Why on earth didn't you tell this to the police? They need to find whomever Carla was talking to. If he didn't kill her, he might have seen something that would help them figure out who did."

"They could arrest me for trespassing if I told them I went inside the building. Gordon would fire me the minute he heard. No one else in this town would hire me if I got sent to prison."

I snatched my milk shake off the side table and

sucked down a large gulp, trying to quell my anger. I slapped the cup back down. "People don't go to prison for trespassing, Gretchen. Besides, you're missing the bigger picture. If the police can find the man you overheard talking to Carla, then the detective can verify that she was still alive when you were there."

At this, Gretchen looked up.

"Don't you see?" I said. "You'll be in the clear. Everyone will know you couldn't have killed Carla. You've got to tell the police." And if she didn't, I would.

Hope lit up Gretchen's face. "I never thought of it that way."

"Talking to the cops is your best choice. Look, I don't know what they'll do when they find out you lied to them, but it'll be easier to come clean now than to let the cops find out later on their own. I can give you Detective Palmer's number. I'm sure I have one of his business cards in my purse."

"Wait, I might have one." Gretchen rose with renewed energy and dug around the shelf of the hostess stand until she pulled out a card. "He left it with me last time we talked." She studied the small white rectangle. "I'll give him a call. I hope he isn't too mad."

I rose and gave her a hug. "You'll feel so much better once you get this off your chest."

Gretchen picked up the handset. "I'll call right now, before I chicken out."

"Good idea. I'll leave you to it." I grabbed my lunch bag and milk shake and left the tent, my mind already processing Gretchen's new information. Who was the mystery man talking to Carla? Brittany had told Ashlee that Carla was alone when she left work that night, so when did the guy show up? If Miguel was her boyfriend, it made perfect sense that he might slip in the back door to say hello. But what happened after that? What exactly had they been arguing about, and why would he kill Carla?

Or maybe Miguel wasn't the man Gretchen had overheard. Maybe Ricky had stopped by unannounced and had tried to convince Carla that he was a good enough guy to date Erin. Had Carla insulted him, and had he lashed out by killing her?

Then again, maybe the argument Gretchen had overheard had nothing to do with Carla's death. Maybe the guy had left, and the real killer had shown up right after that. Either way, identifying the mystery man could give the police vital information.

Still mulling over the possibilities, I entered the farmhouse through the French doors, cut through the dining room, and went straight into the office, shutting the door behind me. By now, I was famished, but before I scarfed down my cheeseburger, I sent a quick text to Jason to tell him I'd learned new details about Carla's murder. We exchanged a few texts before he asked me to dinner. I readily agreed, relieved that I wouldn't have to stop by the grocery store after work.

My dinner plans settled, I pulled my cheeseburger from the bag and ate, grimacing with each bite. Cold cheeseburgers were not nearly as tasty as hot cheeseburgers. At least the milk shake was still yummy, even if the consistency was more akin to chocolate milk at this point.

I finished my meal, such as it was, and turned to the computer. After spending the afternoon polishing a newspaper ad, helping Esther with the laundry, and cleaning the pool, I was ready to call it quits. I washed my hands at the kitchen sink and listened to Zennia and Esther, who sat at the kitchen table, discussing the menu for the rest of the week.

"I still say a nice, juicy rib-eye steak would hit the spot," said Esther. "And a baked potato smothered with butter and sour cream, like Arthur used to love when he was alive."

I glanced over my shoulder at Zennia. She looked three shades paler than normal. "Think of the saturated fat," she whispered.

"How about chicken?" I asked as I turned off the faucet. "That's healthier. But don't tell Berta I'm the one who suggested it. I swear that chicken already hates me."

Esther smacked her lips. "Chicken's good. Zennia, do you know how to make sausage gravy?"

Zennia shuddered at the question. I finished drying my hands and said good-bye to them both, ready to head home.

At the apartment I picked up Ashlee's shoes and sweatshirt from the floor and tossed them in her room, loaded the dirty dishes into the dishwasher, and went to my room to get ready for dinner with Jason. After taking a quick shower and blow-drying my hair, I donned a long, flowy top, black leggings, and short black boots, then applied a swipe of mascara and a dab of lip gloss. Ashlee hadn't come home from work yet, and I was thankful for the quiet as I got ready.

At six sharp the doorbell rang. Jason stood on the other side of the door, looking handsome in crisp jeans and a dress shirt.

He eyed me appreciatively. "Seeing you is definitely the best way to end the day." He kissed me firmly on the lips, sending a jolt of pleasure through me.

I gathered my jacket and purse, and he held the door while I walked out of the apartment.

After the quick drive downtown, we dined at the Breaking Bread Diner, where I ordered the fish and chips, and he ordered a tri-tip sandwich. While we ate, I filled him in on everything I'd learned that day. When we left the restaurant, the sky was still light but the air was cool.

"How about a walk?" Jason asked.

I patted my stomach. "Sounds good to me. I need to burn off some calories after that meal."

Jason wrapped an arm around me and pulled me close. "If it's calories you want to burn, there are better ways than walking."

"Aren't you full of ideas." I laid my hands on his chest and kissed him. We broke apart when a couple walked past on their way into the restaurant. "Let's stick with the walk for now."

We strolled down the sidewalk, arm in arm. When we stopped at the corner to wait for a car to drive by, I poked him in the belly. "Hey, I just realized that while I told you all sorts of tidbits about Carla's murder at dinner, you haven't said a single word about what you've uncovered."

"What would you like to know?"

"Everything."

He gave my waist a squeeze. "How about I skip over all the boring minutiae and tell you only what matters?"

"Even better. Let's hear it."

We walked down the block and stopped outside Going Back for Seconds, the consignment shop where Mom worked. The shop was closed for the night, and we took a seat on the bench in front of the store.

"Let's see," Jason said. "Did I mention the official cause of death was asphyxiation?"

I shivered, imagining Carla's final moments as she gasped for air but could suck in only thick, viscous mud. "What a horrible way to die."

"No kidding, although apparently the blow to her head probably knocked her unconscious first. With any luck, she didn't suffer."

"I hope not. Any idea what the killer used to hit her?"

A car sped past, most likely someone on their way home from work. The world didn't stop because someone was murdered, but it would be nice if it slowed down for a minute.

"Nothing positive," Jason said. "One of the employees remembers a statue on a shelf in Carla's office. From the description, it sounds like a Chinese foo dog. But she's the only one who remembers it, and she saw it only one time. Employees weren't generally allowed in the office."

"Would Erin know? She must have been in Carla's office before."

"She doesn't remember a statue being there at all, so she was no help."

Or else she was playing dumb because she was the one who hit Carla and then removed the evidence. "If Gretchen overheard Carla arguing with a guy in her office, how did she wind up in the mud room?" I asked.

"Is she sure the two people were standing in the office when she overheard them?"

I replayed our conversation in my head. "Now that you mention it, she never said one way or the other. I assumed that's where they were since Brittany saw Carla in her office when she left for the night. But Gretchen stepped only into the hall when she stopped by later. She never even saw the people."

"I'm sure the police will be able to determine where Carla was during the argument. Providing Gretchen called them, like she told you she would."

Gretchen had better have called Detective Palmer. I didn't like being lied to, and the police would take an even dimmer view. The longer she waited, the worse off she'd be. "Have you learned anything more about Miguel?"

"Not much. I discovered his last name is Ruiz and he works in public relations for the public works department. I left him a voice mail about a possible interview, but he hasn't called back. I'll try again."

While we'd been talking, the evening sky had grown dark. I watched as streetlights up and down Main Street came on one by one. As if by mutual consent, Jason and I rose when the lamp closest to us popped to life.

"We didn't burn off much of that dinner sitting on the bench," I said. I surreptitiously tugged at my waistband, which was much tighter than before dinner. Maybe Brittany was right, and I should be concentrating on bikini season. Naw, I'd worry about it when I had to buy bigger pants.

Jason gave me a devilish grin. "I told you my way is a lot more effective."

"You have a one-track mind," I said. "Let's keep walking. It's still early. But let's cross the street. I'd rather not walk past Carla's place right now."

We crossed to the other side and headed back up the street, glancing in the store windows. A miniature wooden plow and a collection of Raggedy Ann dolls filled the display window of the antique store. A single customer stood at the counter of the Get the Scoop ice cream parlor.

As we passed the empty storefront for what was once a short-lived wine bar, I looked in the window, surprised to see a light on in the back. The place had closed down several months ago, and I hadn't heard about any plans to open a new business in the spot.

I stopped walking and gestured toward the store. "Why's that light on?" I dropped my voice to a whisper. "Do you think someone's broken in?"

"They wouldn't turn the light on," Jason said, not bothering to lower his voice. "They'd use a flashlight. Plus, I don't think there's anything left to steal."

He had a point. I'd looked in the window a while

back, and the previous owners had cleaned out the place, not leaving so much as a spare nail. "Think we should call the police, anyway?"

Jason shook his head. He didn't seem nearly as concerned as I was. "Maybe the light was always on, and we never noticed before. Maybe someone is thinking of renting the place."

That was possible, but the light gave me an uneasy feeling. Was someone back there, and if so, why would they break in? Was this the same person who'd snuck in the back door of Carla's spa and killed her? No, that was absurd. Blossom Valley didn't have some random killer on the loose, going around and trying the back doors of all the businesses, especially considering this store was out of business.

I jiggled the handle of the glass door. It turned in response. I guessed there was no reason to lock the door, with nothing to steal. "We should still check it out, don't you think? Make sure things are okay."

Jason shrugged. "If it'll make you happy."

I pushed the door inward, and Jason followed me inside, the rustling of our clothing sounding much too loud in the silent room. The glow from the nearby streetlamp and the light in the back room showed me that the room was completely bare. I stepped toward the back but froze when I heard voices.

Jason bumped into me from behind. "What?" he asked at regular volume.

"Shh! I heard people talking."

I listened. I didn't hear any more voices, but now I heard footsteps. They were coming this way. I tensed and leaned into Jason as I waited to see who came around the corner. Jason placed a hand on my shoulder, but his grip was far too relaxed.

Why wasn't he more worried? Who was in here with us?

What if it was the killer?

Chapter 15

As the footsteps got closer, I thought about making a run for it.

Jason moved up beside me. "Are you all right?"

I started to shush him again, but just then, Stan and Patricia came around the corner from the back. I laughed in relief when I saw them.

Patricia swatted Stan's chest with the back of her hand. "See, Stan? I told you someone was out here."

"You're always right, dear." Stan squinted at us in the dim lighting. He pointed at me. "Dana, right?" He shifted his finger to Jason. "You're the reporter. Jason, is it?"

"Right," Jason said. "We were walking by and saw the light on in the back. We wanted to make sure everything was all right."

I liked the way he said that. He made us sound like Good Samaritans, not the nosey parkers with crazy imaginations that we really were. Well, I was, at least.

"Everything's great," Patricia said. "I've decided to

open a craft store here. We were discussing the amount of space and the layout."

"Congratulations," I said. "How exciting."

"New businesses are a big deal around here. I could run an article in the *Herald,* if you're interested," Jason said.

Patricia clapped her hands together. "I'd love that. I want the whole world to know."

"It'll be a huge success," Stan said. "If anyone knows their way around hot glue guns and scrapbooks, it's my Patricia." He gave a hearty laugh, and I noticed how much younger it made him appear. He must have been quite the looker back when he wooed Patricia.

"This place will be a crafter's dream, with drawers of beads and sequins and top-quality card stock, not to mention all the workshops I'm planning to teach. I know what I'm doing," Patricia said. "To think Carla didn't want to be my business partner."

Was that it? Had Carla's refusal to allow Patricia into the spa business spurred her on to open this place? Maybe she couldn't let the rejection go and decided she could do a better job alone.

"Yes, well, now that we know you're not a burglar, we'll be on our way," I said.

"Have a nice evening," Jason added.

"Be sure to stop by for the grand opening in a month or two," Stan called after us as we stepped out onto the sidewalk. I pulled my jacket tighter against the rapidly cooling night air, and we walked back up the street, toward the Breaking Bread Diner and Jason's car.

"Do you think Patricia decided to open her own store before or after Carla's death?" I asked.

"Hard to say," Jason said. "Maybe she'd been toying with the idea once her offer to Carla fell through, and Carla's murder made her realize she shouldn't wait. Unexpected death has a way of making people take a closer look at their lives."

"Or maybe she held out hope that Carla's business would struggle, and Carla would beg Patricia to invest, after all," I said. "Once Carla was gone, that plan disappeared with her, but the motivation to open her own business stayed." Another thought struck me. "You don't suppose Patricia was so bitter about Carla not wanting to be partners that she killed her and opened this place as a kind of after-the-fact, in-your-face retaliation, do you?"

Jason stuffed his hands in his jacket pockets. "If it was revenge she wanted, it'd make more sense to open the store right away so she could make sure her business was more successful than Carla's."

"True."

We reached his car, and Jason held open the door for me. I slid into the passenger seat and waited for him to shut the door and walk around to his side. "How long does it take to open a new business, anyway?" I asked as I clicked my seat belt into place. "Maybe you're right that Patricia planned all this a while ago, but Carla was killed before Patricia could bring the idea to fruition."

"Odd that she didn't tell us about the craft store before now." Jason turned the key in the ignition, and the engine purred to life. "Did she say anything to you?"

"At the Celebration of Life, she made reference to big plans. This must be what she meant." I leaned my head against the leather seat and closed my eyes. Thinking about murder all the time was exhausting.

We rode to my apartment in silence. When we got there, Jason walked me to the door.

"Interesting night," I said as I dug out my keys.

"Every night with you is interesting."

"That must be why you hang out with me."

I turned to face him, and his eyes traveled up and down my body. "That's one reason."

He leaned in, and we locked lips. My whole body sizzled.

When we broke apart, Jason brushed my bottom lip with his thumb, his gaze lingering on my face. "I'll call you tomorrow," he said, his voice husky.

I smiled. "If you don't, I will."

He headed down the stairs to his car, and I went inside the apartment. Ashlee was sitting in her usual spot on the couch, watching TV. She looked up when I entered.

"Hi, Carol Brady. How was your date night with Mike?"

"Carol Brady, huh?" I hung my jacket on the back of a chair.

Ashlee chuckled. "You two are such fuddy-duddies. I know you're gonna get married someday and have a bazillion kids like on *The Brady Bunch*. Live in some nice house out there in suburbia. It's only a matter of time. So now I'm calling you guys Mike and Carol."

I looked at the shoes and socks that littered the floor

in front of the television. "Guess that makes you Alice. Why don't you clean something?"

"Nice try. I'll clean when I'm ready."

"I'll be living in suburbia with all those kids before that ever happens."

Ashlee stuck her tongue out at me. She was immature enough to be one of my imaginary kids right now. I sat down on the couch next to her, ignoring the TV and thinking about what I'd learned today.

"Hey, do you know Erin's boyfriend at all?" I asked. If Miguel wasn't the one arguing with Carla the night she was killed, Ricky was the next most likely choice. Maybe Ashlee could give me some insight into what kind of guy he was.

"I don't even know Erin, let alone her boyfriend."

"Oh." There went that idea.

"Brittany talked about him once. Said he stopped by the spa for Erin, and Carla had a fit. But Brittany says he's an okay guy. She heard his mom's sick and he works as a mechanic to help support her. She's got MS or some disease like that."

My image of Ricky was only getting murkier. Was he a bad-news thug or a teddy-bear sweetheart? "Why did Carla dislike him so much?"

"I don't know. I didn't know Carla, either." Ashlee studied her fingernails. "His friends are kind of shady, so maybe Carla lumped him in with them. Or it could be that wicked car he drives. You know how old people hate those things."

Carla was only in her forties at the time of her death, and not exactly a Social Security candidate, but Ashlee might be right about the car. It wasn't the type of vehicle a respectable, career-minded man typically drove.

I pushed myself off the couch. "I'm spent. See you tomorrow." I went into my bedroom, changed into my pajamas, and replied to a good-night text from Jason. I barely managed to crawl into bed before I fell asleep.

The next morning I headed into the kitchen for breakfast. An empty space in the cabinet showed where the new box of Pop-Tarts should have been. I grabbed the cereal box and sighed as I shook the box and listened to the few flakes bounce around the bottom. I guessed Ashlee hadn't made it to the store yet. Now I had no Pop-Tarts and no cereal. Grumbling under my breath, I searched the refrigerator but came up with only an alarmingly stiff piece of pizza and two wrinkled lemons with bluish-green spots on them.

I thought about waking up Ashlee to tell her how irritated I was, but instead decided to turn rotting lemons into lemonade and treat myself to breakfast. I grabbed my keys and purse and drove to the part of town with the fast-food restaurants and gas stations that the tourists stopped at on their way to the Mendocino coast. With little traffic on the road, I slowed down and cruised past the restaurants. I'd eaten on this strip so many times over the past month that I knew all the menus by heart, but I was hoping I'd feel a pull toward one or the other. I passed McDonald's and shook my head. I'd eaten there three times last week.

As I made my way down the street, I observed a guy

in a dark blue sedan going the other way. If I wasn't mistaken, it was Miguel, Carla's boyfriend. I watched in my rearview mirror as he pulled into the McDonald's parking lot. Well, one more meal under the golden arches wouldn't hurt. Maybe I'd get lucky and discover a little gossip to accompany my hash browns.

I slammed my foot on the gas and cranked the wheel to flip a U-turn, flinching as a delivery truck bore down on me. I offered a hurried wave, swooped into the parking lot, and screeched to a stop in the slot next to Miguel's car. He'd already gone inside the restaurant, and I hurried after him.

Miguel stood in line at the counter in dark gray slacks and a white dress shirt. I got in line behind him and stared at the back of his head, silently willing him to turn around. When that didn't work, I said, "Hi."

This time, he turned and flashed me a smile that almost made me swoon. Of course, Jason would look this fantastic when he hit fifty, too. I was sure of it.

"Well, hello again," he said.

"Funny running into you so soon," I said. Never mind that I'd cut through traffic and clipped the curb to make it happen.

"I don't normally eat at places like this, but I'm in a hurry this morning, and I work right down the street." He laid a hand on his flat stomach. "I hate to miss breakfast. Gotta fuel the old body at my age. I'm a runner." Then he cringed. "Though my leg's been acting up lately."

Seeing an opening, I stepped right in. "You should stop

by the O'Connell Organic Farm and Spa. Our masseuse, Gretchen, sometimes treats athletes for muscle problems."

"Thanks. I might do that."

There was a pause. I spoke before I lost my nerve. "I'm sure your wife appreciates you keeping in shape."

Miguel gave me a funny look. "Wife? I'm not married." As he said this, he slipped his left hand into his pants pocket.

I feigned confusion. "I'd swear someone told me you were married. Guess I heard wrong."

The line moved forward, but Miguel stayed where he was. "I thought you knew I was dating Carla. Why would you think I was married?"

I felt my cheeks heat up. "Some guys don't let marriage stop them from dating." Yikes. Had I actually just said that?

"I'm not one of those guys," he snapped. He turned his back on me and stepped up to place his order.

He'd sounded so insulted that I had to wonder if all those rumors were wrong. Even Sue Ellen had gotten conflicting reports on Miguel's marital status. But why had he hidden his hand when I commented on his wife? And if Miguel wasn't married, did he have another motive for murdering Carla?

The cashier next to Miguel's opened up, and I moved over to order a biscuit sandwich, hash browns, and coffee. By the time I had paid for my meal and had gone to wait by the pickup area, Miguel already had his food and was heading out the door. He didn't wave good-bye, not that I expected him to.

My order came up right then, and I grabbed my take-out bag and coffee and returned to the parking lot in time to see him pull out of the lot. I settled into my car and sipped my coffee while I thought about Miguel. If he didn't have a jealous wife causing problems, I couldn't imagine another reason for Miguel to kill Carla.

What dark secret could he be harboring that would result in murder?

And if such a secret existed, how could I find out?

Chapter 16

Stowing questions about Miguel in the back of my mind, I pulled into traffic and drove to the farm. Half a dozen cars sat in the parking lot. A man and a woman were loading a suitcase into the trunk of their compact.

I took the back path and entered the farmhouse through the kitchen door. Zennia stood near the stove, cracking eggs into a bowl. A large plate of bacon strips lay on the counter.

Even though I was already holding breakfast in my paper take-out bag, my mouth instantly watered at the sight. "Zennia, I didn't know you ever fried up bacon." I set the bag and coffee cup on the oak table and hurried over to the counter.

"It's not real bacon," she said. "It's facon."

My hand froze over the glistening strips. I glanced at Zennia and saw the hint of a smile. "Facon?"

"Right. It's made from textured vegetable protein. You crisp it up, and it tastes exactly like real bacon."

Somehow I doubted that. I let my hand fall to my side. "I should eat my own breakfast. Don't want to waste money." With a last look at the faux pork product, I sat down at the table and pulled my egg-and-sausage biscuit sandwich out of the bag.

Zennia took a whisk from a drawer and started beating the eggs. She nodded toward the sandwich I was unwrapping. "My bacon isn't any faker than the food in that sandwich. For heaven's sake, the scrambled eggs are folded into a square."

"The eggs come from very uptight hens." I took a bite, savoring the salty sausage flavor. Way better than facon. "Have you seen Gretchen this morning?"

Zennia leaned the whisk handle against the inside of the bowl and used two hands to set a large cast-iron skillet on a burner. "Not yet. I don't know if she called Esther, either, although I'm sure Esther would have mentioned it when I saw her a minute ago if Gretchen wasn't coming in."

"Well, she showed up yesterday afternoon to track inventory and clean up, so I imagine she'll be here."

"I didn't realize she'd even stopped by." Zennia turned the dial on the stove. Blue flames popped into view under the skillet. "With the spa so far from the kitchen, I don't see her every day."

I'd have to stop by after breakfast and see if Gretchen had followed through on her promise to talk to Detective Palmer. I hated to be the one to report how she lied about entering Carla's spa that night, but the police needed to know about the man she'd overheard Carla arguing with.

Zennia turned to me, her face tense. "Has Jason said anything to you about whether the police have any new suspects? I'm worried about Gretchen. She's taking these visits from that detective very hard."

"It would stress anyone out. Jason didn't mention a new suspect, but he doesn't always tell me the inside scoop."

"What good is having a reporter boyfriend if he won't share with you?"

I waggled my eyebrows at her. "He has plenty of other qualities to make up for it."

"Like those dimples." Zennia gave me a wicked grin. "And that cute butt."

My mouth dropped open. "Zennia!"

Zennia swatted me with a dish towel. "Don't tell me you've never noticed."

I felt my cheeks flame hotter than the stove burner. "Well, sure, but he's my boyfriend."

"That doesn't mean the rest of us can't look. We just have to make sure we don't touch."

I took a sip of coffee to keep from laughing. "I appreciate that. Speaking of boyfriends, I did run into Carla's boyfriend this morning, when I stopped for breakfast."

"Did Carla have a boyfriend? I don't know anything about her."

"Yes, and I've heard rumors that he's married. He might have killed Carla to keep his wife from discovering the affair. Of course, Miguel swears he's single."

Zennia turned toward the stove. I heard the eggs sizzle as they hit the hot pan. "He wouldn't be the first guy to try to cover up an affair," she called over her shoulder. "I can name countless politicians who refuted everything right up until there was no room left to maneuver. Even then, they still tried to lie."

"It's just that he seemed so hurt when I suggested it." I pulled out my hash brown patty, crumpled up my sandwich wrapper, and stuffed it in the bag. "Then again, he instantly tucked his hand in his pocket when I asked about a wife, like he didn't want me to see a wedding ring."

"Sounds guilty to me." Zennia grabbed a spatula from a drawer and shoved the eggs around the skillet.

"I have to admit, he does remind me of a politician," I said. "He can be quite the charmer. Of course, it doesn't hurt that he's easy on the eyes."

Zennia hefted up the skillet and dumped the eggs onto a large white platter. "What's Miguel's last name?"

I closed my eyes to concentrate. What had Jason said? "Ruiz, I think. He works for the public works department."

"Oh, I know him."

My eyes popped open. "You do?"

"Well, rather, I knew him. He attended a meeting that I protested at a few years ago over an increase in water rates. Water is a necessity of life, for both plants and animals, including us humans. They were proposing a thirty percent rate hike. This town has a lot of low-income seniors who couldn't afford that." Zennia looked like she was winding up to embark on quite the rant. I hurried to get her back on track.

"What do you remember about him? Any chance he brought his wife to the meeting, and she had bright green hair and was covered in tattoos?" At this point, I was looking for any concrete proof that Miguel was married, no matter how outlandish.

Zennia laughed, the water rates forgotten. "I'm sure that would ring a bell, but even now I'd almost swear he had a wife. One of my friends was complaining that all the good ones were taken." She tapped her chin. "Come to think of it, she'd even attended their wedding. I remember she refused to come to the meeting, because she felt the situation would be too awkward if she protested against a friend." She nodded. "Yes, that was it."

The loser.

Miguel was married, after all.

He could deny it all he wanted, but now I knew he had the perfect reason to kill Carla. Where was he the night Carla was murdered?

Esther bustled into the kitchen, humming quietly. "Morning, you two." She turned to me. "Dana, I had the most wonderful idea while I was taking out the recycling last night."

"What's that?" I asked.

"I'd like to teach a composting class."

I worked to hide my surprise. Esther had never been overly involved in activities at the farm, preferring to leave the day-to-day management to Gordon. I had always thought she'd enjoy the business more if she could see how much the guests liked the place, but she seemed to prefer taking a backseat. I rose and gave her a hug. "Esther, that's a fantastic idea. I'm so proud of you."

"Oh, gracious," she said, blushing, "you make it sound like such a big to-do, but I'm not talking anything fancy, just a little class to teach newbies the basics. I was thinking once a month would be plenty. We can always add more if enough people sign up."

"Whatever you want," I agreed. "We can nail down specifics before I draft up some ads for the *Herald,* even the *Penny Saver.* And, of course, I'll blog about it on our Web site."

"And I'll tell all my friends in my meditation circle," Zennia said. "Most of them already compost, but we've had some new, younger members join recently who I'm sure would be interested."

Esther patted her gray curls. "Gosh, my little plan might work out. Dana, let me sit on this a spell and figure out all the nitty-gritty. Maybe we can get together after lunch."

"Let me know whenever you're ready," I said.

Esther hummed her way back out of the room, while Zennia popped two slices of sprouted wheat bread into the toaster.

I drained the rest of my coffee, sorted my breakfast trash in the containers under the sink, and said good-bye to Zennia. Time to find Gretchen.

The air outside was cool, but the morning sun warmed my head and shoulders as I wound my way past the pigsty. I stopped at the fence, and Wilbur wandered over to stick his snout between the wooden boards. I patted his head, almost giggling as the coarse bristles tickled my skin, and he snorted his thanks.

I continued on my way, nodding to Berta and the other chickens before cutting past the cabins.

Inside the spa tent, Gretchen was in one of the partitioned areas in the back, folding towels and singing softly. When she saw me, she broke off from her singing and smiled. I noticed her cheeks held more color than they had yesterday afternoon. "Dana, good morning."

"You seem in good spirits."

She shook a towel out and began folding it. "That's because I did what I said I would. I talked to the police."

"You called Detective Palmer?"

"Better. After you left, I decided to go down to the station. I thought the police might be more understanding if we could talk face-to-face and they could see how sorry I was for not telling them everything before." She finished folding the towel and added it to the stack on the massage table. "Of course, I was so nervous, I ran a red light and almost hit a bus on my way down, but I finally got there."

"And everything went okay?"

"Yep. I mean, sure, he was mad when I first told him. Talked about obstructing justice, interfering with police duty, stuff like that. It was total gibberish to me, but then he calmed down and asked me a bunch of questions about that night. He seemed happy with my answers."

I grabbed a loose towel off the stack of laundry and snapped it open. "What exactly did you tell him?" I folded the towel in half.

"About the fight I overheard, what little I remembered of it, anyway. He kept asking me about the man's voice, how deep it was, if he had an accent, but I'm afraid I wasn't much help."

"You never know. Just the fact that you heard a man there is important." I picked up another towel. "That reminds me. Could you tell what room Carla was in when you heard her talking?"

Gretchen shrugged. "I have no idea. I'd never been inside the spa before. I could tell the voices were somewhere on the right, but that was about it."

I tried to remember which rooms were on the right when Carla gave me the brief tour, but most of the doors had been closed. Was it important to know where Carla was during the argument? Somehow, I thought it was.

"What happened then?" I asked.

"He sent me home. Said he might call me back with more questions later, but that was it. I think everything's fine now."

I hadn't realized how anxious I was about Gretchen's situation until I felt relief flood through me. My fingers and toes tingled. "I'm so glad, Gretchen. I knew telling him was the right thing to do."

She held a towel to her chest, keeping her eyes downcast. "I know I should have told him sooner. I could have saved myself a lot of grief."

"At least you told him now. That's the important thing."

A "Yoo-hoo" sounded from the front of the tent

before she could say more. Gretchen dropped the towel back on the laundry pile and hurried toward the lobby area. I added my towel to the stack of folded ones and followed her.

A middle-aged woman in pumpkin-colored stretch pants and a long yellow T-shirt waited at the hostess stand. Her face brightened when she saw us. "Gretchen, I can't tell you the terrible week I've had. Thank goodness you had an opening this morning."

I could almost guarantee her week hadn't been as bad as Gretchen's. Based on the wink Gretchen gave me, I had a feeling she was thinking the same thing.

"I'll talk to you later," I told her. I smiled at the woman and walked out of the tent. I took a moment to breathe in the fresh morning air and enjoy the deep blue of the cloudless sky. An unusual amount of rain had hit Blossom Valley over the winter, and I was glad to see the sunny days returning.

Off in the distance, I saw a man near the vegetable gardens, walking along the path toward the spa. As he got closer, I recognized Detective Palmer. Worry twisted my insides. Maybe he'd changed his mind about arresting Gretchen for lying to him. Maybe he was here to cart her off to the county jail.

Gretchen and I might have celebrated too soon.

Chapter 17

I stood my ground and waited for Detective Palmer to get closer, wondering if there was anything I could say to keep him from hauling Gretchen away in handcuffs. When he was within earshot, I called out, "Detective Palmer, isn't it great how Gretchen decided to help you guys with your investigation?"

I heard a sigh escape his lips as he reached me. He crossed his arms over his navy blue polo shirt. "Exactly what do you know about it?"

"I know she told you how she overheard two people arguing in the Pampered Life right before Carla was murdered."

His frown deepened. "You knew this before I did?"

I stood there under his unrelenting gaze. The sun felt much warmer all of a sudden. In my efforts to help Gretchen, I might have landed in water hotter than the farm's Jacuzzi. "The minute Gretchen told me what she'd heard, I insisted she contact you," I assured him.

"Good. I'm sure you know better than to keep information from the police."

"Absolutely." I glanced back inside the tent, but Gretchen was nowhere in sight. She must have taken her client to one of the sections in the back. Still, I lowered my voice. "You're not here to arrest her, are you?"

Detective Palmer's eyes locked on mine. "What makes you think that?"

I shifted my weight. "Why else would you be here?"

"That's police business."

"Do you have any solid suspects at least?"

"We're exploring several avenues."

I'd noticed a long time ago that the detective had a knack for never actually answering my questions. Today was no exception. "Well, it sounds like you've got the situation well in hand." I smiled.

He didn't smile back. "Is Gretchen in the spa right now?"

"Yes, but she's with a client."

"I'm sure she understands that a homicide investigation comes before her customers."

I held up my hands. "Of course. Only, I was thinking about the gossip that would start if people find out you were visiting her at work."

"I'll be discreet. Now excuse me."

He moved past me into the tent. I was tempted to follow him, but I knew he'd order me right back outside. Besides, he'd implied that he wasn't here to arrest Gretchen, and even if he was, there wasn't anything I could do to stop him, as much as I'd like to think I could.

With no work to keep me outside, I returned to the house. As I crossed the patio area, I could see a few people still eating breakfast in the dining room. Zennia was in the kitchen, sprinkling minced chives on a pile of scrambled eggs. A fresh pile of facon waited on paper towels on the counter. I almost snagged one of the salty brown strips, but then I remembered it was a processed vegetable product and left it on the counter.

"Need me to serve?" I asked.

Zennia wiped some egg bits off the plate's rim. "That's all right. I'm working on my last two orders right now."

"Okay. I'll be in the office if you need me." As I passed the doorway to the dining room, I could hear people talking while they ate their eggs and facon. I wondered if they knew what they were really eating.

In the office Gordon was hunched over the printer. As I watched, he pressed several buttons on the control panel and then slapped the top of the printer.

"Printer acting up again?" I asked from the doorway. "It kept jamming on me last week."

He whirled around and scowled. "The stupid thing keeps telling me it's out of cyan. I'm trying to print an inventory list in regular black ink, but it won't let me."

I stepped into the room and pulled open the supply drawer. "I'm guessing we don't have a new cyan cartridge?"

"No. I forgot to order a replacement when I installed the last one." He checked his watch. "Look, I hate to ask, but could you run to town and get a new one? One of our suppliers is coming out any minute to discuss pricing, and I can't leave. You'd be doing me a huge favor. I'd owe you one."

Gordon had to be in dire straits if he was practically begging for my help. "I have time."

"Thank you." He walked out of the office, while I grabbed my keys and removed some money from the petty cash container. Before I stepped into the hall, I texted Jason to let him know I was running into town on an errand and to ask if he wanted to meet up for a quick cup of coffee.

Without waiting for his reply, I walked to my car and drove into town. At the supply store, I had a moment of panic when I saw an empty space on the shelf where my printer cartridge should have been. After some frantic searching behind all the other colors, I found a single remaining box. Who knew cyan was so popular?

My phone chimed as I was leaving the store. Jason was finishing an interview with Patricia at her new craft store. With the store only a couple of blocks away, I texted him back and asked him to wait. I quickened my steps.

When I got to Main Street, I turned the corner and made my way up the block past the Breaking Bread Diner. On the other side of the street, I could see Jason standing outside the vacant store, chatting with Patricia. I cut across to join them. Jason gave me a peck on the cheek under Patricia's watchful gaze.

She opened her mouth, as if to ask about our relationship, but I spoke before she could. "How is your shop coming along?" I asked.

"I have a contractor scheduled to come in. He and his crew need to make some repairs before he starts installing a counter and putting in shelves. Of course, I still need to order inventory. Plus, there's plenty to set up, but with any luck, I'll be open within a month."

Jason turned to me. "Plenty of residents will want to hear about the new store, so I decided to cover it in the paper now. I'll do a follow-up article for the grand opening."

I thought about Mom's continual quilting and sewing projects. "My mom will probably be first in line."

"I know a few ladies who might knock her out of the way to get here first," Jason said.

Patricia put a hand to her chest. "I can only dream my store will be so popular." The words sounded humble, but her superior smile and upturned chin made me think she was quite confident her place would be a success.

The roar of an engine interrupted our conversation. Patricia's gaze settled on something over my shoulder, and her smile disappeared. I turned in time to see Ricky speed past in his muscle car.

"There goes trouble," Patricia said.

Jason gave her a questioning look, and I realized that he didn't know who had driven by. While we'd talked about Ricky, Jason had never seen him. When he arrived at Carla's memorial service, Ricky had already left.

"That was Ricky, Erin's boyfriend," I told him. "The one Carla didn't approve of."

Jason jerked open his notebook. "That's Erin's boyfriend?" He flipped through the pages rapidly, moving toward the front of the notebook. He stopped on a page and ran his finger down the paper. "He's Richard Donovan."

"Ricky is probably short for Richard. Did you do a story about him?" I said.

Jason looked up at me. He still held his finger to the name. "You don't understand. He's the guy who got in the car accident last week." He took two swift steps in the direction Ricky had driven, as if hoping to catch up to him.

"And?" I asked, prodding. I had no idea what had Jason so wound up.

He spun around. "The accident happened here on Main. He was only a block away from the spa the night Carla was murdered."

Chapter 18

I gawked at Jason as his words sank in. Ricky was downtown when Carla died. Had he gotten in the accident as he was speeding away from the crime scene? Had he killed Carla?

Beside me, Patricia spoke up, as if reading my mind. "I thought he could be the killer. I'm not surprised one bit."

"What do you know about him?" I asked. It was clear Patricia didn't like the guy, but I was curious to know exactly why.

"Carla told me plenty." She glared down the street, as if Ricky might feel her disapproval from here. "All about how poor his family is and how he hangs out with hoodlums all day. She knew Erin could do better—a lot better—and hated to see her settle for someone with so little."

"Being poor isn't a crime," I said, bristling at the statement.

"Has he ever been arrested?" Jason asked.

Pink tinged Patricia's cheeks. "Well, not that I know

of, but he could have done plenty that no one's heard about. I've hardly talked to the boy, except once or twice, when I was visiting Carla and he was picking up Erin."

"How did he act around you?" I asked.

"Polite as can be, although I wouldn't expect anything else. You know how criminals can be such smooth talkers when they need to be. But he's a bad apple. You can tell."

What I could tell was that Patricia was a snob. Still, I couldn't ignore the fact that Ricky was near Carla's spa around the time of the murder. That was an awfully big coincidence.

Jason stuffed his notebook in his pocket. "I need to get back to the office."

"And I should head to the farm," I said.

Patricia held out her hand to Jason, and he took it. "Thank you so much for interviewing me," she gushed. "If this place is a success, I know who to thank." She nodded to me. "Be sure to tell your mom that I'll be open soon." With a wave over her shoulder, she went inside the store.

"She's something else," I said when she was out of earshot.

"Yeah, I'm just not sure what," Jason said. "I'll have to take a rain check on that coffee, but at least let me walk you to your car."

My eyebrows shot up. I knew he couldn't wait to get back to the office and follow up on this latest information. "I'm parked a couple of blocks from here. I don't want to keep you from your work."

"That's okay. I need to tell you what I learned."

Intrigued, I waited for a break in traffic and crossed the street. Jason fell into step beside me. When we reached the curb on the other side, he started talking.

"I didn't want to say anything in front of Patricia, but Richard—I mean Ricky—might not have been alone in that car the night of the accident."

I stopped and looked at him. "Who was he with?"

"I never found out. Witnesses to the accident mentioned a girl running from the scene, but no one got a good look at her. Ricky swore to the cops that he was alone."

"Do you think it was Erin? She could have skipped class that night and gone out with Ricky. If she was in the car at the time of the accident, that would mean she was also near the spa when her aunt was murdered. Maybe she's the one who killed her, and then she panicked and called Ricky to pick her up."

"It's entirely possible. Before I knew about Carla's murder, I assumed Ricky had an underage, drunk girl in his car or another situation that would cause him trouble. But your suggestion makes a lot of sense."

I started walking again, mentally running through the scenarios. "The problem is that Gretchen heard Carla arguing with a man right before she was killed. That would put Ricky at the scene, not Erin."

"Is Gretchen sure it was Carla who was arguing?"

My thoughts sped up, and my feet hurried along with them. "I don't see how she could be positive. She'd never met Carla, so she wouldn't recognize her voice. Maybe she overheard Ricky and Erin, which means Gretchen might have gotten there right *after* Carla was killed, not before. Of course, this is all guesswork on our part, but it makes you realize how little we know. Let's hope the cops are having better luck."

Jason skirted a fire hydrant. "Just in case, I'll pass this information along to Detective Palmer."

"Do me a favor and bring up my name when you talk to him. It never hurts to stay on the good side of a police detective." Especially after he thought I had withheld information about Gretchen. Maybe this would convince Detective Palmer that I wanted only to help.

Jason put his arm around my waist and pulled me close. "Well, you're always on *my* good side. In fact, you can be on any side of me you want."

My face suddenly felt so hot that I almost started fanning it. Jason always had that effect on me.

I heard a store bell jingle nearby and then my name called. I stepped back from Jason and turned around. Mom stood in the doorway of the Going Back for Seconds clothing store. I'd been so wrapped up in talking to Jason that I hadn't even noticed we'd passed it.

"Hi, you two," she said. "Dana, I thought I saw you walk by the other way a few minutes ago, but I was helping a customer and you seemed to be in a hurry."

"Hi, Mom. I didn't realize you were working this morning."

"That's because you never call me." She pressed the back of her hand to her forehead in the style of a theatrical Southern belle. "Now that she's moved into her new place, it's like she's forgotten all about her poor mother," she told Jason. I felt my face redden and opened my mouth to protest, but before I could say anything, Mom started laughing. "I'm only teasing. You've always been a wonderful and conscientious daughter, although I am curious why you're not at work right now."

I held up my bag. "I needed printer ink, and Jason happened to be covering the new craft store that's opening soon."

Mom looked up the street, toward Patricia's store. "Sue Ellen mentioned that a craft store was going in where the wine bar closed. I can't wait."

A woman walked toward us, heading to the entrance of the store. We all shuffled to the side to make room, and she squeezed past us and through the door.

"I should see if she needs any help," Mom said. "Say, Dana, why don't you come over for dinner tonight? You too, Jason. I'm making chicken."

I wasn't surprised in the least. She cooked chicken at least four times a week, sometimes more. When I lived at home, I'd started to hate the smell of roasted chicken. Now I thought about all the processed foods I'd been eating the past few weeks. A home-cooked chicken dinner sounded downright delicious.

"I'd love to," I said.

Mom beamed.

"I'm afraid I have other plans," Jason said, "but thank you for the invitation."

"Another time, then." Mom turned to me. "See you

tonight." She went back inside the store, the bell jingling after her.

Jason and I resumed walking. We turned at the corner, getting close to where my car was parked.

"Gee, what are these other plans you have tonight? Not a date, I hope." I smiled to let Jason know I was teasing.

"I limit my dating to hot girls who work at organic farms." He winked at me. "I'm getting together with one of my buddies. We'll probably drink beer and watch ESPN."

"You'll have a blast." Sitcoms and the occasional singing competition were more my style, but to each his own. We reached my car, and I unlocked the door.

"The only thing missing will be you." He gave me a kiss that made me all woozy inside. "I'll call you later." He headed back the way we'd come, no doubt in a hurry to start working on his article.

I drove back to the farm and found several cars parked in the lot, although the lobby was empty when I entered. Even Gordon wasn't at his customary post. I went into the office, replaced the ink cartridge, and then opened a marketing file I wanted to update.

Esther came into the office while I was working and sat down in the guest chair next to the bookcase. I took my hands off the keyboard and swiveled around to face her. "Hi, Esther. How's your day been going?"

"It's right as rain now that I've finished talking to Gretchen." She plucked at a button on her denim blouse. "You know how much I like her, and she had me awfully worried when I last spoke to her. Now everything seems okay, thank heavens."

I didn't know how much Gretchen had told Esther, and I certainly didn't want to share any troubles she might want to keep private, so I merely nodded. "Yes, she's back to her old self."

Esther leaned forward and patted my knee. "And how is your job going?"

"Fine. I'm working on a new brochure to highlight Zennia's cuisine. I've added plenty of photos of the vegetable and herb gardens. Would you like to see it?" I turned around, grabbed the sheet I'd been marking up, and gave it to Esther.

She looked it over, her head bobbing up and down in silent agreement. She handed it back. "Such pretty pictures. Between this and the other spa brochures you've created, we should see a whole slew of new customers."

"Let's not forget your composting class. That's sure to bring in more people. Which reminds me, are you ready to discuss the details?"

"I guess we could do that." Esther fiddled with one of her buttons again and glanced at the office wall, her gaze lingering on the photos of the farm back when she and her husband used to raise crops, long before she'd turned it into a bed-and-breakfast. "I only hope people are interested in what I have to say."

"Esther, you're an expert. You were composting before composting became popular. Anyone who attends the class will hang on your every word." I turned toward the computer and brought up a blank Word document. "Let's make a list of everything you might talk about."

Esther straightened up in her chair. "Well, I imagine most folks who come to my class will be beginners, so first I could talk about the benefits of composting, like how compost can add a host of nutrients to the soil and help plants thrive."

"Perfect. Love it," I said as I typed. "I know very little about composting, so one thing I've always wondered is where you even start a compost pile."

"Most people can find a nice spot in their yard that's out of the way, or they can build their own bin or buy one. It's easy as pie."

I typed up the information. "Good. What else will you talk about?"

"They'll need to know what they can compost. I add most any table scraps to the pile, although I leave out the meat and bones. They attract all sorts of pests you don't want. But any leftover fruits and vegetables are good, plus pastas or breads, even coffee grounds and used filters. All those break down real easy."

"Don't I see you putting your rose clippings and other trimmings on the pile sometimes?" I asked while I typed.

"I throw in all my yard waste. You need a good mix of dried matter, like twigs and dead leaves, and wet material, like food scraps and grass clippings. The combo helps break everything down to make nice compost."

I smiled at her. "See? I knew you were an expert."

She blushed and waved her hand. "Oh, stop."

We spent a few minutes discussing other topics she could cover. After reviewing several key points, I had all the information I needed to draft an ad.

"I think we've got everything," I said.

Esther stood and straightened her shirt. "You know, this might be kind of fun. Think I'll go tell Zennia about it." She toddled out of the room.

I returned to the computer and got started on the ad. Between working on the file, helping Zennia with lunch, and arguing with Gordon over how large an advertising budget we needed for the farm, the afternoon whizzed by. At five o'clock sharp, I updated my time card and gathered my belongings. It was time for dinner at Mom's house.

And after that, I could give more thought to why Ricky had been so close to the Pampered Life the night Carla was killed. And to the identity of the mystery girl who had been in his car. Whoever she was, I wanted to know exactly what she was running from.

Chapter 19

I pulled up to Mom's house and killed the engine, listening to the mysterious parts under the hood tick and pop. As I got out of the car, I glanced at the front door and smiled. Even though it wouldn't be dark for a while, Mom had already turned on the porch light. When Ashlee and I were teenagers, the porch light was always Mom's sign that she was waiting up for us.

The smell of herbs and onions greeted me in the entryway when I walked in the door, and I inhaled deeply. I really needed to cook more in my new place, maybe even a dish that didn't require a can opener.

I went into the kitchen. Mom stood before the open door of the oven, studying the contents of a casserole dish. I could see chicken breasts nestled in a bed of brown rice, with bright green broccoli florets peeking out between the grains.

Mom closed the oven door and laid the mitts on the counter. "Dinner will be ready here in a few minutes."

I set my purse on a chair and shrugged out of my coat. "Need any help?"

"No, dear. You're a guest tonight. Sit down and relax." She reached into the cabinet above the counter and pulled down three dinner plates. "I asked Ashlee to join us. She'll be here as soon as she gets off work."

Mom set the plates on the table, while I went to the drawer to grab the silverware. She tried to shoo me away, but I ignored her.

"She doesn't have a date with Chip?" I asked. "Then again, he hasn't been hanging around the apartment lately, so maybe she's through with him."

"Ashlee did mention she was losing interest. But I'm sure she'll find a new boyfriend soon. She's so popular."

Mom said she was "popular"; I said she was "not particularly choosy." Mom set three glasses on the table, while I retrieved the napkins. I was laying the last one next to a plate when the front door banged open.

Ashlee came into the kitchen, her blond hair up in a ponytail, her makeup freshly applied. "Hey, my peeps. Is dinner ready yet?" She tossed her purse on the chair with mine and dropped down onto an empty one.

"You're just in time," Mom cooed as she rushed to the oven and removed the casserole. I took the seat opposite Ashlee at the table. Mom set the dish on a trivet and sat down at the head of the table. For a second, I felt as if I'd traveled back in time a few weeks, to when we'd all been living together. A wave of nostalgia washed over me.

We made short work of eating dinner. When we were finished, I rose from the table and carried my plate to the sink. I placed it in the dishwasher and dropped my fork in the silverware caddy. Mom and I cleared the rest of the table, while Ashlee checked her reflection in her dinner knife.

"How about a quick game of cards?" Mom asked as she wiped down the table with a damp rag.

"I'd feel terrible taking all your money after you made such a tasty dinner," I said.

"Who says I won't beat the pants off both of you?" Ashlee asked.

I went into the hall and opened up the game closet, then removed the poker chip case from the shelf. I carried it back to the table and unlatched it. "How about you put your money where your mouth is?"

We all sat down, and I divvied up the chips.

"Let's play for more than a penny a chip tonight," Ashlee said. "I've got my eye on a new pair of shoes."

Mom pursed her lips. "The pennies are for fun, not to turn you into a professional gambler."

"You know what's fun," Ashlee said, "is strip poker."

I rolled my eyes, and Mom sighed. We all placed our ante in the middle of the table, and I pulled out the deck of cards. While I shuffled, Ashlee rattled on about some new guy she'd met at the vet's office where she worked when he brought in his sick turtle. She paused in her rhapsodizing about how gorgeous the guy was to say, "Dana, we should get a turtle. They're super easy to take care of."

"I think a turtle still falls under the no-pet clause in our lease. But you could date this guy and take care of his turtle when you're over at his place."

Ashlee rearranged the cards in her hand and then

folded. "Not a bad idea. That'll show him how caring I am."

"Does this mean you're no longer seeing that other boy?" Mom asked as she tossed a chip onto the stack.

Ashlee scrunched up her nose. "I might still see him sometimes, but I don't see any kind of future with him."

That tended to happen with all of Ashlee's boyfriends after the first month or two. "Well, good luck with this next one," I said. Ashlee squinted at me to see if I was being sarcastic, but I simply smiled at her.

"So, Dana," Mom said, "what else do you know about this new craft store? My bunco buddies and I are very excited about the opening. Esther and I might try making a quilt together."

I folded my own hand of mismatched cards and watched as Mom swooped in and pulled the pile of chips over to her stack.

"Patricia Porter is opening it," I said. "She's the one who threw the Celebration of Life for the spa owner that I told you about. She plans to include workshops, although she didn't tell me exactly what lessons she'll offer. Considering how excited she is about opening the store, I'm sure she'll teach people anything and everything."

"I can't wait," Mom said as she started to shuffle. "Patricia Porter . . . Why does that name sound familiar?" She paused in her dealing and looked at Ashlee. "Didn't she have a daughter in your grade?"

"Porter's the last name? Not that I know of." She looked off into the distance, absentmindedly fiddling with her poker chips. "Wait, now that I think about it, there was a girl named Dawn Porter, but she was in all the advanced classes, so I didn't hang out with her much. Her mom was always on her case about her grades and getting into the top colleges. She could have relaxed more if she'd gone to some of the parties the other kids were throwing, but she was always such a stress case."

"What parties?" Mom asked.

Ashlee's eyes grew wide, and I could see her trying to think up an answer. Even with our childhood long behind us, nobody liked getting caught misbehaving. "Oh, you know, study parties at the library, that kind of thing."

Yeah, right. I was pretty sure that Ashlee had never actually stepped inside the Blossom Valley library the entire time she'd been in school, except maybe to use the bathroom.

Mom set the rest of the deck down and picked up her hand of cards. "Nice try. Anyway, now that you mention Dawn, I remember her mom. She used to be a member of the PTA when you were in elementary school. She was the president, in fact. Ran that association like one of those controlling dance moms you see on TV."

"I've spoken to her only a few times, but she definitely comes across as the take-charge type," I said as I set two cards facedown and Mom dealt me two new ones.

"She told me once that since she never finished college and started her own career, she'd made raising her children to their highest potential her new career. Of course, she ran off almost everyone who belonged to the PTA. Membership was at an all-time low the second year she was president. People got tired of being roped into all her fund-raisers and projects."

I wondered if Stan had ever attended those meetings. I could see him being her biggest fan. "I take it PTA president isn't a position that people elect someone to?"

"By the time the next election came around, the only members left were people who liked her or those who were afraid of her."

"That's one way to win." I fanned out my cards and tried to keep the smile off my face as I realized I had a flush. I cleared my throat. "Think I'll try three chips this time," I said as I tossed them into the middle.

Ashlee threw down her cards. "I'm out. You always clear your throat when you have a big hand."

"I do not," I said. Did I? I guessed I needed to work on my poker face.

We played for another hour, until Mom had amassed a huge pile of chips and Ashlee and I were both down to tiny stacks.

"Looks like you're the big winner tonight, Mom," I said.

Ashlee stuck her lip out. "Guess those shoes will have to wait until payday."

"And until after you've paid me your share of the rent money." I started putting the chips back in the case. "How much do I owe you?" I asked.

"I'll let you girls off the hook this time," Mom said.

"It's so nice to have you home again, even if it's only for one evening."

Eating dinner and playing games with Mom and Ashlee had felt so much like old times, that for a moment, I considered asking to sack out in my room for the night, under the Hello Kitty comforter that still graced the twin bed. But I shook off the feeling. My apartment was my new home.

I stowed the poker chip case and the cards where they belonged. "Guess I should get going," I said. I pulled on my jacket. "I've got work tomorrow."

Ashlee said, "Me too."

I said good night to Mom and walked out with Ashlee. As I started my car, I felt one last wistful pull toward the house before I drove off into the night.

The next morning I stood in the middle of the kitchen and cursed the empty cupboards. I'd have to stop by the store and at least buy milk and cereal if I ever wanted to eat at home again. With no time to shop before work, I picked up a breakfast burrito at a fast-food joint on my way through town and drove out to the farm. The morning was unusually warm, and I decided to take ten minutes and sit at the picnic table on the patio to eat breakfast. The sparrows and robins accompanied my meal with a steady stream of chirps and trills, begging for a nibble. While I ate, I watched a dragonfly flit around the pool surface before zipping away.

As I popped the last bite in my mouth, one of the

French doors to the dining room opened, and Miguel walked out. His appearance was so unexpected that I involuntarily gulped. I swallowed twice more to force the lump of burrito down my throat.

He saw the take-out bag and smiled, his perfect white teeth gleaming. I guessed he wasn't harboring any ill will from yesterday's encounter. "A fast-food breakfast two mornings in a row. You must like them."

"Mostly, I don't like to grocery shop." I wadded up the greasy wrapper and dropped it in the nearby trash can, saving the paper bag to place in the recycling bin when I got to the kitchen.

"I can relate. If it wasn't for my trying to eat healthy as much as possible, I'd never shop for groceries again. The gentleman in the lobby said the spa is back here." He pointed toward the cabins. "Is that it?"

I shook my head. "Those are the guest cabins. The spa is farther down the trail." I rose from the table. "I'll show you."

Miguel put up his hands in protest. "I don't want to put you to any trouble. I'm sure you're busy."

"No trouble at all." Plus, this would give me the opportunity to talk to him privately about Carla.

We moved past the pool and toward the guest cabins. I was careful to keep my pace slow, but not so slow that he might notice.

"Have you heard anything from the police lately about Carla's murder?" I asked, wondering if they were focusing on Miguel as a possible suspect. Did they know he was married? Surely the police had easy access to court records.

"They have stopped by more than once to ask questions but haven't told me anything. I'd like to at least know they're getting somewhere with their investigation. Carla deserves justice."

"I'm sure they're making progress." I spotted a fuzzy caterpillar inching its way across the path. I used my paper bag to scoop the caterpillar up and move it to a patch of grass off to the side. A bird might eat it for a snack later, but at least no one would step on it. When I straightened up, I found Miguel smiling at me. "How did you two meet, anyway?"

His smile wilted. "At a chamber of commerce meeting. We got to talking and found we both had similar backgrounds in project management and business administration. We hit it off right away."

"Sounds like a perfect match." If only one half of that match hadn't already been married. I tried to sneak a peek at his ring finger, but I was walking on the wrong side. He probably took the ring off the minute he left the house in the morning, anyway.

"Yes, and we both valued our independence. We wanted to keep the relationship casual."

A casual relationship was about all Carla could expect given the circumstances.

"I only wish I'd had a chance to say good-bye." Miguel's regretful tone caught me off guard, and I glanced over. His expression was unreadable, but his eyes were moist.

I softened my tone. Even if he was a no-good cheating scoundrel, he could have still cared deeply for Carla. "I think everyone has that thought when a loved one dies unexpectedly. I felt the same way when my father passed away."

"Things were going so well between us," he said. "I realize now that I assumed we'd go on like that forever."

We were nearing the spa, and I felt like I hadn't learned anything useful on my little walk with Miguel.

"Did you ever visit Carla at the Pampered Life?" I asked, making a last-ditch effort.

"A few times. Of course, her place was open only a couple of weeks before she . . . well, you know." He cleared his throat and looked away. After a moment, he spoke again. "I'd stop by after work sometimes, and we'd go to dinner or get coffee."

A piece of the puzzle snapped into place. "Did she leave the back door unlocked for you?"

His head swiveled in my direction. "How did you know?"

"Just a hunch." I wondered how many other people knew about this habit. Was her murder planned around this easy access, or did the killer catch a lucky break? "Were you supposed to have dinner with her that night?"

"No. I had a meeting."

I almost groaned aloud in my disappointment. Here I'd pegged him as the most likely suspect, and he had an alibi.

"But I think she left the door unlocked all the time, in case I stopped by." He jerked to a halt. "My God, do you think the killer knew that Carla normally did that?"

"It's possible."

He rubbed a hand over his face. "She wanted me to

skip my meeting, you know. Said I'd have more fun with her. She was right, but I had already missed the last meeting and felt I had to go. If only I'd listened to her." He turned away from me and swiped his eyes.

He seemed to be honestly grieving her loss. My heart seized up at his obvious pain. "Even if the killer used the back door to gain entry, you can't blame yourself."

"I need to blame someone."

"Then blame the person who killed her," I said.

He looked at me, and I saw a flash of anger in his soft brown eyes. "Trust me, I do."

We'd reached the entrance to the spa. "Here we are," I said.

Miguel smoothed down his hair, rubbed his eyes one more time, and stepped inside the tent. I heard him say, "I'm Miguel, your nine o'clock appointment."

"You're the one with the possible torn muscle?" Gretchen asked. "Right this way." Their voices faded as they moved away from the entrance.

When I could no longer hear anything, I retraced my steps toward the cabins, thinking about my conversation with Miguel. It struck me as odd that he had used the back entrance to the spa for his clandestine meetings with Carla, and yet he had attended her Celebration of Life, as if he had nothing to hide.

At any rate, he was clearly crushed by Carla's death. But were those tears based on grief over Carla's untimely demise or guilt over killing her?

Chapter 20

When I returned to the farmhouse, I forced myself to concentrate on finishing my write-up for Esther's composting class so I could post it to our Web site. After that, I fine-tuned the ad I planned for the *Blossom Valley Herald*. When I was satisfied, I called the paper to talk about prices and placement. That accomplished, I headed for the kitchen. Lunch was fast approaching. Since I didn't have any additional marketing work at the moment, I'd see if Zennia needed my help.

I sniffed the air as I walked into the kitchen. The aroma was tangy and sweet. At the stove, Zennia was stirring something in a pot. I crossed the room and peered in.

"That smells scrumptious. What is it?" I asked.

"Mustard sauce to pour over the tilapia I'm serving for lunch. It has almost no fat but still manages to taste truly decadent."

"I'm sure the guests will love it." I was continually impressed by Zennia's wealth of food knowledge. That didn't mean I always wanted to eat what she was offering, but this particular recipe description made my mouth water. "If there's any extra left over from lunch, could I have it?"

Zennia's mouth fell open a little, but she recovered quickly. "You're volunteering to eat my food?"

"Just this once. I promise not to make a habit of it." I looked at the kitchen counters and noted the absence of any side dishes. "In the meantime, do you need any help?"

"I'm not expecting very many people, but I do need to finish the entrée. Think you could make a quick garden salad? Only if you don't have other work, of course."

"I'm all yours at the moment." I went to the refrigerator and gathered a head of red-leaf lettuce and a couple of cucumbers and carrots.

We worked in companionable silence. While I washed the lettuce, sliced the cucumbers, and peeled and shredded the carrots, Zennia stirred and seasoned her sauce. When twelve o'clock arrived, I filled individual salad bowls, drizzled on some homemade poppy seed dressing, and carried two bowls into the dining room. Only four people sat at the tables. We normally drew a larger lunch crowd with our spa and lunch combos, and I wondered where everyone was.

I went back to the kitchen for two more bowls, and then I stood inside the door of the dining room, filling the occasional request for extra dressing or more water. Out the French doors, I saw two women sit down at one of the picnic tables. I grabbed two sets of silverware rolled in napkins from the sideboard and went to the kitchen for two more salads.

I carried everything outside and set it before the women. As one of the women unrolled her napkin, she dropped her knife on the cement. I bent down and retrieved it.

"Let me run inside and get you another one." I glanced up as I spoke and recognized the thirtysome-thing brunette and her blond companion as the same two who had dined here a few days ago, the ones who had first mentioned Carla dating a married man. What else might they know?

I hurried inside for another knife and brought it out-side. After I handed the knife to the woman, I lingered a moment to see what they'd talk about, but they were discussing a television show they'd both watched the night before. Disappointed, I moved back inside to make sure the other diners didn't need anything.

For the next few minutes, I stayed busy as I brought requested items and cleared away plates. While I moved around, I kept my eye on the two women sitting outside. They hadn't stopped talking once, but every time I went out to the patio, they were discussing celebrity gossip. By the time I went outside to remove their plates, I'd about given up hope.

Then the brunette at my elbow brushed some dan-druff off her shoulder and whispered to her companion, "Turn around. There she is."

The little hairs on my neck prickled. As the blonde craned her head to check behind her, I looked up in anticipation and felt my stomach plunge. Gretchen was approaching the pool area from the direction of the spa. She was undoubtedly the target of the woman's remark.

The blonde turned back around and tapped her fingers on the table. Her penciled-in eyebrows were raised so high, they almost reached her hairline. "I can't believe this place hasn't fired her yet. She might have killed that lady."

"I bet they can't fire her until the police arrest her. You know how everyone sues the second they get canned nowadays."

"Still, you'd think she'd quit. The humiliation alone would keep me hiding in my house."

During this little exchange, I'd been moving the silverware around, stacking and restacking the plates, and doing anything else to appear occupied. The blonde cleared her throat and jerked her head in my direction, as if I somehow wouldn't notice the movement. They both stopped talking.

"Care for any dessert?" I asked.

"Just coffee," the brunette said. She ran her tongue over her teeth and brushed at her shoulder again.

"Coffee would be good," agreed the other. "I'll need the caffeine to keep me awake this afternoon."

I carried their dirty plates into the kitchen, wondering if I should have defended Gretchen to those two busybodies. But what would be the point? They'd believe what they wanted to believe, regardless of what I said. Besides, arguing with customers wasn't good for spa business. They seemed like the type who would complain to all their friends. And to Gordon, too.

Zennia was already washing the lunch dishes at the sink, and I added the two I was carrying to her stack. I filled two cups with the fair trade organic coffee she always had brewing and set them on a tray with a sugar container and the creamer.

When I got back outside, the women had stopped talking about Gretchen and had moved on to Ricky, if the one comment about that "scuzzy little boyfriend of Erin's" was any indication.

"He can't be that bad," the brunette argued. "I heard he got a partial scholarship to one of the UC schools, but he couldn't afford to go even with the extra help."

"I'm not surprised," the blonde groused. "His mom is dirt poor."

She sounded exactly like Patricia, and I had to wonder if that was who she was getting her information from. I rolled my eyes in disgust at her haughty tone as I went back inside.

The dining room had emptied out, and I cleared the few remaining forks and coffee cups. By the time I'd stripped the tables and put the linens in the washing machine, I was starving. Zennia was still washing dishes, but she refused my offer to help, so I made myself a plate of fish with mustard sauce and sat down at the kitchen table. I took a bite. It was fantastic. I resisted the urge to gobble up the entire plate at once and wondered what other dishes I had missed out on by refusing Zennia's offerings.

As I was scraping up the last bits of fish, Zennia sat down across from me.

"Well?" she demanded.

I pretended not to know what she was asking. "Well, no problems with the lunch service. Everything went like clockwork."

Zennia wagged a finger at me. "You know what I'm talking about. How was the sauce?"

I dabbed at my lips with a napkin. "I'll admit, it was good. I'd eat it again."

She clapped her hands together. "I knew you'd like it."

I couldn't help but smile. Zennia loved it when people enjoyed her cooking.

After I washed and dried my plate, I returned to the office to catch up on correspondence. The newspaper had sent an e-mail confirmation for my order, and several people had commented on today's blog about making your own air freshener gels. I spent the rest of the afternoon helping to clean the guest cabins and manning the front desk while Gordon ran an errand.

When the workday wound down, I removed my purse from the desk drawer and pulled on my sweater, mumbling to myself, "Don't forget the milk. Don't forget the milk," over and over. Otherwise, I'd drive right past the Meat and Potatoes supermarket without stopping, and no way would I go back out again once I was comfortably seated on my couch at home.

In the lobby Gordon was hunched over a spiral-bound notebook that lay open on the counter. He turned back a few pages and then forward again, his frown deepening. I realized he was studying the spa's appointment book, and my throat tightened a notch.

When he saw me, he held up a hand, signaling me to stop. I slowed my steps, though not without some hesitation.

"I've been looking through the spa's bookings," he said. "Our appointments are down significantly. Gretchen used to struggle to fit everyone in. Now she has huge gaps in her schedule."

I couldn't stop my grimace. I didn't like where Gordon was heading. "Maybe it's the time of year," I suggested. "With spring here, people might prefer to spend time outdoors rather than inside a spa." I took two steps toward the door, hoping Gordon would let the topic drop.

"Nonsense," he said. "It's those rumors that Gretchen killed the lady from the other spa. I told you her murder would be our undoing."

I aborted my attempt to leave and walked over to the counter. "Don't jump to conclusions. The drop in appointments could easily be a coincidence. With tax time around the corner, people might be watching their money more closely."

Gordon flipped more pages back and forth, making a snapping sound as he whipped the paper to and fro. "That doesn't explain everyone. Look, I know you're friends with Gretchen. I like her, too." He rested his hand on the appointment book. "Tell you what. Rather than firing Gretchen, I can put her on leave and hire a temp worker until these rumors blow over. And if they don't, then I may need to let her go."

His comments instantly transported me back a few months, to when he'd tried to get me ousted from my job, as well. The stress and uncertainty at the time had been crushing, and I knew Gretchen would feel the same way.

"You can't do that. It would destroy her, and she's in bad enough shape as it is. Gretchen loves this job."

"And she's good at it, but she's only one employee here. I have to think about all of you, plus the welfare of this farm." He looked at his watch. "I won't bother to run my idea past Esther tonight. But if the number of appointments doesn't increase soon, I may have no choice. Now I need to get to the high school. Tonight is the first meeting for that business club I told you about."

I was so busy worrying about Gretchen that it took me a moment to even remember he was planning to start a business club. "Did a lot of students sign up?"

"Six, at last count. I'm sure once word gets out, membership will increase. If people want to succeed in business, they need to start young, and I've got the expertise to help them." He slapped the appointment book shut. "I'll put this back in the spa, on the off chance someone calls to book a session. Let's hope someone does, for Gretchen's sake." He strode out of the lobby and in the direction of the spa tent.

I watched him through the window, gnawing on my lower lip. I knew Gordon wanted only what was best for Esther's place, but Gretchen would be devastated if she got laid off.

Still, Gordon was right that people were gossiping about Gretchen. I'd overheard those two women myself at lunch. Plus, Brittany had mentioned the rumors about Gretchen's involvement in Carla's murder at the Celebration of Life. This town thrived on speculation.

I slapped my hand on the counter in frustration. Gretchen was my friend, and I knew there was only one way to stop the rumors. The police had to find Carla's killer. And if they didn't, I would.

Chapter 21

As I drove toward town from the farm, I barely noticed the spring blossoms covering the pear tree branches in the orchards. I ignored the rows of grapevines marching toward the hills in the nearby vineyards. Most evenings I found the drive charming, but Gretchen's potential suspension weighed heavily on my mind.

I exited the highway and drove down Main Street, studying the Pampered Life on my way by. Someone had propped the front door open. Were the police still searching the spa for clues? If so, where was the police car? The side lot next to the spa was empty, as was the parking space at the curb. If it wasn't the police, who else could it be?

I was so distracted by the spa's open door that I almost blew past the side street for the Meat and Potatoes market. At the last second I hung a right, drove down the block, and pulled into the parking lot. Once through the automatic doors, I grabbed a basket and went in search of the cereal section. The market was busy with the after-work crowd. People shifted and spun around each other like we were all part of a synchronized dance.

In the breakfast aisle I narrowly avoided getting hit by a woman pushing a cart with a screaming toddler but bumped into a man as he moved out of the way of an elderly lady in a scooter. "Excuse me," I said without looking up, my gaze focused on the brightly colored boxes of sugary cereals. Which one cost the least but still held the best prize?

"Fancy running into you here," the man said.

I turned toward the voice and discovered that I'd bumped into Stan. He was dressed in a slightly wrinkled blue shirt and striped tie, clearly on his way home from the office. He smiled at me, and I caught a glimpse of boyish charm peeking through his grown-up exterior.

I smiled back and automatically peeked in his basket. I saw a package of steaks, a box of tampons, a bottle of red wine, and a bouquet of white and yellow daisies. He followed my gaze, and his cheeks reddened.

"Running an errand for Patricia," he mumbled.

"I'm sure she'll love the flowers." No need to mention the tampons. I studied the cereal selection once more and grabbed the box advertising a glow-in-the-dark yo-yo inside. "How's she feeling these days?" I asked as I placed the box in my basket. "I'm sure all the work on the craft store is helping to distract her from Carla's death."

Stan shifted his own basket from one hand to the other. "That store has been a blessing. We were both so shocked when Carla was killed. Who would do such a thing? She was a beautiful, vivacious woman. I can't imagine anyone disliking her enough to kill her."

I wondered if he'd use those same words to describe Carla in front of Patricia. She seemed like the jealous type. "The police may find that she was killed during a robbery gone bad. The killer might not have known what a wonderful person she was."

Stan's face drooped. "That would almost be worse, to snuff out such a lovely life with no thought as to how her death would impact those around her. And with Erin packing up everything at the Pampered Life, soon no one in this town will even remember Carla was here."

"Is that who was at the spa just now? I saw the front door open, but I thought perhaps the police were still combing through everything."

"The police said they're finished with that part of their investigation." He switched hands for the basket again. Patricia was probably wondering where her steaks were. "Carla was renting the space for the spa, and the landlord's already asking what will happen with the business. Erin's moving everything to Carla's house so she doesn't have to pay another month's rent. She can't do much else until probate closes."

"Is she in charge of handling Carla's estate?"

"Her mother is, Carla's sister. But she doesn't get out much, what with her penchant for drinking, so Erin's stuck with the work. Of course, Patricia's offered to help out." Stan glanced at his watch. "Speaking of which, I need to get going. Can't keep the little lady waiting."

He hustled toward the checkout stand like he could

feel Patricia breathing down his neck. I went back to my shopping, grabbing other essentials besides my cereal, including milk, orange juice, and the Pop-Tarts that Ashlee never remembered to buy. Then I threw in a bag of cheese puffs for good measure.

As I wandered the aisles, a nagging sensation followed along with me. I didn't know why the idea of Erin packing up the spa troubled me, but it did. The police must have uncovered everything they needed for their investigation, or they wouldn't have let her inside. But what if they'd missed something?

Even if they hadn't, I wanted answers to some questions that had been troubling me. Namely, when Gretchen overheard Carla arguing with someone in the spa, which room had they been standing in? I'd assumed Carla had been arguing with a man in the office, but what if I was wrong? If it turned out that Gretchen had overheard people arguing in the mud room, then it might not have been Carla at all. It could have been Ricky and Erin whom Gretchen had heard. After one or both of them had killed Carla.

With such disheartening thoughts on my mind, I grabbed three candy bars while in the checkout line. I didn't know if chocolate would make everything better, but it certainly couldn't hurt.

I paid for my groceries and carried them to the car. With the bags stowed on the passenger seat, I made my way out of the lot and back over to Main Street. As I turned the corner, I saw Erin walking toward the Breaking Bread Diner. I slowed to a crawl and watched as she opened the door to the restaurant. Must be grabbing dinner while she packed up her aunt's things.

The car behind me honked, and I snapped to attention. On impulse, I turned at the next corner, doubled back, and drove past the Pampered Life. The front door still stood open. I thought about parking across the street from the spa, so my presence wasn't completely obvious, but I wasn't planning on being there that long. Instead, I whipped into the parking lot and pulled into a space.

Erin might dine at the restaurant, but even if she decided to bring dinner back to the spa, I knew from experience that the place was slow with to-go orders. Nothing was ever ready when they said it would be. That delay could give me enough time to run in and verify the layout of the spa so that I could figure out exactly where that argument had happened.

Heart thumping, palms already sweating, I got out of my car and headed for the front of the building. At the doorway I looked down the block one last time. The sidewalk was clear. No sign of Erin. This might be my one chance to take a look before Erin closed the place for good. But why hadn't Erin locked the door before walking to the diner? Was Ricky in the spa?

"Hello?" I called from the doorway.

No answer.

"Hello?" I said more loudly.

Still nothing. Maybe Erin didn't expect to be gone long, which meant I needed to hurry.

I darted inside before I lost my nerve, and stopped just over the threshold. The artwork had been taken off the walls and stacked together. The small tranquility fountain with the spinning ball had been unplugged and drained of water. Half-full boxes sat in a corner.

With a sense of apprehension, I stepped into the hall. Down at the other end, I could see the back door through which Gretchen had entered the night Carla was killed. If I was remembering correctly, she'd heard the voices to her right. That meant those doors would be on my left now since I was coming from the opposite direction.

I walked over to the first door on my left, which had been closed on my one and only visit to the spa. I turned the knob and pushed the door open. A long massage table covered in towels sat in the middle of the room. Swiftly shutting the door, I moved down the hall. The second door was open, but I barely glanced inside. I already knew from my previous visit that this was the manicure room. That left only one room on this side of the hall.

I opened the door to that room. Yep, the office. A glass and metal desk occupied one side of the room. A stiff-looking office chair was parked in front of it. By one wall sat a filing cabinet, and by the other, a potted palm. Someone had placed a mostly full cardboard box in the corner, and I went over to peek inside. Picture frames and knickknacks, all the things that added a personal touch to an office, filled the box. I poked around to see if I could find anything noteworthy, but nothing caught my eye.

I thought about taking a quick look in the desk drawers, but I was already pressing my luck. Erin could be back at any minute, and God knew what she'd do if she found me here. As it was, the empty rooms and silent hall were creeping me out.

But the visit wasn't a total loss. I now knew where the office was located, straight across from the mud baths, with the back door in between. If Gretchen had entered through the back door, there was no way she could have mistaken where the voices were coming from. That meant Carla was definitely in the office, probably arguing with Ricky. There was an outside possibility that she'd been arguing with someone I didn't even know about, but I didn't think so. With the employees gone for the day and the front door locked, the person must have been familiar with the spa and Carla's habit of leaving the back entrance unlocked. Erin would have known about that, and she could have easily told Ricky, intentionally or not. Another check mark against Ricky.

I heard a sound coming from the front of the building and froze. Someone had come inside. I could hear them moving around the lobby. If the rustle of a plastic bag was any indication, it was Erin, back with her dinner.

I'd waited too long.

Now I was trapped.

Chapter 22

Panic coursed through me as I thought about Erin finding me in the spa. My breath came in hitches as I spun around in a circle, looking for an escape route.

Other than the door, the only way out was a single window set in the back wall, but it was covered by venetian blinds. I couldn't possibly get through the window without making a full-on racket. Erin would be on me in an instant. Considering that she'd stabbed her mother's boyfriend, I didn't expect a welcoming bear hug when she walked in the office and saw me here.

Could I dash out the office door and make it out the back exit before Erin spotted me? What if the door was locked? Why, oh why, did the Breaking Bread Diner pick this one night to be fast with their service? My only hope was that Erin ate her dinner in the lobby, which might give me an opportunity to sneak out the back.

I took several deep breaths to steady my nerves, then crept across the room and pressed my back against the doorjamb. With a silent prayer that Erin wouldn't be standing right outside the office, I slowly turned my head until I could see into the hall.

Empty. I released the breath I'd been holding and listened to the sounds still coming from the lobby. I pictured Erin taking her dinner out of the bag and rummaging around for the plastic utensils, which always seemed to hook on to the bottom of the bag.

I turned toward the back door. It wasn't more than ten feet away, but it felt like a hundred.

Not giving myself a chance to chicken out, I tiptoed across the thinly carpeted floor, my arms held out to the sides, as if I were navigating a balance beam. After pausing once to listen for Erin, I reached the door and gently pushed down on the bar.

The bar didn't move. I pushed again and then again, a little more frantically each time. Nothing. The door was locked. How was I going to get out of here? Could I find a place to hide until Erin left? How long was she planning to be here?

"What the hell do you think you're doing?" Erin asked from directly behind me.

I sucked in my breath. I'd been so wrapped up in my thoughts, I hadn't heard her approach. I took one last look at the door, clinging to the ridiculous idea that it might pop open by magic, and then slowly turned around, my heart hammering.

Erin was no more than three feet away. In one hand, she held a wickedly sharp pair of office scissors. Chills broke out all over my body.

"Erin, hi," I said with fake cheer, taking care not to stare directly at the scissors.

"I asked what you were doing," Erin said.

"I was driving by and saw the door was open. I thought I'd stop to see if you needed any help." That almost sounded plausible and was even partly true. I waited to see if she believed me. My hands were clenched so tightly into fists, I could feel my nails cutting into my flesh.

Her eyes narrowed. "Then what were you doing in the office?"

I tried to smile but couldn't. "Looking for you, of course. I'd already checked the other rooms, and the office was the only one left." In my panicked state, I couldn't remember how long it had been since I'd heard her come in. Would it have taken me that long to walk down a single hallway and look in a handful of rooms?

Her face struggled through a series of emotions, from disbelief to acceptance to confusion, like she wanted to believe me but couldn't. She began pacing before me, gripping the scissors. "Didn't you hear me come in? Why didn't you come right up front?"

"I, uh, well, I got distracted by that box of photos. I guess I didn't hear you."

Erin pointed the scissors at me. They were so close, I could have grabbed them, but I was frozen to the floor. "When I came down the hall," she said, "it looked like you were trying to escape out the back door." The words came slowly, as if she was thinking things through as she spoke. She frowned. "That doesn't sound like someone who stopped by to help me."

I was hoping she hadn't noticed that part. I tried to think up another lie, but my mind was blank. Outside, a loud rumble came from the direction of the street, and I felt a burst of hope. As noisy as the sound was, the front door must still be open. Would anyone hear me if I screamed? Was anyone even out there?

A self-satisfied smile spread over Erin's face as the rumble abruptly stopped. "Sounds like Ricky is here to help me deal with you."

I was already afraid to move, and now even my breathing stopped at the mention of Ricky. Was she right? Would Ricky back up Erin and her craziness? Or would he somehow give me a chance to escape?

I wasn't sure if my situation had just gotten better . . . or a whole lot worse.

Chapter 23

My hands tingled as I faced Erin and her twisted smile. I'd be smiling, too, if I were her. Not only was she holding a deadly pair of scissors, but now Ricky had arrived to help her, too.

From down the hall, I heard the faint sound of whistling growing louder. Then Ricky's voice drifted toward us. "Erin? You in here?"

Erin's grin grew wider. "I'm back here. Come see what I caught."

Ricky came into view over Erin's shoulder as he entered the hall from the lobby. With Erin's back to him, I didn't think he could see what she held in her hand. He saw me and gave a nod like everything was fine.

"Hey, I remember you. You're popping up all over the place." He stepped up next to Erin and glanced down. His eyes locked on the scissors clutched in her hand, though he seemed more befuddled than anything. "What are you doing with those?"

"Protecting myself," Erin said, her voice high. "I saw

them in one of the drawers earlier, so when I heard a bunch of noise, I grabbed them and came back here to find out what was going on. Good thing I did." She gestured toward me, and I flinched as the scissors swung near my face. "I caught this one snooping around. She must have walked right in while I was off getting my dinner. Who does that?"

"You left the door open," I said.

Erin looked like she was about to say something, but Ricky spoke first. "Did you call the cops?"

"Great idea," I said. "Let's call the police."

Erin took a step away from Ricky. "Not yet. I'm still waiting for her to tell me what she was looking for."

I turned my attention to Ricky, hoping I could reason with him, since Erin wasn't cooperating. "I already told Erin I wasn't looking for anything. I noticed the door was open when I drove by, and decided to stop in and see if she needed anything. I was back in the office when she came in because I'd already looked in the other rooms, but she wasn't there."

Ricky looked at Erin. "She might be telling the truth, you know."

"Why was she back here so long?" Erin asked. "And why did she even come in? She's just like Patricia, always sticking her nose in other people's business."

Ouch. That hurt. I jutted my chin out. "I'm nothing like Patricia."

Erin gave me a withering look. "Right. That's why you came inside as soon as you saw the spa door was open, even though I hardly know you."

Ricky placed a hand on Erin's arm. "None of that

matters. You need to put the scissors down before someone else walks in. I don't want you to be the one who gets in trouble. She's the one who broke in."

Tears sprang to Erin's eyes, and her face turned a mottled red. "That's exactly what would happen, too. I'm always getting blamed for stuff that isn't my fault. It's not fair." She lowered her arm and let it hang limply at her side.

That was definitely a good sign, but I couldn't allow myself to relax yet. She could still stab me with one solid thrust.

Ricky must have been thinking the same thing. "Why don't you give me the scissors?" he said softly. "I don't know why you even have them."

She whirled on him. "Because there's a killer out there! Someone murdered my aunt, and I need to defend myself. What if they come back?"

Ricky held out his hand. "I'm here now. You don't need them anymore."

Erin looked at the scissors, then at Ricky. I held my breath. After several excruciating seconds, she laid the scissors in his palm.

My body sagged in relief as he reached over and set the scissors next to a fern on a small table nearby. "I'm sorry I upset you," I told Erin. "I never should have come in here."

"You got that right," she huffed. "You should've at least let me know you were here, instead of scaring me like that. I've totally been on edge after what happened to Aunt Carla."

She'd calmed down considerably now that Ricky was

here, and I couldn't help feeling bad for her, never mind the danger I'd been in.

"We're all on edge," I told her.

"But I have the most reason to worry," Erin said. "My aunt is the one who was killed, and nobody knows why. What if I'm next?"

"No one's coming after you," Ricky said. He slid an arm around her waist and pulled her close. "I'll protect you."

I studied the two lovebirds. A pair of innocent victims or the dynamic duo of death? Now that Erin was no longer threatening me with bodily harm, I couldn't resist the urge to try to weasel a little information out of them both. "Maybe you witnessed something the night Carla died that could help the police find the killer."

Erin shrugged out of Ricky's embrace and put her hands on her hips. "What do you mean? I was in class when she was killed."

Ricky was studying me closely. I thought of the scissors, which were still within easy reach for him. At least the front door was open. Maybe I could sprint past these two if things got out of hand.

"What are you getting at?" he asked.

"I heard Erin was with you when you had a car accident right down the street that night."

Erin gasped, her eyes wide as she turned toward Ricky. "How did she—"

"Quiet," he said.

"Look, your accident was covered in the newspaper, only I didn't make the connection that you were the driver until recently." Actually, Jason had realized that Ricky and Richard were one and the same, but I didn't want to drag his name into the situation right now.

Ricky shrugged like he didn't care, but his shoulders were stiff. "So I got in a little fender bender. No big deal."

"But witnesses said you had a female passenger with you, and she ran off. That's kind of a big deal when a murder happened right down the street."

Erin's hand crept up to her mouth. "I knew I shouldn't have run."

Ricky turned to face her. "I told you to hush."

Erin pointed at me. "But if she knows, the police must know. The one time I cut class—"

"She's only guessing."

They glared at each other, seemingly locked in a silent argument. I used the temporary distraction to turn my body and sidle along the wall toward the lobby. I was close enough to smell the cigarette smoke clinging to Ricky's clothes, and I hurried my steps. I didn't like having my exit blocked. Ricky and Erin were too unpredictable.

Once I'd moved past them, I spoke again. "Aren't you worried that if I guessed Erin was with you, other people will, too?"

Ricky jerked his head and exhaled sharply. "Man, you really do butt into people's stuff. I should have listened to Erin."

Erin gave me the same snarky look that Ashlee used to give me when Mom sided with her during an argument.

"The police aren't idiots," I said. "Why not admit

you were there and see if you can help catch Carla's killer?"

Without warning, Ricky swung his arm up and slapped the wall next to him with a thud. I jumped, while Erin reached for his hand. She bent over his palm to take a look, cooing at him as if he were a small child with a scraped knee.

"Look, lady," he said to me, "I already told the cops I was alone. I can't change my story now, and neither can Erin. You need to mind your own business."

I backed up a couple of feet closer to the lobby. "You're not some teenage girl," I said to Erin. "And you're old enough to drink, right? So why run?"

Erin dropped Ricky's hand and leaned into him. "Because of Aunt Carla. With the accident so close to the spa, I was worried she might drive by on her way home and see me with Ricky. We'd already gotten in a huge fight that afternoon about me dating Ricky. She said she'd kick me out if I didn't break up with him. I couldn't let her see us together."

My eyebrows came together. "But I thought you had already told her you were moving out because of Ricky."

"That's what I said, but I was only bluffing. I needed a place to stay until I can graduate."

Ricky wrapped his arms protectively around her, his anger gone. "I already said you can stay with me."

Erin shook her head. "Your mom has so many medical problems. She wouldn't want me underfoot in the trailer all day."

"She wouldn't mind. She'd probably like the extra help."

I could feel them slipping into their own private conversation. "Once you found out Carla had died, why not tell the cops the truth then?" I asked.

"For what?" Erin asked. "So they would know I was basically outside the spa at the very minute my aunt was murdered?" Erin sneered. "Why should I give them a reason to suspect me? Patricia would love to hear about that."

Ricky scowled. "And with her big mouth, you know she'd tell them about your mother's—"

Erin cut him off, her eyes flashing. "We don't talk about that."

"Sorry."

I could only assume he'd been about to mention how Erin had stabbed her mother's boyfriend. Maybe not, though. Maybe Erin had even more to hide.

"If you want to talk about something," Erin said, "how about the way Aunt Carla offered you that money for—"

"Knock it off," Ricky growled.

They fell silent, the discussion evidently at an end. I would have loved to know what Erin was about to say, what money Carla had offered Ricky and why, but in that moment I realized exactly how exhausted I was. Being threatened with a pair of scissors did that to a person.

"I'm gonna take off now," I said. "Sorry again for the misunderstanding."

Erin nodded, while Ricky gave me a two-fingered

salute. I left them in the hallway and made my way outside, breathing in deep lungfuls of cool evening air, feeling like I'd never get enough. I stood for a moment and watched cars drive up and down the street. No one would ever guess that I'd been trapped in the spa just now. Main Street had probably looked much like this the night Carla was murdered.

Hands still shaking slightly, I climbed inside my car and locked the door behind me. I pawed through my grocery bag until I located one of the chocolate bars I'd bought earlier. Peeling back the wrapper, I took a bite and let the chocolate soften and melt in my mouth. Then I glanced back at the building and stopped. Why on earth was I still sitting here? Erin had threatened me with scissors! I needed to go.

I threw the rest of the chocolate bar in the bag, started up the car, and backed out of the space. As I pulled out of the parking lot, I noticed the spa door was still wide open. The lingering remnants of sweet chocolate turned sour in my mouth.

Erin had done a fine job convincing Ricky and me that she'd grabbed the scissors because she feared for her life. But if she was so scared, why had she left the door open when she'd gone down the street for dinner? If it had been me, I'd have locked the place up tight before stepping outside. Better yet, I would have asked the diner to deliver so I wouldn't have to bring my food back to an empty spa where my aunt had been murdered. For a woman living in fear, the open door seemed awfully careless.

Maybe Erin wasn't as afraid as she wanted Ricky and

me to believe. Maybe she'd played the sympathy card so she didn't come across as a nut job who threatened innocent people with office supplies. She might have intended to use those scissors on me, after all, and Ricky's arrival messed up her plans.

That idea made me clutch the steering wheel even tighter, and I almost pulled over and finished the candy bar. If Ricky hadn't shown up when he had, I might have been Erin's next victim.

Chapter 24

By the time I got to my apartment, my neck was stiff and my hands ached as I thought about what an idiot I'd been to go inside the spa alone.

I clenched my teeth together to keep them from chattering as I grabbed my groceries and locked the car. I had run the heater for the entire drive home, but I still couldn't ward off the chill that had settled in my gut. The milk I'd bought at the Meat and Potatoes market felt warmer than I did at this point.

Once I'd lugged the bags up the stairs, I unlocked the front door and entered the dimly lit apartment. I flipped on the light and saw a message on the magnetic refrigerator pad, letting me know Ashlee was on a date with Chip. Perhaps their relationship wasn't kaput quite yet.

After putting away the groceries, I sat on the couch and squeezed my hands between my knees to try to warm them. I listened to the refrigerator hum. From outside, the sound of a car motor reached me. Then a new sound, a popping noise, came from the direction of the bedrooms.

I sucked in my breath as I pictured someone outside my bedroom window, trying to find a weak point to gain entry into the apartment. Maybe Erin had changed her mind and decided I was a threat, after all. Another popping sound came, and my brain recognized it as water dripping in the shower. I exhaled loudly, disgusted with myself.

I snatched up the TV remote and turned on the TV, increasing the volume until it blocked out my thoughts. The reporters for the evening news were covering a recent spike in crime in San Francisco, and I immediately clicked through the channels to find lighter fare. I tried to concentrate on the TV, but every time I thought I heard a strange noise, I'd mute the volume and freeze like a rabbit caught in the beam of Esther's flashlight when she checked the vegetable garden at night.

After another minute I tossed the remote on the couch and walked around the apartment, inspecting each room in turn, flipping on the lights as I went. I knew no one was here, but I still had a case of the creepy crawlies. My little encounter with Erin had shaken me more than I cared to admit.

When I finished looking under the beds and behind the shower curtains, I headed for the kitchen to throw together dinner. As I passed the coat closet by the front door, I couldn't resist opening it again, even though I'd already looked inside once.

Still empty.

Feeling silly now, I shook my head and poked through

the kitchen cabinets. My cell phone trilled from its place on the counter, and I snatched it up, thankful for the distraction.

"How's my favorite girl?" Jason asked when I answered.

"To tell you the truth, I've felt better." My skin prickled, and I looked over my shoulder, swearing to myself it was the last time.

Concern filled his voice. "You're not sick, are you?"

"All I'm suffering from right now is a case of an overactive imagination."

"Then I've got the perfect cure. Come over tonight. I'll make you dinner."

I hesitated. The idea of walking out to my car, even if it wasn't quite dark yet, filled me with trepidation. The parking lot was full of cars and trucks, plus two Dumpsters, creating dozens of hiding places. Then again, getting out of the apartment held more appeal than sitting here and jumping every time a neighbor slammed a door or a driver on the street honked a horn.

"Sounds great," I finally said. "Give me thirty minutes?"

"See you then."

I hung up and went into the bathroom for a quick shower. After blow-drying my hair, I dressed in dark jeans and a lightweight cream sweater and applied a touch of makeup. Satisfied with my appearance, I went into the kitchen to erase Ashlee's message on the fridge and replace it with one of my own. I turned off all the lights except the kitchen one, grabbed my purse, and left the apartment, locking the door behind me. I twisted the knob several times to make sure it stuck.

Prepping for my date had definitely improved my mood, but I still paused at the top of the stairs and studied the parking lot. As I watched, a neighbor I knew vaguely by sight pulled in, and I used the opportunity to trot down to my own car and get in while I wasn't completely alone.

I drove across town to Jason's home in a quiet residential neighborhood that was a mix of retirees and young married couples. Everyone mowed their lawn and trimmed their hedges, and an ice cream truck cruised through the neighborhood most summer evenings. I pulled to the curb in front of the two-story duplex where Jason rented one side, and shut off the engine, humming to myself as I got out of the car. Jason opened the front door before I even got up the walk.

I eyed his black apron with the words *Kiss the Chef* stitched across the front. "Is that a direct order?" I teased.

"Absolutely," Jason said.

We kissed, and then I stepped into the house. Jason motioned for me to follow him to the kitchen, where his oval oak table was covered by a white tablecloth. Two candles, already lit, stood in silver candleholders. An opened bottle of chardonnay and two glasses waited off to one side.

Jason poured a glass of wine for each of us and handed me one. I took a sip and wandered over to study what was on the counter. Piles of chopped vegetables covered the bamboo cutting board. Two fillets of delicate, pale fish lay on a paper towel–lined plate to the side of the sink.

"What's with all the vegetables?" I asked suspiciously.

"I'm making ratatouille." Before I could protest, he went on, "Don't worry. I know it's a lot of vegetables, but you'll love it. Trust me."

"What's the occasion?" In all the time we'd been dating, Jason had cooked for me only once, and that meal had involved a jar of spaghetti sauce, a package of dried spaghetti, and a loaf of frozen garlic bread, reflecting my own style of cooking.

"As much as I loved those chili dogs you served the other night, I wanted to make a dish that was a little more, um, sophisticated."

I put one hand on my hip. "Are you mocking my chili dogs?"

"Never. But I wanted to show you my own talent in the kitchen." He led me to the living room, where I could hear a current R & B song coming from small speakers near the TV. "Enjoy the music, and I'll start cooking the vegetables."

I shook my head. "I can't sit around while you do all the work."

"I want you to. I'll be done in five."

I settled on the supple leather sofa and sipped my wine, tapping my foot along to the music. I could hear Jason puttering around the kitchen for a few minutes, before he came into the living room and sat down next to me, his glass of wine in one hand.

He placed his other hand on my knee, his expression

one of concern. "You sounded upset on the phone earlier. What's going on?"

I focused on the blank TV while I thought about how best to phrase my answer. I knew Jason would be unhappy that I'd put myself in danger. "I had a little run-in with Erin at the spa."

Jason leaned toward me, almost spilling some wine. "What kind of run-in?"

Careful to keep my gaze on the TV, I said, "The spa door was open when I was driving home, so I decided to pop in for a minute to see if Erin needed any help."

"Why would you think Erin was there?"

"I ran into Stan at the supermarket. He told me she was packing up Carla's things. Anyway, when I got inside, she wasn't there, so I thought I'd take a quick look around. She caught me in the office and thought I was snooping."

I risked a peek at Jason. He was frowning. "You shouldn't have gone in there alone like that. A woman was killed at that place, in case you forgot."

"I didn't forget. But like I said, Erin wasn't there when I first went in. And the spa is on a public street. The door was open. People were constantly going by." A slight exaggeration, but he didn't need to know that.

"It was still a stupid thing to do," Jason grumbled.

I stiffened. "Look, Gordon's worried about how this murder is affecting the spa. He noticed appointments are down, and he might lay off Gretchen because of it. She doesn't deserve that."

"Of course not, but that doesn't mean you have to put yourself in harm's way." Jason vigorously rubbed the back of his neck, clearly frustrated. "What happened then?"

Based on Jason's already negative reaction, I decided to skip right over the part where Erin threatened me with the scissors. "Ricky showed up."

"What?" Jason yelled. Apparently, that answer wasn't any better. He used his free hand to grab my shoulder, startling me with his intensity. "You were alone in the spa with two murder suspects?"

"Only briefly. Plus, the door was open." Now that I was sitting safely on Jason's sofa, I could afford to be dismissive. I'd never let him know how scared I'd been at the time. I pointed toward the kitchen. "How's the ratatouille coming along?"

He looked at me like he'd never heard the word before. Then he jumped up from the sofa. This time, wine sloshed over the side of his glass. "Damn it!" He held his glass aloft and disappeared into the kitchen. I heard muttering and the sound of pots banging before he returned, his wineglass freshly topped off. He took his seat beside me.

"Now that you've calmed down, would you like to know what I found out?" I asked.

"Who says I've calmed down?"

"I do. Eating ratatouille on an upset stomach is bad for digestion."

"Maybe more wine will help." He drank half the glass in one giant gulp. "So what did you find out on your foolhardy errand?"

I ignored the little dig. "Erin and Ricky admitted that Erin was in the car when Ricky had his accident."

"No surprise there. I was positive she was the one, and I'm pretty sure Detective Palmer knows it, too."

"Then why doesn't he arrest her?"

"He would if he had more evidence. He still might bring her in for further questioning."

I scooted forward on the sofa. "Speaking of Erin, she said something interesting about Carla offering Ricky money. What do you suppose that's about?"

Jason swirled the remaining wine in his glass. "No idea. Think she was trying to buy him off to leave Erin alone?"

"It's a possibility. Of course, Ricky might not have taken too kindly to that idea and might have killed her."

"Seems easier to simply refuse the money."

"I guess." I set my wineglass on the table, thinking. "That's two people who could have committed the crime, now that Erin's alibi is no good." I snapped my fingers. "That reminds me. I ran into Miguel at the spa today, and he was at some meeting when Carla was killed."

Jason leaned back on the sofa, a knowing gleam in his eyes. "That's what he told you and the police, but I asked around, and no one remembers him at the work meeting he supposedly attended. More than one person noted his absence, in fact. What do you want to bet his alibi is as phony as Erin's?"

I stared at Jason as his news sank in. *Son of a seaweed wrap.* Miguel had lied to me.

Chapter 25

I slammed my fist down on the coffee table, rattling the wineglasses. "I knew it. I knew Miguel was hiding something. Worse yet, he lied to me, and I fell for it." I didn't know if I was madder at Miguel for being so dishonest or at myself for being so gullible.

"Don't forget he lied to the police, too," Jason said. "Not just to you."

I stood and paced the confines of the small living room. Jason watched me with a bemused expression. "He had such a sob story," I said. "All about how he was partly responsible for Carla's death because she'd wanted him to skip the meeting that night and he'd insisted on going, anyway. How if he'd only met with Carla, she might still be alive." I threw up my hands. "And I fell for that malarkey." I stopped pacing. "If he wasn't at the meeting, then where was he?"

"Who knows? Detective Palmer mentioned a follow-up visit once he realized Miguel's alibi was questionable, but I haven't heard anything." He held up one finger. "Hang on a sec. I need to check the fish." He disappeared into the kitchen, while I resumed my pacing.

After a moment he came back in, holding the half-empty bottle of wine, and I joined him on the sofa, trying to calm myself. "Speaking of Detective Palmer, did he ever find that dog statue you mentioned?" I asked, picking up my glass.

"No. It wasn't in the office, and the police didn't find it when they searched Carla's home, either."

"So it probably is the murder weapon."

Jason drank some wine. "*If* the statue even exists. The police don't want to speculate."

I set down my glass and rubbed my hands on my thighs. "I'm not sure it matters, anyway. Anyone could have grabbed the statue while arguing with Carla, so it doesn't point us to one particular person." I drummed my fingers on my knee. "Okay, so far we have Miguel, Erin, and Ricky as people who could have killed Carla. Anyone else?"

Jason refilled my wineglass and topped off his own before setting the bottle on the table. "Patricia and Stan," he said.

"Stan?" I'd almost forgotten about the guy. While he was as good a suspect as any, he struck me as so . . . unremarkable. Plus, he and his assistant were working the night Carla was killed. "But he has an alibi."

Jason stroked his goatee. "I'd forgotten. Although everyone's alibi seems iffy at this point."

I considered this as I sipped my wine. Thinking about Stan's alibi reminded me of Miguel's. How had I not questioned it? Was it because those crocodile tears had looked so real?

Jason cleared his throat. "I hate to bring this up. . . ."

My stomach tightened at his tone. "Yes?"

"Is there any chance Gretchen could have killed Carla? A witness did see her at the spa around the time Carla died, and Gretchen admitted to being there." He was studying my face.

I shook my head. "I won't even consider it. Gretchen is too kind to murder someone. If she says she's innocent, then I believe her."

"She started working at the spa only a few months ago. How well do you know her?" Jason said, pressing.

"Well enough."

A timer dinged in the kitchen. I was grateful for the interruption.

Jason rose from the sofa. "Dinner's ready." He held out a hand and helped me up. "If you feel like you might faint from my amazing cooking, give me some warning and I'll rush you right into the bedroom to lie down," he said, obviously trying to lighten the mood.

I took his arm and leaned into him. "Ha! I may have to faint on purpose."

We walked out of the living room and over to the table, where he pulled out a chair at one of the place settings. I smiled up at him as I sat down; then I set my wineglass by the silverware.

Jason grabbed both clean plates and took them to the stove. When he returned, the plates were covered with vegetables and fish. He put one before me and took the opposite seat, staring at me expectantly.

I looked around the table for any seasonings or condiments I was supposed to add, but didn't see any. "What?" I finally asked.

"I'm waiting for you to take the first bite."

Picking up my fork, I speared a cube of eggplant and added a piece of fish. I put the bite in my mouth, feeling Jason's eyes on me the entire time. After I'd swallowed, I said, "Delicious. Absolutely delicious."

Jason smiled. "See? Vegetables aren't your enemy. I bet you'd even eat this again."

"Only if you make it for me."

He laughed. "At least you're open to the idea." He picked up his own fork. "Now let's eat."

Two hours later I was back in my car, and Jason was watching me pull away from the curb. We'd lingered over dinner before cleaning up the kitchen and spending some time getting cozy on the sofa. After we parted, I drove through the quiet streets of Blossom Valley. Only the Get the Scoop ice cream parlor and the Breaking Bread Diner appeared to be open this late.

At the apartment complex I pulled into my parking space and shut off the engine. The sound of my footsteps accompanied me as I crossed the lot and started up the stairs to the apartment. Off to my right, a cricket chirped from a nearby bush. The scent of wood smoke filled the air.

When I was halfway up the stairs, I felt more than heard a rhythmic beat coming from my apartment. As I got closer, I could feel my insides vibrate in time with the rhythm. *Uh-oh.*

I trotted up the last couple of steps and flung open the unlocked door. Loud music poured over me in waves, the pulse pounding away. Ashlee sat on the couch, the fingers of one hand splayed out on the coffee table. Across from her, Brittany sat on the floor, painting Ashlee's nails.

I rushed across the room to the stereo and cranked down the volume. Blissful silence fell on my ears.

"Hey," Ashlee barked, whirling around, "I was listening to that."

"So was everyone else in the complex. We don't want another complaint from the neighbors."

Ashlee made a pouty face but didn't protest further. I walked over to the couch and looked at Brittany's handiwork. "Black fingernail polish? I didn't know you liked the Goth look."

Ashlee stuck out her bottom lip. "I'm in mourning."

"Did someone die?" She didn't look terribly upset, but you never knew with Ashlee.

Brittany paused with the nail polish brush hovering over Ashlee's pinkie nail. "She and Chip broke up. We're having a closure ceremony."

"Closure ceremony?" How had I never heard of this before?

"You know," Brittany said, "she updated her relationship status on Facebook, deleted his contact info from her phone, and now I'm painting her nails. After that, we're going to eat a pint of Ben & Jerry's. Each."

Ashlee sniffed. "We're saying good-bye to what I thought was a supergood relationship."

I sat down next to Ashlee and patted her knee. "I had no idea you cared about Chip so much. I thought you were getting tired of him."

"I was, but I still planned to see him sometimes, when no other guys were free. I'd tagged him as my backup boy, but when I told him that, he said I could forget it. Now he's gone."

"How tragic," I said with a straight face.

Brittany lifted her head. "I know, right?" Without waiting for an answer, she bent back over Ashlee's hand.

Ashlee turned to me, careful not to move her arm while Brittany worked. "How was dinner with your hubby?"

Brittany glanced up. "When did you get married, Dana? Hey, Ashlee, we should live together when your sister moves out. We could turn it into a bachelorette pad." She giggled.

"Hey! I just moved in," I said. "Besides, I'm not married."

"Might as well be," Ashlee mumbled.

Brittany stuck the brush back in the bottle and twisted the top. "I'm never getting married. No man is ever telling me when I need to have dinner ready and on the table."

"Actually, Jason made dinner for me tonight," I said.

Ashlee snickered. "Man, you have him trained like a puppy."

I swatted her arm. "I do not. And at least I have a man."

"Ooh, burn," Brittany said as she scrutinized Ashlee's nails.

Ashlee stuck her tongue out at me. "Did he rub your feet while you two talked about rainbows and kittens?"

"For your information, we spent most of the night talking about murder."

"Carla's murder?" Brittany asked.

I nodded. "We found out some interesting stuff about Carla's niece, plus her boyfriend, Miguel." I was careful not to provide Brittany with too many specifics. I wasn't sure how much of what Jason had told me needed to be kept quiet.

Brittany leaned forward. "That hot guy was her boyfriend? I thought she was seeing some old dude. At least that's what I heard."

"Well, Miguel isn't terribly old, but he is in his early fifties, I think."

"Sure doesn't look it," Brittany gushed.

I had to agree with her on that point. Even with the lines around his eyes and the silver streaks in his hair, or maybe because of them, he was a good-looking man. I noticed Brittany staring at my hands, and I knew she was critiquing my nails. I curled up my fingers.

"Let me paint those," she said, reaching for my hands.

I instinctively pulled back. "I don't think black nails would go over well at the farm, especially with Gordon, the manager."

Brittany dug around in her tote bag and pulled out a bottle of pale orange polish. "How about Peach Fizz?"

I tried to remember the last time I'd taken the time to

paint my nails. Between cleaning the cabins, feeding the animals, and completing all the other odd jobs I did around the farm, I usually made it my main goal not to *break* any nails.

"Sure. Why not?" It might feel nice to be the pampered one for a change. It would be the finishing touch after the dinner Jason had cooked for me.

Brittany squealed with delight and whipped out a nail file.

Ashlee jumped up from the couch. "While you two are yammering, I'm getting the ice cream. You want some, Dana? We got extra."

The fish and ratatouille had filled me up, but I could always find room for ice cream. "Sure, I'll take a scoop."

Ashlee went into the kitchen, while Brittany started filing my thumbnail.

"What were we talking about?" she asked as she worked.

"Trying to figure out who might have killed Carla. Patricia and her husband are two more possibilities."

"I don't know her husband, but you gotta watch out for that Patricia."

A kink formed in my shoulder from holding my arm out, and I tried to shift around to find a more comfortable spot while Brittany held tight to my hand. "She comes across as a little controlling, but she's always been perfectly pleasant to me."

Brittany finished filing my nails, wiped down my fingers, and shook the bottle of polish. "I met her only a couple of times, but I could tell she's one of those phonies. Talks all nice to you, and then she does stuff behind your back. Like, she didn't even show up for the ribbon-cutting ceremony at the spa. Told Carla she had some huge stomach bug and could barely get out of bed, but I saw her that night eating dinner at the diner."

"Maybe she made a speedy recovery," I said, though I doubted it. Why wouldn't she show up for her best friend's big moment? Was she still bitter about not being a partner?

Brittany unscrewed the cap and applied a coat of polish to one nail. "Plus, every time she came in the spa, she'd make little comments about the place. She'd gush about how beautiful the colors were, but she would never have picked those for herself. Or she'd say the chairs were super comfy and there must be another reason her back was acting up. Stuff like that. And we had a surprise inspection by the health inspector the third day we were open. He said he'd gotten a call about our cleaning practices. I don't know for sure that it was Patricia, but I bet she's the one who called." Brittany had been talking faster and faster while she'd been painting my nails, and now the brush slipped off one nail. A trail of Peach Fizz ran up to the first knuckle of my ring finger. "Oops." She giggled as she grabbed a napkin and wiped off the polish.

Ashlee came back with three spoons and a stack of ice cream pints, using her chin to keep the tower from toppling. She gingerly set the cartons on the coffee table and dropped onto the opposite end of the couch. "Hurry up, you two."

"I'm going, I'm going," Brittany said. As soon as she

finished the last nail, she shouted, "Ice cream break!" She hopped up from the floor. "I get the banana and fudge one." She grabbed the pint.

"I'll take the one with the brownie bits," I said as I grabbed the carton, careful not to smear my polish. "And I'm eating it straight out of the carton." I handed it to Ashlee to open. She did and passed it back before handing around the spoons. We all dug in.

Back on the floor, Brittany moaned. "This is so good. But only three more bites, or I'll have to spend a week at the gym to work it off."

"It's worth it," I said as I shoveled another bite into my mouth.

Ashlee rolled her eyes. "Dana doesn't worry about staying slim," she said to Brittany out the side of her mouth.

Brittany studied me. "I didn't think so." She saw me open my mouth to protest and hurried on. "Hey, it's not that you're fat. It's just that you're not really thin, like Ashlee here."

"I've checked the charts. I'll have you know my weight is in the normal range for my height," I said. "Besides, men like women who have a little meat on their bones. Together, you two couldn't make up one quarter-pound burger patty." I took another bite of ice cream to show them how much I didn't care what they thought about my weight. Even if I did just a little.

Ashlee shook her head as she dug her spoon into her pint of Cherry Garcia. "Guys say that only because they think chunky women won't sleep with them otherwise."

"They do not," I said. "You want to believe that men

love skinny women, because otherwise, all those years of skipping dessert were a total waste."

"Not true," Ashlee said.

I savored another spoonful before carefully putting the lid back on the carton, not sure if my nails were dry yet. "I'd love to argue with you some more, but I've got work in the morning. Thanks for the ice cream."

I stuck the carton in the freezer and the spoon in the dishwasher, and then I headed to my room. After I got ready for bed, I lay in the dark and thought about what Brittany had said. Was Patricia behind the call to the health inspector? She'd claimed not to be upset about Carla refusing to make her a partner, but between what Brittany had told me tonight and what Erin had said before, she must have been angrier than she was letting on.

And I couldn't forget Stan. The only motive I could think of was that he killed Carla to defend his wife's honor, but that idea seemed ludicrous. This wasn't the eighteen hundreds. There would be no duel.

Still, someone had murdered Carla, and I needed to focus on eliminating the people on my list. If I could cross off one name at a time, then eventually, there would be only one left: that of the killer.

Chapter 26

The next morning I stood at the gate to the pigsty. I'd already posted the day's blog and helped Zennia with the breakfast service. Now it was time to clean up after the pigs.

Wilbur saw me pull on the rubber boots that were kept near the sty and open the gate. He lumbered to his feet and ambled over as I slipped inside and latched the gate behind me. With his curlicue tail wagging, he reminded me of a dog waiting for a treat.

I could only shrug and offer my empty hands. "Sorry. I've got nothing for you. But I am cleaning your stall." This particular chore definitely wasn't my favorite part of working here, and technically, it wasn't even my responsibility, but Esther couldn't always get to it and I knew the pigs appreciated it, even if they didn't show it. Plus, I kind of liked the little fellows.

I picked up the rake and got to work, chatting with Wilbur as I cleaned. "Anything new with you?" I asked.

He shook his head. I wasn't sure if he was answering me or if he had a fly buzzing around his eyes.

"I'm starting to get used to living with Ashlee," I told him. "Of course, I'd like it more if she went grocery shopping on occasion or cleaned up after herself. Talk about being a pig."

Wilbur snorted loudly.

"No offense," I said.

I finished cleaning out the old straw and grabbed the hose. Wilbur watched me.

"You guys sure have a peaceful life out here," I said. "No worries at all." I saw Gretchen near the spa entrance and nodded in her direction. "Not like poor Gretchen. I don't believe the police suspect her of killing Carla anymore, but some of the townspeople do." Wilbur tilted his head as if he was actually following what I was saying. "I'm sure the police will figure things out soon. They must know by now that Miguel lied about his alibi. And how Patricia was supposedly Carla's best friend, but she's not always that nice."

Wilbur pawed at the ground and sniffed the dirt, then snorted again.

"An excellent idea. I *should* talk to her again."

I finished cleaning the sty and returned the tools to their proper places before scrubbing my hands and forearms at the outside faucet like a doctor prepping for surgery. Then I hosed down the boots before going inside the kitchen to scrub my hands again, trying to stay out of Zennia's way as she dished up lunch. No matter how much I cleaned my hands after working in the sty, I'd swear I could still smell the muck.

The rooster clock on the kitchen wall showed it was already past noon. Cleaning the sty had taken longer than I'd expected. As I toweled off my hands, my stomach growled so loud that even Zennia heard it.

"There's plenty of seaweed soup," she said as she ladled a spoonful into a bowl. "The guests are all raving about how delectable it is."

I leaned over the bowls full of broth and sniffed. If seaweed tasted anything like it smelled, no way would I ever try it. "What is it with you and seaweed lately?" I asked.

Zennia set the bowl down and wiped up a puddle of soup on the counter before filling another bowl. "I told you how healthy seaweed is, with all its vitamins and minerals, plus all the nutrients from the other vegetables I add. It's like a health food store in a bowl."

I knew there was a reason I avoided health food stores. "Thanks, but I have an errand to run in town. I'll grab lunch there."

"Let me know if you change your mind." She picked up the bowls of soup and hustled toward the dining room.

Once she was gone, I went to the stove and looked into the pot, noting the dark green squares floating on top of the broth. My head filled with visions of seagulls circling over the ocean surf. I wrinkled my nose. No seaweed soup for me.

I retrieved my purse from the office, cut through the lobby, and sidestepped the ducks on my way down the sidewalk. Once in my car, I drove to town and pulled into a slot directly in front of Patricia's store. I could hear hammering the moment I opened my car door, and it only got louder as I approached the shop.

Through the plate-glass window that covered most of

the storefront, I could see two workmen moving around inside. One was patching a hole in the wall, while the other constructed what looked to be a counter. Off to the side, Patricia watched them, wearing spotless white coveralls and holding a clipboard in her hand, reminding me of Gordon when he was supervising one of us at the farm.

As I stepped inside, Patricia caught sight of me. "What a nice surprise, Dana," she said, though judging by the way she scrunched up her face, I had to assume she was more annoyed than pleased.

"Hi, Patricia," I said, raising my voice over the din. "I wanted to see how your shop is coming along. My mom's been bugging me for an update." Totally untrue, but a little buttering up never hurt.

"Oh, she's so sweet." She waved me over. "Not much has changed since the last time I saw you, but come on back and we can talk." She turned toward the man measuring the counter. "I'll only be gone a minute."

He nodded, and she led the way to the back room. The space was mostly empty, save for an old wooden desk that someone had polished to a glossy sheen and a plush black office chair on wheels. In one corner someone had flipped over a straight-backed chair and had rested the seat on a worktable so that the legs pointed toward the ceiling.

"There now. It's much quieter. I can't stand to yell over that racket," Patricia said. She sat in the cushioned chair and set the clipboard down. "You can tell your mom everything is on track. I still hope to open in another few weeks."

"You must know what you're doing."

The hammering ceased, and Patricia popped up

from the chair. She stepped around the corner, and the hammering resumed. She returned to her seat and shifted her weight a few times to get settled. "My job is to keep everyone else in line at this point. As soon as the construction work is finished, I can start getting everything else ready."

With the only other chair resting upside down on the worktable, I had nowhere to sit. Instead, I moved around the room, noting the scratches and chips in the walls, which I was sure Patricia would soon cover with a fresh coat of paint. I walked to the overturned chair and saw thick gobs of glue where the legs met the seat. The sharp smell of glue was evident in the air. "Sounds like you've got everything under control. Is Stan helping you?"

Patricia sighed. "In a roundabout way. He's picking up the slack at home so I can devote more time here. Considering all the years I've taken care of him, it's only fair."

"Still, that's awfully nice of him. Some guys are so spoiled by their wives that they become completely useless. You've got quite a husband there." I couldn't resist the urge to reach out and wiggle one chair leg. It moved easily in my hand. I glanced back in time to see Patricia grimace.

"Guess that hasn't finished drying," she commented.

I felt myself flush and dropped my hand. "Sorry." I switched topics. "So what do you think about Erin packing up the Pampered Life? I'm assuming you already know about it, since I heard the news from Stan."

Patricia gave me a sharp look, as if Stan was not allowed to speak to anyone without his wife present.

"I ran into him at the supermarket," I added.

She smiled, though the expression looked strained. "That explains it. Excuse me a minute." She disappeared around the corner, and I heard her talking to the men. When Patricia returned, she settled back in the chair. "I offered to help Erin pack. I figured it was a big task for one person, but of course, she didn't want my help. She never does."

"I'm sure she's still grieving over Carla's death. She might have wanted time to go through her aunt's belongings in solitude."

Patricia shook her head. "She's too stubborn to ask for help. I can't wait until she comes crawling to me when she can't figure out how to empty the mud baths. I already have the number of a guy who can do the job, but I won't be giving her my help until she wants it."

I couldn't tell if Patricia was upset that Erin had refused her help because Patricia didn't like being excluded from things or because she truly cared for the niece of her best friend. "Think you'll see any more of Erin now that Carla's gone?"

"I doubt it," she practically spat. "I feel an obligation to look after her for Carla's sake, but if she rebuffs me at every turn, I don't see how I can. I'm sure Ricky will knock her up any day now, and she'll move into that trailer with him and his mother."

All righty then. Good to know Patricia had such high aspirations for Erin. "He's probably a decent guy. He's still young enough that he has time to pick a career."

"If he bothers. Did you know Carla was all set to loan that kid money to go to school?"

So the money wasn't a bribe to buy Ricky off. I

perched on the edge of the desk. "That was awfully generous of her. I thought she didn't like Ricky."

Patricia picked up the clipboard and scanned the top page. "It was stupid, if you ask me. He never would have paid her back. But she had this crazy idea that if he went to college, he'd make something of himself. She didn't want Erin dating a bum."

"I heard he's a mechanic. That's a good profession."

"I wouldn't know about that. All I know is that the next time I talked to Carla, the deal was off. She wasn't planning to offer him any money, after all, and, boy, was she mad. She never did tell me what got her so upset."

Interesting. What had made Carla retract her offer to help Ricky pay for school? Had she uncovered a secret about his past that had made her turn against him? I might need to find some way to track him down and ask him. So long as I wasn't trapped with him in Carla's spa again.

Patricia was tapping her pen on the desktop and watching me.

I rose. "I should get out of your way."

"I'll walk you out," she said. "I could use the fresh air." We passed through the front room, and Patricia stopped to point out a flaw to one of the workmen before continuing on.

Once we were outside, I looked down the street. From where I stood, I could barely make out the green-and-white awning of Carla's former spa. I already knew how Patricia felt about Erin's boyfriend, but how did she feel about Carla's? "Miguel came by the spa the other day. He's still shaken up over Carla's death."

"Miguel is such a dear, sweet man. I keep inviting him to dinner, knowing he must be heartbroken, but he prefers to suffer his grief in private. He has such a strong spirit."

Funny how Erin was a selfish ingrate when she snubbed Patricia's invitations, but Miguel was a noble warrior. "He was especially upset that Carla had invited him over that night," I said, "but he'd chosen to go to a meeting for work. Is that what he told you?"

"Yes, the poor thing. Can you imagine the guilt he must be feeling? I would never be able to live with myself if I were him."

So Miguel was telling everyone the same story about this work meeting. I guessed that once you lied to the police, you'd better make sure you didn't change the details. Patricia's head kept swiveling between me and the shop. She was clearly anxious to get back to supervising the workmen.

"I've gotta run," I said. "Good luck with your business."

"Thanks, but luck will get me only so far. Determination and smarts will get me the rest of the way."

I had no doubt Patricia possessed both. I watched as she strode back into the shop and immediately started talking to the men.

But as smart as Patricia was, she hadn't seen through Miguel's phony alibi any more than I had. Where had Miguel been the night of Carla's murder? What was he hiding?

Chapter 27

The end of my lunch hour was rapidly approaching, but instead of returning to my car, I walked across the street. As long as I was downtown, I might as well see if Mom was working today. Now that I'd moved out of her house, I was continually amazed at how little we saw of each other. I missed the chats we used to have.

The bell chimed as I entered Going Back for Seconds, and I stopped in the doorway to let my eyes adjust to the dim lighting. I spotted Mom in a back corner, talking to a customer. While I waited for her to finish, I browsed the nearby racks. For being second-hand, the merchandise was in impeccable condition. Most of the items were fancy dresses and silk pantsuits, and I had to wonder if the women had worn the outfits for special occasions and then had decided to sell them, knowing they'd never wear them again.

The customer Mom was helping disappeared into one of the dressing rooms in the back, and Mom came over to where I was looking through a collection of cocktail dresses. She plucked a little black dress off the rack. "This would be perfect for a date with Jason."

I took the dress and held it against myself to see how long it was. The hemline hit mid-thigh. "He'd certainly like it."

"Keep it in mind for the next time he invites you to a special night out." She hung it back up. "What brings you into town? Are you off work today?"

"No, I'm on my lunch break and thought I'd stop in and see how you're doing."

The customer came out of the dressing room, and Mom rushed over. As the lady spun before the tri-fold mirror and watched the skirt twirl, Mom oohed and aahed in appreciation. The woman took one last look, nodded at her reflection, and went back to the dressing room.

Mom returned to where I waited. "That emerald-green color is stunning with her complexion." She lifted a jacket and fussed with the shoulders until the material hung straight.

"It looks like you're enjoying this job," I said.

"I couldn't be happier. How's work at the farm?"

"The spa side has been slow lately, but I'm sure business will pick up again. And Esther is teaching a composting class in a couple of days."

"Good for her." Mom lowered her voice and leaned in, keeping one eye on the dressing room area. "I don't want to upset you, but Sue Ellen is hearing a lot of tittle-tattle about your masseuse. People are convinced she's involved in that murder. More than one person has told Sue Ellen they won't go to the spa as long as she's working there."

I squeezed my eyes shut and rubbed my forehead. "I've heard similar remarks. Unfortunately, this kind of talk won't die down until the police make an arrest."

"I just hope they don't arrest your masseuse," Mom said. "That'll damage the reputation of Esther's place."

"Sounds like the damage has already started." I felt worry gnaw at my gut. "Say, Mom, maybe you could ask your friends to book a session at the spa? Only until the police clear everything up, of course."

"That's a wonderful idea. So many of my friends love being pampered. They'll jump at the idea. Consider it done."

The woman came out of the back area, dressed in her original clothes and carrying the emerald-green dress like it was a priceless heirloom.

"I need to ring her up," Mom said.

"And I need to grab my lunch before my hour is completely gone. I just wanted to say hi."

"I'm glad you did." Mom gave me a quick hug before she hurried to the register.

I went out the door and back across the street to where my car waited outside Patricia's shop. As I climbed inside, I could see the workmen moving around through the window. I didn't see Patricia, but I suspected she was lurking nearby.

I stopped on my way out of town for a fish sandwich and fries to go. As I drove back to the farm, I thought about what Mom had said about people avoiding the spa. Gordon had already commented that appointments were down. If he found out the situation was even more serious than he believed, he'd insist that Esther fire

Gretchen immediately. There'd be no way Gretchen—or I—could change his mind.

I parked the car and followed the path to the kitchen. As I walked through the back door, I heard Zennia gasp. She jumped up from where she was sitting at the kitchen table and dashed over to open the trash can. I heard the crinkle of cellophane as she threw something in.

"Is anything wrong?" I asked her.

She whirled around, rapidly chewing whatever was in her mouth. She squeezed out a muffled "No."

Not sure why Zennia was acting so oddly, I moved over to where she stood and lifted the trash can lid. On top of the pile of detritus sat a familiar wrapper. I slapped a hand over my mouth. "Zennia, are you eating a Twinkie?"

She held up a hand while she finished swallowing. "Now, I know what you're thinking," she said as soon as she could speak.

I felt a huge grin spread over my face. "I'm thinking that for all your lectures about how the food you put in your mouth determines whether your body thrives or fails, you like the occasional unhealthy treat as much as the rest of us."

She pushed the trash can lid down. "I do not. It's only this one time. I gave in to a childhood treat, is all."

After the grief she'd given me over the past few months when she caught me eating anything deep-fried or sugar filled, I couldn't resist teasing her. "I don't know that. You could be in this kitchen all day long, stuffing your face with Ring Dings and miniature powdered doughnuts."

She swiped at her mouth, as if telltale crumbs might still be lingering there. "Twinkies are my one weakness. My grandmother used to keep a supply at her house for my after-school snack. Eating one always brings back those wonderful memories. Plus, I had a bowl of seaweed soup first to counterbalance all that sugar."

Her mention of the seaweed soup reminded me of my fish sandwich. I grabbed a plate out of the cupboard and a napkin out of the holder. "Is it my imagination, or are you cooking foods that are almost normal lately? Even the seaweed soup looked a bit tame, compared with other dishes I've seen you make."

"I had an epiphany," Zennia said. "As much as I love introducing guests to new dishes, not all my creations have been well received. I've decided the most important thing is for people to eat healthy, even if they stick with the more tried-and-true foods."

I set my lunch on the table and sat down while Zennia washed a dish in the sink. "If your other creations are anything like that fish with mustard sauce you made the other day, count me in." I bit into my sandwich.

As I swallowed my bite, Gretchen came in the back door, singing to herself. She broke off when she saw us, and said, "Hey, guys." She went to the refrigerator and started poking through the contents on the shelves, eventually pulling out a carton of yogurt. "So I did have one more in here."

I gestured to the chair across from me. "Care to join me?"

She grabbed a spoon from the drawer and sat down. "For a minute."

Zennia dried her hands and glanced at the rooster clock. "Wish I could stay, too, but I've got an herb garden to tend to." She went out the back door while Gretchen pulled the foil top off her yogurt.

"Busy afternoon coming up?" I asked. Surely not all of her clients had abandoned her, even if Sue Ellen seemed to think so.

"I've got a session in ten minutes with that one guy, Miguel. Thanks for pointing him in my direction, by the way. He told me you were the reason he called for an appointment."

From the way she spoke, I realized Gretchen didn't know exactly who Miguel was or his relationship to Carla. I was curious to know her opinion. "What do you think of him?"

Gretchen shrugged noncommittally, but her cheeks took on a pink tinge. "He seems nice. Um, he did suggest we might have dinner sometime."

My nose twitched. Something suddenly stank, and it wasn't my fish sandwich. "Gretchen, I don't know how to break this to you, but Miguel's married."

"What?" Gretchen asked in disbelief. "Why do I always attract guys like that?"

"Not to mention he was dating Carla before she was killed."

Gretchen almost dropped her spoonful of yogurt. "You gotta be kidding me. And now he's asking me out? What's wrong with that guy?"

"Good question." I chomped down on my sandwich, taking out my disgust on the fish fillet.

Gretchen shoved back from the table and rose. "I can't wait to get this appointment over with. I'm not sure I want him as a client anymore after what you told me."

"Maybe once his leg heals, he won't come back."

"Or maybe I'll make sure I'm booked solid whenever he tries to schedule a session."

I chuckled. "That's another solution. In any case, let me know if he says anything interesting while he's here. You know, like how guilty he feels about killing his girlfriend."

"Don't I wish. Then all my problems would be solved." She rinsed out her yogurt container before tossing it in the recycling bin, dropped her spoon in the sink, and trudged out the back door.

I pushed thoughts of Miguel from my mind while I finished my lunch and then went into the office to grab the digital camera from the desk drawer. I tried to update the farm's Web site every few weeks. While I could reuse some of the vegetable garden photos from the brochure, I wanted to capture the vivid reds and yellows of the spring flowers that had recently bloomed.

After taking half a dozen photos of the daffodils that lined the path leading to the guest cabins, I moved on to the wildflowers that grew among the shrubs, managing to capture a photograph of a bee as it landed on a bright orange poppy.

At the corner of the first cabin, a purple flower caught my eye. I'd just squatted down to get a close-up shot when I heard, "I'd use my camera on that cute guy over by the tent."

I glanced behind me to find an attractive woman in her late forties standing nearby. I'd seen her visit Gretchen for various spa services before, but I didn't know exactly who she was. She was staring off into the distance, and I rose from my crouched position to follow her gaze. I saw Miguel at the entrance to the spa tent, talking to Gretchen.

"Man, is he smokin'," the woman said. She saw my raised eyebrows and laughed. "He's probably too old for you, but he's right in my ballpark. I've had my eye on him for a while now."

"Do you know him?" I asked.

She winked at me. "Not as well as I'd like to. I'm friends with one of his cousins. I bump into him every now and again at family gatherings, things like that. I haven't seen him in a few months, but now that he's single again, I might have to try my luck."

Single? What about his wife? Or did she see Carla's death as her big opportunity to snatch up Miguel for a little side action, never mind his wife? "Aren't you the least bit upset that the woman he was seeing was murdered?" I asked. I couldn't keep the judgmental tone out of my voice.

The woman's eyes widened. "Who are you talking about?"

"Miguel's girlfriend, Carla. Isn't that who you were talking about when you said he was single again?"

The woman raised a hand to her chest. "He has a girlfriend? I was talking about his wife."

"His wife?" I said stupidly.

"Yeah, he finally divorced the old battle-ax. I figure he's ready to jump in the dating pool again. But you're saying he already has."

She kept talking, but I tuned her out. Miguel was divorced? What did that mean for Carla's murder?

I was more confused than ever.

Chapter 28

I struggled to come to grips with Miguel's marital status. I needed to rethink everything I thought I knew about the guy. No wife meant no motive. He was a freewheeling single male who could date whomever he wanted. There went all my theories about why he might have killed Carla.

"You okay?" the woman asked me.

I brought my attention back to her and shook my head. "Guess I got lost in my thoughts."

She nudged me with her elbow. "He's coming this way. How do I look?" She smoothed down her hair and stuck out her chest.

Miguel reached us before I could answer.

"Hi, Miguel," the woman sang, thrusting her chest out even more. She'd better watch it, or she'd throw her back out.

Miguel flashed his straight white teeth. "Why, Valerie, it's been far too long. Where have you been hiding yourself?"

"Oh, here and there. I've been volunteering at my son's school. You know how I love working with children."

"It's one of your sterling qualities." He nodded toward me. "And, Dana, you're looking lovely, as always."

I considered my navy blue polo shirt and khakis with fresh dirt stains on the knees. "Um, thanks." Now that I knew Miguel was divorced, I was looking at him in a whole new light. He wasn't some sleazy married guy with no morals. He was a single guy playing the field. No law against that.

Valerie stepped up to Miguel's side and laid a hand on his arm. I noticed she managed to lean a boob against him, too. "Will I be seeing you at Patty's birthday party next weekend?" she cooed.

"I'm planning to stop by. I'll look for you."

"Be sure that you do," Valerie gushed as she squeezed his arm. I felt like I was getting a free lesson in Flirting 101.

Miguel patted her hand and shifted away from her. "I must bid you ladies adieu. Work calls." He strolled down the path, hands in his pockets.

Valerie turned back to me, feeling her cheek. "Does the spa have chemical peels?"

"No, but we do offer facials with all-natural ingredients."

Valerie waved her hand. "Yeah, yeah, that's all well and good, but it won't get rid of these wrinkles before that party. Guess I'll cancel my massage. I don't have much time to whip myself into shape."

I wanted to tell her that all the time in the world wouldn't turn back the clock and make her a twenty-something vixen, but she'd already rushed off to talk to Gretchen.

When she was out of sight, I pulled my cell phone from my pocket. I was about to hit Jason's number when one of the nearby cabin doors opened. A couple emerged, laughing and talking. They said hello on their way by, and I decided that the middle of the path was not the best location to make a private phone call.

Still holding my phone, I cut past the cabins and followed the Chicken Run Trail, careful not to walk too far in among the trees. Reception tended to be spotty farther along the path. I stopped under an oak tree and listened for any sound. Other than the hum of insects and an occasional bird chirping, the area was silent.

Certain I wouldn't be overheard, I made the call.

"Hey, Dana," Jason said when he answered. His words were slightly distorted.

"Did I interrupt your lunch?" I asked.

"I'm eating a sandwich at my desk, but I'd much rather talk to you."

At his words, I got that warm, fuzzy feeling that was becoming a regular sensation anytime I talked to Jason. "You'll never guess why I called."

"You won a free cruise, and I'm the lucky guest?"

"No."

"You've secretly been taking striptease lessons and need to practice on me for homework?"

"No." Although that one did sound tempting.

"Too bad," Jason said. "I give up. Why'd you call?"

My grip tightened as I pictured how excited he'd be at my news. "Miguel is divorced. He wasn't cheating on a jealous wife, after all. Or even a wife who wasn't jealous. That means he had no reason to kill Carla."

"Huh."

I hadn't expected Jason to drive straight over to celebrate my discovery, but I had anticipated a little more enthusiasm. "That's all you have to say?"

"Sorry. You did an excellent job finding out Miguel is single."

"Don't patronize me," I said, not hiding my irritation.

I heard typing over the phone. "I'm not, but even if Miguel doesn't have a wife, he still lied about his alibi. I have to wonder why."

In my excitement over the divorce, I'd forgotten about Miguel's nonexistent alibi. "Let's think. Maybe he panicked. Maybe he doesn't have any way to prove where he was that night, and was worried the police would arrest him if he couldn't establish his whereabouts."

"They'd need a lot more than that," Jason said. "Lots of people can't provide evidence of where they were on any given day."

"He might not know that. Spouses and boyfriends are usually at the top of a cop's suspect list." But it did seem odd. Where had Miguel been that night? Assuming he wasn't the one who killed Carla, why else would he need to lie?

Jason broke into my thoughts. "Okay, let's say Miguel has no motive. Who does that leave us with?"

I used my free hand to count off the suspects. "Erin, of course. Carla didn't approve of her relationship with

Ricky and threatened to kick Erin out of the house. Ricky, for the same reason . . . Plus, Carla withdrew her offer to give Ricky a loan for school." I paused for breath. "Then there's Patricia, who wanted to partner with Carla on the spa, but Carla turned her down. Plus, Stan, who . . ." My voice trailed off. I still had no ideas about Stan.

Jason read my mind. "Even without a motive, we gotta keep him on the list."

"Yeah, we should. You know, I was talking to Patricia, and she got all bent out of shape when I mentioned I'd spoken to Stan. Remember how I told you I ran into him last night at the grocery store?"

"Yes, that was right before you went to the spa by yourself, and Erin caught you," he said dryly. "I remember."

I kept talking before he got sidetracked by my lack of judgment. "Anyway, I thought it was some weird control thing that she didn't like people talking to her husband when she wasn't around, but maybe that wasn't the reason. Maybe Patricia knows Stan killed Carla for whatever reason, and she's afraid he'll bust out with a confession if she's not there to stop him."

The phone was silent for so long that I thought my call had been dropped. Then Jason spoke again. "Does Stan strike you as the type to have emotional outbursts?"

I visualized Stan in his conservative suit, buying his wife's feminine hygiene products. "Well, no. He's definitely a steady Eddie. Aren't most accountants? But maybe the guilt's getting to him."

"Sorry. I'm not buying it."

I sighed. "Me neither. Especially since he has an alibi."

I heard whistling behind me and whirled around, my heart thumping. I wasn't sure who to expect, but it was only an older gentleman, whom I recognized as one of the guests. He wore a straw hat on his head and had a pair of binoculars around his neck. He carried a book about birds in one hand.

"Oops. I gotta go," I told Jason.

"Me, too, but let me know if you find out anything else."

"Right back atcha." I clicked off, said hello to the man, and headed back to the house.

I waved to Berta and the chickens on my way past the chicken coop and cut through the hedge near the redwood tree. A man was soaking in the Jacuzzi, a glass of wine nearby. Another man and a woman were playing Scrabble at one of the picnic tables. I slipped in the French doors of the dining room and crossed the hall to the office.

Once in my chair, I downloaded the scant few photos from the camera onto the computer and realized I needed to take a lot more before I could update the Web site. I spent the rest of the afternoon wandering the farm, taking photos of anything interesting that caught my eye and trying to get the pigs and chickens to cooperate. They had an uncanny knack for turning around right when I clicked a photo, giving me plenty of shots of their backsides. I deleted those.

By the time I finished sorting through the pictures

and picking the best ones for the site, it was time to go home. I decided to leave through the kitchen door so I could say good-bye to Wilbur. I followed the path to the pigsty and stopped a moment to give him a friendly pat before moving on. As I passed the spa entrance, Gretchen came out, pulling on her jacket. I slowed my steps and waited for her to catch up before I resumed my regular pace.

"Heading home?" I asked.

"Yep. Did my last facial a few minutes ago."

A fly buzzed in my ear, and I swatted it away. "Before I forget, I learned this afternoon that Miguel isn't married, after all. Turns out he's divorced."

"So he's not a total scumbag," Gretchen said. "I probably should have been nicer to him during our session, then."

I laughed. "Maybe he'll think you were playing hard to get." We stopped at my car. "I don't suppose he said anything about Carla's murder while he was here."

"Not a word. I tried to work it into the conversation a couple of times, but he always changed the subject. The guy's slick."

"I've noticed that myself." I unlocked my car door. "Thanks, anyway, for trying to get him to talk."

"I only wish I'd learned something to help. Oh, well, see you tomorrow."

"See ya."

She walked to her car while I climbed in mine. The drive home was mercifully short. As soon as I got in the apartment, I kicked off my shoes and sank onto the couch, doing my best to ignore the open magazines, the half-full bowls of cereal, and the flip-flops that covered the coffee table. I'd leave all that for Ashlee. I closed my eyes and let the day melt away.

I was starting to drift off when a sound penetrated the fog in my brain. I heard someone clomping up the outdoor stairs and then a key being inserted in the lock. I opened my eyes and groaned. Ashlee was home.

She bounced into the room and kicked the door shut behind her. "Hey, Dana. Brittany's coming over in a minute."

I sat up and surveyed the room. "That doesn't give us much time to clean up this mess."

"Who says we're cleaning anything? It's only Brittany."

"Still, we should make an effort," I said. "And since this is your mess, I'll let you start."

Ashlee made a face but moved toward the coffee table. "Fine, whatever." She swept the magazines into a stack and picked up a cereal bowl. She pointed at the table. "I knew it. Isn't that your napkin?"

I held up the napkin by two fingers and inspected it as if I was a detective at a crime scene. "I don't see my fingerprints on it, but I'll throw it away, anyway."

"See? I knew this mess wasn't all mine."

"You're right. That one napkin is obviously what ruined the whole look." I carried it to the kitchen and dropped it in the trash can under the sink.

Someone, presumably Brittany, knocked on the door. I went to answer it, but Ashlee said, "Wait!" She scurried into the bathroom, probably to make sure her makeup hadn't moved since the last time she checked.

Another knock sounded, and Ashlee yelled, "Coming!" Before I could reach the door, she brushed past me and flung it open. Brittany waited on the other side.

"Well, don't just stand there," Ashlee said. "Get in here." She grabbed Brittany's wrist and pulled her into the room.

Brittany giggled. "Good to see you, too." She looked at me. "Hey, are you coming with us tonight?"

Before I could ask where they were going, Ashlee piped up. "Yeah, you should come. We're going bowling."

"The two of you?" I asked. Usually Ashlee went bowling only with her latest love interest. She swore the lighting in the place made her look like Heidi Klum.

"One of my friends spotted a bunch of hot guys there last time she went. Now that I've got a slot open in the boyfriend department, I thought I'd try my luck," Ashlee announced.

Ah, that explained it. I considered my exciting plans for a Friday evening, which involved a frozen meal and watching TV. I needed to get out more. Plus, bowling was fairly cheap. "Sure, I'll go."

"Cool. Let's hurry up and get ready," Ashlee urged. "I want to stake out a spot at the alley before the after-work crowd shows up."

I went to my room to get cleaned up. Twenty minutes later I'd showered, dressed, and primped. I found Brittany on the couch by herself, reading one of Ashlee's fashion magazines. Apparently, the poor girl had been left to entertain herself while Ashlee and I had both gotten ready. We really needed to work on our hosting skills.

"Ashlee's not done yet?" I asked, though I already knew the answer. I'd never known Ashlee to be ready before me.

"Haven't seen her."

"Can I get you a soda or anything?"

Brittany flipped the magazine closed. "I'm good."

I sat on the other side of the couch. "Are you searching for a new job now that the spa's closed?"

"Naw. My uncle's got a dentist office in town. His admin's having a baby, and I'm filling in for her while she's out on maternity leave. With any luck, she'll stay out and I can work there full-time." Brittany giggled. "Don't tell my uncle I said that. He thinks she's the best admin he's ever had."

"What about that other girl who worked with you at the spa? What was her name? Jessica?"

"She had to move back in with her parents in Oakland. I'm sure she'll find a gig down there."

Ashlee came out of her room. "Okay, girls, let's go find some guys."

I studied her miniskirt. "How will you bowl in that?"

She self-consciously tugged the hem down. "I'll be fine. And this skirt guarantees that every guy in the place will have his eyes on me."

"Well, sure. It's a free peep show."

Ashlee rolled her eyes. "Whatever. Let's go."

We all tramped downstairs and piled into Ashlee's car. I hurried to buckle myself in as she revved the engine and floored it in reverse. She took the turn out of the driveway too fast, and I grabbed the back of Brittany's headrest to steady myself.

"This will be way cool," Ashlee said from the driver's seat. "Dana, since you're already stuck with Jason, you can be my wingman, or wingwoman, if you'd rather call yourself that."

I leaned forward in my seat. "I'm not helping you pick up guys. I'm there to bowl."

"You can do both. But be sure the guy's cute. And when you're talking me up, try to mention that I used to be a cheerleader. Then he'll know how limber I am."

I threw myself against the car seat, too disgusted to reply. I was no one's pimp.

Ashlee adjusted the rearview mirror so she could wink at me. "I'm kidding about the cheerleading. I mean, you can talk about it if you want, but it's not totally necessary. There are so many other fabulous things you can say about me." She watched me in the mirror, waiting for my reply.

"Stop sign!" Brittany shrieked.

Ashlee slammed on the brakes, and the car shuddered to a stop, the nose of the Camaro well over the line. "Sheesh, when did they put that there?"

"Back when we were in elementary school," I said.

She stomped on the gas, and we surged forward. "That can't be right. I would have noticed it before." She looked at me in the mirror again. "So will you help me?" She stared at me so long that I began to worry she'd run another stop sign.

I threw up my hands and said, "Fine. I'll help you."

She nodded and returned her eyes to the road.

A few minutes later we arrived, relatively unscathed, at the bowling alley. Brittany got out and popped the seat forward so I could slide out and join her. The three of us marched in together. The guys playing at the nearby lanes and seated in the snack area all watched our grand entrance. It helped that we were the only girls in the place.

"Eat first or bowl first?" I asked, raising my voice to be heard over the techno music beating out of the speakers.

Ashlee scanned the crowd. "Definitely better odds at the snack bar. We'll start there."

Like some sort of coordinated man-hunting routine, she brushed her long blond hair over her shoulder, while Brittany patted her own shorter style. Together, they sashayed to the snack bar. I trailed behind at a slower pace, giving them room to maneuver.

They stopped before the giant menu board posted behind the counter and looked at it, nudging each other and giggling from time to time. I had no idea what was so hilarious about nachos and corn dogs, so I tuned them out.

When they didn't edge any closer to the counter, I moved around them to place my order. Whoever was working the snack bar had his back to me as he bent down and shoved packages of napkins into a storage area under the counter. When he'd finished emptying the box, he stood up and turned around.

I almost fell back a step. It was Ricky. If he was already working as a mechanic, what was he doing here?

Chapter 29

Ricky's eyes widened when he saw me, his expression probably a mirror image of my own startled one.

"Oh, hey," he said. "How's it going?" He grabbed a nearby rag and started wiping the counter.

"I didn't realize you worked at the bowling alley. Someone told me you were a mechanic."

He grunted. "I wish. I sweep the floors for the mechanic is more like it. He's supposed to train me one of these days, but I had to get a second job if I wanted to eat."

I nodded in sympathy. Even with Ashlee and me both working full-time, I still worried about all those extra bills that showed up unexpectedly, like car repairs and doctor visits. "At least this is a cool place to work." If you liked loud music and even louder bowlers.

Ricky finished wiping the counter and tossed the rag underneath it. "It's all right, and the food's free."

"Can't beat that." I leaned on the counter, wondering how I could find out more about why Carla had offered Ricky money for school and then had changed her mind. If he couldn't afford to buy food, he'd definitely need Carla's money to pay for his classes.

Ricky looked past me. "Are you gonna order?"

I turned around. Not only had Ashlee and Brittany gotten in line behind me, but so had three other people. Our little conversation would have to wait. I hurriedly read the board. "Give me a corn dog and lemonade."

He turned to fill my order while I dug money out of my pocket. By the time I extracted the right bills, he'd placed my lemonade and wrapped corn dog on the counter. I tried not to think about how long that corn dog had probably been lying in the heated case. I handed him the money, took my change, and stepped to the side to wait for Ashlee and Brittany.

After ordering, they came away with a bottle of water for each of them and an order of fries to share. That was their dinner? That wouldn't keep me full for fifteen minutes, let alone the whole night.

We found an empty booth that looked like it was older than all of us combined, and sat down to eat. We were done in five minutes.

"Ready to do some bowling?" I asked as I wiped mustard off my fingers.

Ashlee scanned the snack area. "Yeah, there's only a bunch of old guys in here now. Maybe the hot guys are already bowling."

I slid out of the booth and tossed my trash in the can. Ricky was still busy helping customers. I'd have to wait to speak with him. With any luck, everyone would run out to see Ashlee bowl in her ridiculously short skirt, and I could talk to him in private.

We paid for our games and got our lane assignment, then moved over to the shoe rental. Ashlee immediately rejected the brown-and-white saddle shoes the guy offered her, and insisted on a black-and-white pair. She held them up for me.

"These match my outfit," she declared.

"Fantastic," I said.

I took the first pair the guy gave me, and we made our way to our assigned lane. I swapped out my shoes before hunting for the lightest ball on the racks that I could find. A bright pink number at the end of the row drew my attention. I tested the weight before I returned to our spot.

When I got back, Ashlee was sitting with some guy I didn't know. They had their heads bent together, and Ashlee was twirling her hair, while he kept rubbing the stubble on his chin and nodding. Brittany was lacing up her shoes at the other end of the row of chairs, and I took a seat beside her.

I gestured to the cozy couple. "Who's that?"

Brittany straightened up and tipped her foot first one way, then the other, frowning at the bowling shoe. "I think he said his name's Zach. He came over right after you left. He thinks Ashlee's hot." She giggled.

How did Ashlee do it? I'd been gone for five minutes to pick out a ball, and she'd already snagged a guy? At least she didn't need me as her wingwoman anymore.

I entered our information into the console and bowled first. Gutter ball. On my second roll, I knocked down two pins. Brittany didn't fare much better. We waited for Ashlee to take her turn, but she was busy smiling and whispering with Zach. I went over to the two lovebirds and tapped her bowling shoe with my own. "You're up."

Ashlee gave a start, as if she'd forgotten we were even at the bowling alley. She batted her eyelashes at Zach. "Gosh, it's been so long since I bowled."

He stood and offered his hand. "Let me show you how."

Oh, gag.

They went over to the ball return, and Zach picked up a ball and handed it to her. Then he stood close enough behind her that I couldn't have wedged a shoehorn in between them. At least no one could see how short Ashlee's skirt was with Zach blocking the view. He guided her arm as she swung the ball forward and released it. My stomach roiled as I watched them.

Beside me, Brittany giggled. "Aren't they the cutest couple ever?"

I settled back and got ready for what would turn out to be the longest bowling game in history. Every time it was Ashlee's turn, I'd have to remind her. Then she and Zach would bowl together like conjoined twins. After each turn, Ashlee would have to tug down her skirt so she didn't get arrested for indecent exposure. Then Brittany and I would bowl. In between turns, I checked on Ricky at the snack bar. A steady stream of customers kept him busy.

Finally, the tenth frame arrived. I was so happy to see the end of the game, I bowled a spare. Brittany closed out her round, followed by Ashlee and her new friend. All our scores were abysmally low.

"Another game?" Brittany asked.

I couldn't imagine sitting through another ten frames of Bowling with Lovers. "Let's take a break."

Zach's eyes lit up, and he put an arm around Ashlee's waist. "I can show you my crazy skills in the arcade," he told her.

"Okay," Ashlee said a little too brightly. I knew Ashlee hated dating guys who spent time playing video games rather than paying attention to her. Maybe Zach wasn't such a catch, after all.

"I need to freshen up my makeup," Brittany said, grabbing her purse off the seat.

That left me to stake out the snack bar. I loitered near the napkin dispensers while Ricky waited on the two customers in line. Once they left and no new customers appeared, I stepped up. Ricky placed his hands on the counter and looked at me.

With my corn dog still sitting in my belly, I ordered a small soda.

He set a cup under the dispenser and pushed a button. When the cup was full, he popped on a plastic lid and set the soda on the counter. "Two bucks."

I made no move to get my money out. "Prices have gone up since I was a kid," I said.

He eyed me. "Aren't you in your twenties? You can't be much older than me."

I was getting awfully close to thirty, but who was counting? "I've been noticing how expensive everything is these days. I don't know how Erin manages to pay for school."

"Her aunt helped her out some. And with this extra job, I might be able to give her a hand."

I was touched that he cared enough about Erin that he'd help pay for her school. "I heard Carla offered to help you out so you'd be able to afford a few classes, too."

Ricky crossed his arms. "I'm my own man. No one pays my way."

"Is that what you told Carla?"

"You bet. She accused me of refusing the money because I didn't want to bother with school, but that wasn't true. A guy needs to support himself on his own. I didn't want any help."

Was it that simple? Had Ricky's pride kept him from accepting the loan, or had Carla withdrawn the offer? Did Ricky tell people he'd refused it to save face? Patricia seemed to believe that Carla had retracted the loan offer.

A cough came from behind me. An overweight, balding man had gotten in line and was waiting to order. I guessed my time was up. For now.

I pulled two ones from my pocket and handed them to Ricky. I stuck a straw in my soda and wandered through the bowling alley, sipping my drink. Ashlee was still in the arcade, looking totally bored. At least until Zach talked to her. Then she plastered a smile on her face and nodded at whatever he was saying.

Brittany had finished her bathroom run and was now chatting with a good-looking guy in the lane next to ours. *Score one for Brittany.*

When I'd finished walking the length of the bowling

alley, I tossed my soda cup in the trash and went back to the snack area. Ricky was finishing up with another customer.

When he saw me, he gave me a wary look. "Back again already?"

"Bowling makes me thirsty. Another soda, please." I'd better slow down on the beverages, or I'd spend the rest of the night making bathroom pit stops.

He retrieved my drink and set it on the counter. "You know, I'm glad you came back. Erin feels real bad about pulling those scissors on you the other night. She told me she wants to apologize, but she doesn't know where you live or anything."

And as long as she was a murder suspect, I wasn't going to tell her. "Well, I did surprise her when I dropped by the spa unexpectedly like that. I can't blame her for being on edge after her aunt was murdered there."

"I hear ya, but she'd love a chance to tell you how sorry she is. She knows she scared you pretty bad."

I bristled at the comment. Sure, I'd been petrified, but I didn't want other people to know that. "She freaked me out a little," I conceded, "but I think a lot of that was my own fault. It's just that I heard . . ." I paused, unexpectedly embarrassed to be accusing this guy's girlfriend of stabbing someone. What if it wasn't true?

"You heard she stabbed her mom's old man?" Ricky finished the sentence for me. "Patricia told you that, didn't she?"

"It might have been her," I said.

Ricky banged his fist on the counter. "She loves to spread that story around. Thinks she's making Erin look bad. Never mind that it wasn't Erin's fault. But Patricia lives in her big, fancy house with her white picket fence. She has no idea what the real world is like."

In all his defense of Erin, he had yet to deny the accusation. "So is it true? Did Erin stab her mom's boyfriend?"

He leaned toward me. "Only after he made a move on her. She told him no. When he wouldn't lay off, she stabbed him to protect herself."

I felt like cheering for Erin. "I had no idea that's what happened."

"Her mom didn't want to look like a bad mother, so she convinced the boyfriend not to press charges."

"Is that when Erin moved in with Carla?"

"Yeah. Her drunk of a mom wouldn't kick the bum out, so Erin left."

How sad that her mom had picked a boyfriend over her own daughter. "I'd move out, too."

Ricky's eyes focused behind me, and I knew another customer had arrived. I put my two bucks on the counter and moved out of the way. I didn't have any other questions for Ricky at this point. He'd told me everything I wanted to know.

Now I had to decide if he was telling the truth.

Chapter 30

I returned to our bowling lane. Ashlee was waiting near the ball return, slouched in a plastic chair. She must have ditched Zach, because he was nowhere in sight.

"What happened to your friend?" I asked, setting my soda in a cup holder.

Ashlee shot a glare toward the arcade. "Still playing some stupid video game. I bet he's there all night."

Brittany came up to where we sat, pulling her phone from her pocket and checking her reflection in the mirror app. "You guys up for another game or what?"

I glanced over my shoulder at the guy I'd seen Brittany talking to earlier. He was laughing with his friends, but he let his gaze stray our way every few seconds to see what Brittany was doing. "I thought you found someone new to hang out with."

Brittany looked toward the group of guys and gave a little wave. "I told him we'd hook up after I was done bowling. He wanted to play another round with his friends, anyway."

While I'd mentally vowed never to bowl with Ashlee again, my talk with Ricky had given me enough time to recover from our first game. "Sure, one more game is good."

With Zach no longer giving Ashlee lessons, the second game moved much faster. Before I knew it, the tenth frame was over, and we'd all broken a hundred with our scores. We changed out of our shoes and returned them to the shoe rental area.

On our way out of the building, I spotted Zach still in the arcade. He held a large plastic gun and was shooting at a series of zombies as they popped up on a giant video screen. Two of his buddies stood to one side and cheered every time he shot a zombie in the head.

Ashlee stuck out her chin and tossed her hair over her shoulder on the way past. "He wasn't that hot, anyway," she muttered under her breath.

During the entire ride home, she whined about how immature Zach had turned out to be. Her tirade continued as she made her way up the stairs and into the apartment. I left Brittany to console her and escaped to my bedroom.

As I got ready for bed, I took my phone from my pocket and found that I'd missed a couple of calls from Jason. Too late to call now. Whatever he'd wanted, it'd have to wait until morning.

On my way to work the next day, I stopped by the Daily Grind for a large latte with a double shot of espresso. While I sipped my coffee, I sat in my car in the parking lot and called Jason but reached his voice mail. I'd try again later. I set my coffee in the cup holder and my phone on the passenger seat and drove to the farm.

Once in the office, I uploaded the new farm photos to the Web site. Esther came in as I was cropping the photo of the honeybee. Her blue cotton shirt was wrinkled, and her curly gray hair was uncombed.

"Everything all right, Esther?" I asked as I saved my changes to the file.

She sank into the guest chair. "Gordon and I had a long talk last night."

My fingers froze over the keyboard. "About what?" For a second, I held out hope that Gordon had merely wanted to talk to Esther about something innocuous, like how much food the pigs were eating or how many guests were booked for next week, but that idea died as soon as she spoke.

"He told me how the whole town is talking about Gretchen killing that lady and how our reservations are disappearing because of it. I was up half the night fretting."

"You know how Gordon worries about the reputation of this place. I'm sure we have more reservations than he realizes."

She bit her lip. "I think Gordon might have a point. One of my own friends told me she almost canceled her appointment with Gretchen. If people are too scared to come here, we might need to make some changes."

My stomach sank. While I'd been hoping she'd tell Gordon he was overreacting, this farm and spa was

Esther's livelihood. I couldn't expect her to ignore the rumors altogether. At the same time, though, Gretchen didn't deserve to be fired over gossip. "Esther, a man was murdered at this very farm when we first opened, and we didn't go out of business. If guests are willing to stay here after all that, they won't let a bunch of rumors stop them from visiting."

Esther dropped her gaze to the floor. "I have to think about the farm."

I didn't have the heart to make her feel any guiltier than she already did. "I'm sure you'll decide whatever's fair for both Gretchen and this place."

"Thanks, Dana." She slowly stood and shuffled out of the room. I knew she liked Gretchen a lot, and I didn't envy her decision.

I finished working on the Web site and took a minute to call Jason again. I got his voice mail and hung up without leaving a message. Then I went out the back door of the kitchen to tidy up the patio area. I cleaned up a few pieces of trash the guests had left under the table, then got the pool net out of the shed and skimmed the surface of the water, removing a handful of leaves and dead bugs.

On my way back to the shed, I passed the pigpen and noticed the water trough was muddy. I pointed a finger at Wilbur. "Didn't I just clean that yesterday?"

He sniffed at me and turned away. With a sigh, I leaned the net against the fence, pulled on the boots, and grabbed the hose before letting myself into the pen. I stepped over to the water trough, and my boot slid in the mud. I struggled to keep my balance while Wilbur snorted at me.

"You know, you could always help," I said crossly. "You and your buddies should be a little neater around the trough." Wilbur hung his head, and I felt a pang of remorse. "Never mind. I know you try your best."

I sprayed out the trough and filled it with fresh water. As I dragged the hose back through the pen, one of the pigs bumped me. I felt my feet slip out from under me again, and I flung my arms out to the sides in a desperate attempt not to hit the mud. I felt my weight shift and pull me backward. I jerked forward, overcorrected, and fell to my knees, caking my pants with muck.

"Oh, yuck," I muttered to myself as I pulled myself to my feet. I tried to wipe the big gobs off with my hands but mostly spread the mess around even more. My knees were now coated.

I tromped over to the outside faucet and wiped off my pants as best I could with the nearby towel before washing my hands. I removed the boots and put my own shoes back on, then marched straight to the laundry room and opened the cabinet where I kept a change of clothes.

The shelf was bare. I thought back to how I'd put on those clothes after I'd fallen in the duck pond last month. Maybe I needed to work more on my balance, given the way I was always falling down.

I retrieved my purse from the office and headed to the lobby. Gordon stood at the front counter. He took a step back when he saw me, as if the mud might jump off my clothes and dirty his clean white dress shirt.

"What happened to you?"

"Had a little accident in the pigsty. I need to run home and change."

He waved his hand in front of his face, though I knew he couldn't smell anything. "Don't let the guests see you on your way out."

I looked out the window. A few cars were in the parking lot, but I couldn't see any people. The sidewalk was empty, as well. I glanced around the vacant lobby. I almost asked what guests he was referring to, but didn't. It might remind him of how much our appointments were down. "I'll be careful," I said.

I went to my car, got an old towel out of the trunk, and laid it across the seat. Then I gingerly sat down and brought my legs in after me, careful not to brush my muddy knees against the steering wheel. As I placed my wallet and phone on the car seat, I accidentally brushed the ON button to the phone and saw I had two missed calls—one from Ashlee and one from Jason—and a single voice mail. I accessed the voice mail and hit the speakerphone button.

Ashlee's voice filled the inside of my Honda, her high-pitched tone one note below what only dogs could hear. "Oh, my gosh, Dana, you have to call me! You won't believe what Brittany told me! You're gonna flip out!"

What on earth was Ashlee so excited about? Had Brittany run off with the guy she met at the bowling alley? Whatever it was would have to wait until I got home. I needed to change my clothes before I did anything else.

I sped to my apartment and donned a clean pair of pants, tossing the dirty ones in the tub until I could deal with them after work. I grabbed an extra change of clothes to keep at the office and was rooting around in my closet for a sack to carry them in when my cell phone rang. I snatched it up without checking the display. It had to be Ashlee, still dying to fill me in on whatever had her so worked up.

"Dana, I hate to bother you at work."

It took my brain a second to register that I was talking to Mom, not Ashlee.

"Dana? Is this a bad time?" she asked.

"No. I'm here. Is anything wrong?" Mom rarely called me during work unless there was a problem.

"No, everything's fine. I'm on my break and wanted to call and see if you and Ashlee can come to dinner tonight. I miss having you girls around."

I thought about how much I'd enjoyed our dinner earlier in the week. "I'd love to come over. I already need to call Ashlee back, so I'll ask her if she can make it, too." I grabbed my shoe off the floor and pulled it on. "Say, Mom, could you make that asparagus thing you used to cook? The one with the Parmesan cheese broiled on top?"

"I'd love to," Mom gushed. "I didn't realize you liked vegetables."

I finished tying my shoe. "Neither did I until I stopped eating them. Now I actually miss the occasional bit of green."

"I'll add asparagus to the grocery list. Now I'd better let you go." I started to say good-bye, but she interrupted me. "Oh, before I forget . . . Tell Jason how much I enjoyed his story in this morning's paper."

I had no idea what story she was referring to. "Jason and I have been playing phone tag so far today. Did he have a follow-up article about Patricia's craft store?" I grabbed my other shoe as I waited for her answer.

"No, not that. The story about Stan, of course."

I froze with my shoe partway on my foot. "What about Stan?"

"Don't you know already? I was sure Jason would tell you right away. Stan was arrested for that spa owner's murder."

Chapter 31

The shoe slipped from my grasp and thumped to the floor. I ignored it. "What are you talking about? When did the police arrest Stan?" I asked Mom. Was that why Jason had called last night, while I'd been bowling? Was Stan's arrest what had Ashlee so worked up in the voice mail she'd left me? I pressed the phone closer so I wouldn't miss Mom's answer.

"According to the paper, he was taken into custody yesterday evening. Jason did an excellent job recapping the murder. He's such a good writer."

"I'll be sure to tell him you said so." I picked up my shoe off the floor and jammed my foot inside, then pulled the laces and tied them in one swift motion. "Look, Mom, I have to go. I'll see you for dinner tonight."

"Don't forget to ask Ashlee, too."

"I won't." I hung up and immediately dialed Jason's number.

Voice mail.

Again.

"Call me when you get this. I heard about Stan," I said after the recording finished. I jumped up and paced the confines of my bedroom.

Stan.

Arrested for Carla's murder.

But why would he do it? Because she didn't want to partner with Patricia? That didn't make sense. No one killed a person for such a petty reason.

Mom hadn't mentioned any other particulars about Jason's article, but maybe she'd forgotten something. I needed to read that story myself.

I held up my phone and opened a Web browser. After months of prodding from Jason and everyone else on staff at the *Blossom Valley Herald,* Jason's boss had finally agreed to provide a digital copy of the newspaper online. Now I typed in the Web address, chewing on my bottom lip while I waited.

After a few seconds the newspaper site filled the small screen. The headline screamed ARREST MADE IN SPA OWNER'S MURDER in bold black letters. Below that, a photo of Stan, probably a professional shot taken for his own Web site for his accounting business, peered back at me. I scrolled through the article but didn't find anything I didn't already know. No mention of a motive, either. Darn, I wished Jason would hurry up and call me back.

In the meantime, I needed to get back to work. I grabbed my keys and stuck my phone in my pocket. As I stepped into the hall, the front door opened. Ashlee flew in, scanning the room.

When she saw me, she ran over and grabbed me

by the shoulders. "Dana!" she yelled, even though we were inches apart. "You're not going to believe what I found out!"

I removed her hands from my shoulders and clasped them between my own hands, worried she might hyperventilate if she didn't calm down. "I already talked to Mom. She told me that Stan was arrested for killing Carla."

She pulled her hands from my grasp. "*Everybody* knows that. But I bet you don't know *why* he did it."

Now I felt like grabbing *her* shoulders. "Why? Tell me!"

"Because Stan was sleeping with Carla."

I was so shocked, I literally had to sit down. I barely made it to the couch before my legs gave out. "Wait a minute. Are we talking about the same Stan here? Patricia's accountant husband, who does everything she says? That Stan?"

"I know! I didn't want to believe it, either!" she cried. "But Brittany sent Jessica a link to the story in the *Herald*. When Jessica saw his picture, she remembered him coming by the spa a couple of times. It was always after hours, like he and Carla were trying to keep it a big secret. She called Brittany, and Brittany was about to call me when I called her, anyway, and that's when she told me."

I waited for her to take a breath before I spoke. "Just because Jessica saw Stan at the spa after closing doesn't mean he and Carla were lovers. He could have been there on an errand for Patricia."

Even as I said it, I realized that I might have figured

Carla all wrong. I'd heard from more than one person that Carla had been dating a married man, while other people said she hadn't. She could have easily had two boyfriends, and one of them might have been Stan. I'd considered him a likely boyfriend myself when I first met him, then dismissed the idea when I'd seen how good-looking Miguel was. But Stan was fairly hand-some, too.

Had Carla threatened to tell Patricia, and had Stan killed her to keep her quiet? Is that who Gretchen had overheard arguing at the spa that night? And what about his alibi?

Ashlee shook her head. "Stan wasn't there on an errand for Patricia. He was there for a hookup."

"You could be right," I said, "but I never would have guessed that Stan was capable of an affair. He seems so solid."

"Those are the ones you have to watch out for," Ashlee said knowingly. She clapped her hands together. "Have you talked to Jason? I bet he'd love to know that Stan and Carla were getting it on."

I checked my phone, hoping for a text. Did Jason know? If he didn't, did he know someone who could confirm the affair? "I've been trying to reach him, but I keep getting voice mail. He's probably pestering the cops for more info right now." I stood up from the couch. "But I can't sit around and wait. I should be back at work already." I noted her vet smock. "Speaking of which, why are you home?"

"We're busy this afternoon, so I took an early lunch."

"But it's barely ten o'clock."

Ashlee gave me a look that said I was an idiot. "Duh. That's why I said it's early."

"Fine. Whatever. I'll call you later."

I trotted to my car and roared out of the complex. In minutes I was parking in the lot at the farm. As I barreled through the lobby, Gordon made a show of looking at his watch but didn't say anything. Not that I gave him the chance.

Once in the office I studied the computer screen and tried to focus, but all I could think about was Stan. Good old dependable Stan. Cheating on Patricia was a much better motive than defending his wife's honor when her business deal fell through.

And at least Gretchen was off the hook. Now that an arrest had been made, those evil gossipmongers wouldn't keep whispering about how Gretchen was the killer. Now they'd turn their sharp tongues on Stan. I'd be curious to see how fast the spa's appointment book filled up. Surely, some of those gossipers would feel guilty about spreading rumors and would book massages and facials with Gretchen as a form of penance.

I shut these thoughts out of my head and started working on a new advertisement for the farm. I'd managed to eke out a single paragraph when my phone rang. I jumped at the sudden noise and fumbled to answer the phone, recognizing Jason's ringtone.

"Jason!" I shrieked, no doubt sounding as frazzled as Ashlee had a while ago. I tried to control my voice. "I heard about Stan. When did you find out?"

"Last night, right after they made the arrest. I tried calling early on, but then I got busy."

"No, that's all right. I was out with Ashlee and didn't hear my phone. But she told me the craziest thing a while ago."

"That Stan was having an affair with Carla?"

I stood up with such force that my chair rolled partway across the room. "Then, it's true?"

"Yes. Not only that, but the same woman who saw Gretchen at the spa the night Carla was murdered suddenly remembered seeing a man fitting Stan's description there, too."

"But what about his alibi?"

"They brought his assistant, Alonzo, back in after the witness contacted them. During questioning, he eventually admitted that he left for thirty minutes to grab a bite, which would give Stan a large enough window to drive to the spa, kill Carla, and get back to his office."

I sucked in my breath. "Why would his assistant lie to the police? Doesn't he know how much trouble he's in now?"

"Funny you say that. Alonzo claims he lied to keep *Stan* from getting in trouble. He doesn't believe for a second that Stan killed Carla, so he didn't want the police to suspect him. Clearly, his plan didn't work. Between the affair, the witness, and no alibi, the police had enough evidence for Stan's arrest."

"I wonder if he had the whole thing planned or if it was spur of the moment," I said. "Maybe he hit Carla in a panic, then freaked out and drowned her in the mud. Do the police know what happened? Have they figured out how he got Carla in the mud bath? Was she already unconscious?"

"I don't have those details yet."

"What details do you have?" I asked, settling onto the corner of the desk.

"Tell you what. I've got some stuff to wrap up here, but let's meet for lunch at the Breaking Bread Diner a little after noon. How's that sound?"

I'd have preferred to get together right away, but I knew Jason would be swamped at work. "I guess it'll have to do. See you then."

We said our good-byes, and I dropped my phone in my purse. I was sitting down at the computer when Esther came in.

I almost jumped back up in my excitement. "Esther, did you hear the news? Someone was arrested for killing the spa owner. You don't have to worry about clients canceling their reservations with Gretchen anymore."

Esther laid a hand on her chest. "Mercy me, what a relief. Now I can focus on this composting class I'm teaching tomorrow."

I put a hand to my forehead. "With everything going on, I almost forgot."

She fingered the sterling silver cow on her charm bracelet. "I didn't. I'm so worried that I'll mix up what I'm saying."

"You'll be great, but you can always make a cheat sheet to remind yourself of the key points, if you think that would help."

Esther swallowed. "But I don't know if I can stand up there in front of a bunch of strangers."

I smiled. "Then don't stand. Put a chair up at the front and sit down while you talk. In fact, that will make your entire presentation more personal."

"That's a good idea." She offered me a hopeful smile. "If you're not too busy, maybe I could practice on you?"

I glanced at the time on the computer. I didn't want to miss my lunch with Jason, but I still had a while. "Of course you can."

"Oh, goodie." She dragged the guest chair closer to where I sat. After she'd settled onto the seat, she launched into a story about when she and her husband first tried composting. I nodded along as she spoke, but I was having trouble paying attention as I thought about what Jason had told me over the phone. What had prompted the witness to remember Stan at this late date? Why hadn't they mentioned him before? And what had made the assistant suddenly decide to change his story?

"Does that sound good, Dana?"

I snapped to attention and nodded. "Perfect," I mumbled, though I had no idea what Esther had been saying.

"As long as you don't think it's too boring," she said.

I shook my head, and she started talking again. When she reached the essentials of creating a composting bin, I found my thoughts turning once more to Stan. I could see how the assistant would have confessed to lying once he found out about the witness, but this new information from the witness seemed a little too convenient. I was starting to suspect that someone was trying to frame Stan. But why? Was the real killer worried that the police were getting too close?

"And then I thought I'd finish with a tour of our

composting bin," Esther said. She raised her eyebrows in anticipation.

I nodded. "Sounds like you have everything figured out."

She rose from her chair. "I feel so much better now that I've practiced. Thanks for helping me."

I felt a twinge of guilt. Little did she know I hadn't heard a single word. But I knew Esther's presentation would go fine. She'd just needed an extra shot of confidence.

As Esther walked out, I checked the time. *Five to twelve. Oops.* After running to the restroom to freshen up, I grabbed my phone on my way by the office and found a text message from Jason, letting me know he was running a few minutes late, too.

I drove into town, already thinking up what questions I'd be asking him. Had the police suspected Stan all along? Who was this mystery witness that had conveniently seen Stan? When had the police found out about the affair? Most importantly, what would have driven him to kill Carla, if he was the one who did?

As I cruised down Main Street, I noticed the door to the Pampered Life was propped open again. Erin must be inside, finishing up her packing. I thought about what Ricky had said at the bowling alley, how Erin wanted to apologize for scaring me so badly at the spa. With Jason running late, this might be my only opportunity to talk to her. Once she closed the place down, there was a good chance I'd never see her again.

I parked at the curb and walked inside the spa. Erin had finished packing the lobby since my last visit. The paintings and the tranquility fountain were gone.

The counter was bare. All that remained was a stack of boxes in the corner.

I walked toward the back, glancing in each room as I passed. The first massage room had been emptied out, but the second was still a work in progress. The place was eerily quiet. Remembering what had happened the last time I dropped in on Erin unexpectedly, I called out, "Erin, are you here? It's Dana."

No answer.

I stepped into the office and stopped. Instead of Erin, Patricia was crouched down, placing a pile of papers in a cardboard box. "Oh, hi, Patricia."

Talk about awkward. What did you say to a woman whose husband had been arrested for murdering his mistress? I decided to keep my mouth shut and see if she brought up the topic first.

She straightened up with a groan and reached into her handbag where it sat on the nearby chair. She pulled out her phone and glanced at the screen. "I didn't realize it was lunchtime already." She slipped the phone in her pocket and frowned at me. "What are you doing here?"

I gestured down the hall. "I saw the open door and assumed Erin was finishing her packing."

Patricia snorted. "Erin, ha. That's a good one. As usual, she couldn't finish one little chore, and now I'm stuck with it. If you want a job done right . . ."

I shifted my feet, still not sure what to say. "Don't let me interrupt. I'm sure I'll catch Erin another time." I started to turn away.

Patricia waved her hand. "Sure. Leave. All my friends

are going to. No one will dare be associated with the wife of a killer." Tears formed along her eyelids.

I felt my heart tug. I hadn't always been crazy about Patricia, but I certainly didn't wish such a horrible turn of events on her. "Your true friends will stand by you." I walked past her and over to the desk to grab a tissue out of the box sitting on top.

She accepted the tissue but crumpled it in her hand. "If I even have any. Here, I thought Carla was my best friend, and she was screwing my husband." She squeezed her eyes shut, like she was trying to stop the tears from flowing. "We were friends for over thirty years! Who does that to a friend?"

I lifted my palms, at a total loss. I couldn't imagine the double betrayal of both a husband and a best friend lying to you. "What will you do now?"

"I haven't decided. I'm not sure I want to open my new shop in a town where everyone knows my dirty laundry. I might have to move."

"Where would you go? And what about Stan?"

Patricia laughed a harsh, discordant bark. "Stan's off to jail, right where he belongs. Even if the cops don't find that stupid dog statue, he's got no alibi and the perfect motive. Now I need to worry about myself, like I should have been doing all these years. I've spent my whole life taking care of other people, but from now on, I'll be doing what's best for me."

She prattled on about small towns where she could start fresh and about how she had family in Colorado who would take her in, but I was only half listening. I was still stuck on what she'd just said. Where had she learned about the statue? Jason certainly hadn't written about it in the paper. In fact, he'd said the police didn't know if a statue was even used to strike Carla, since only one employee ever remembered seeing it. How could Patricia know about it? Had Stan told her?

I realized Patricia had stopped talking. She was watching me like an audience member watched a magician while trying to figure out the secret to a trick. I scrambled to think of an appropriate response. "Oh, yes, Colorado is a wonderful state."

"You seem distracted," she said, never taking her eyes off me. "What's on your mind?"

The skin on my back started itching as she kept staring at me. "I'm still in shock that Stan has been arrested. You must be beside yourself." I felt the urge to babble as I waited for her to blink. Or scratch her nose. Or do anything besides look at me. Did she know about the statue because Stan had told her, or was she the one who had killed Carla? Maybe the affair wasn't a total surprise to Patricia, after all. Maybe she knew about it long before the police did.

I took two steps toward Patricia and the open door beyond her, every nerve in my body on high alert. "If there's anything I can do, anything at all, let me know," I said, hoping she couldn't see how scared I was. If I could make it past where Patricia stood, I could outrun her and make it out of the spa.

Patricia wagged a finger at me before I could slip by. "I know why you're upset. I mentioned the statue, didn't I?"

I had no answer, but she wasn't waiting for one.

"See what happens when I don't plan out everything? I make silly mistakes like that."

Before I could rush past her and out the door, she lunged for her handbag on the chair and yanked out something dull and black.

It was a gun. And Patricia was aiming it right at me.

"That's okay." She smiled. "I've got a new plan."

I looked at the gun, pointed straight at my heart, and felt myself start to shake. I didn't know what her plan was, but I did know one thing. I wasn't going to like it.

Chapter 32

I tried to maintain eye contact with Patricia, but my gaze kept drifting to the gun. "What are you doing, Patricia?" I squeaked.

Her grip didn't waver. "A little housecleaning," she said matter-of-factly. She looked down at the gun. "I got this from Stan. Now that I'm opening my own shop, he was worried about robbers."

"Well, I'm no robber, so you can put it away now."

Patricia sneered at me. "You're no robber, but you're a big problem."

I didn't like where this conversation was headed. Could I bluff my way out of here? "I don't know what you mean."

I took another step toward the door. Patricia raised the gun, her finger tightening on the trigger. I moved back and put up my hands, like she was the robber Stan was so worried about.

"Look," I said. "I stopped by to say hi to Erin. I have no idea why you're pointing a gun at me. Why don't you put it away?"

"Too late. I saw your face when I talked about the statue. You must know now that I killed her. But this might work out, after all." She waved toward the room across the hall. "You can die in the mud bath, like Carla. Of course, with Stan in jail, the cops will know he couldn't have possibly done it and will have to let him go, which is a shame, but I bet everyone in town will start spreading rumors about a serial killer on the loose. They'll never suspect me. I'm the perfect citizen. I've never gotten so much as a parking ticket."

"Sure, whatever you say." Far be it from me to argue with a crazy lady holding a gun.

Careful to keep my head still so I wouldn't alert Patricia, I scanned the area in front of me for something, anything, I could use as a weapon.

I saw nothing.

The desk was behind me, and I tried to recall if anything there might help. I could remember only the box of tissues, but maybe I had overlooked an item. I started to shuffle backward toward the desk, but Patricia noticed me moving. I stopped.

"Don't get all cute on me," she said. "I'll shoot you right where you're standing if I have to."

I fought down the panic I felt rising up. Where was Jason? Had he arrived at the Breaking Bread Diner yet? Was he calling my cell phone at this very minute? The phone I'd left in the car?

My car! It was parked at the curb. Maybe he'd notice it when he drove by, and he'd come back to check. Then my momentary optimism faded. Who knew if he'd left work yet? He might still be writing his story and not even realize how late it was getting.

I needed more time, either to come up with a plan on my own or to give Jason a chance to worry that I'd missed lunch and come looking for me. "When did you find out about the affair?" I asked.

Patricia narrowed her eyes into slits. "I had my suspicions that Stan was seeing someone for a while. A good wife knows. So I started following him. When I saw him visit Carla one night after work, I knew."

She squeezed her eyes shut at the memory, and the gun drooped in her hand. With Patricia distracted, I reached behind me and felt along the desk's surface for a potential weapon. I came up empty.

She opened her eyes, and I brought my hand back down.

"He tried to deny it," Patricia said. "Don't all men? Claimed he was giving her some tax advice. Like I'd fall for that old line."

"Maybe he was telling the truth," I suggested.

She waved the gun at me. "I'm not an idiot. He has office hours. There was no reason to see her in the evening. The night Carla died, I started badgering him about it, and he finally admitted everything. Then he ran away like a little girl."

She fell silent again, and I worried that she'd run out of things to say. I still didn't have anything to defend myself with, and Jason hadn't magically appeared. I needed to keep her talking. "What happened then?"

"I did a lot of thinking. About my life and whether I even liked it." She smiled. "And you know what? I do.

I'm opening my own craft store—even if it's not here, after all—I've raised my kids to be full-fledged, successful adults, and Stan . . . well, he's Stan. I can do only so much with him. The real problem was Carla."

"But why kill Carla? Why not kill Stan? He was the married one in the relationship."

"He's also the moneymaker in the family. Why should I lose my nice house and yearly vacations because of his stupid mistake? I'm sure he was flattered when someone as attractive as Carla showed an interest, but he's learned his lesson. He won't stray from me again." She pressed her lips in a hard line. "I didn't mean to kill her. It was an accident."

I tried not to let my disbelief show. "Of course it was. You're not the type of person who'd hurt a friend on purpose."

Patricia nodded. "That's right. I came down to the spa to talk to Carla, woman to woman. Surely, I could reason with her, convince her to stop sleeping with my husband. She owed me for all those years of friendship."

I couldn't help but think that their friendship didn't mean that much if her best friend was sleeping with her husband, but I kept my mouth shut. The last thing I wanted to do was antagonize her.

"When I got down here," Patricia said, "I saw Stan driving away in his car. Can you believe it? The second I find out about him being unfaithful, he runs off to his girlfriend." She jabbed at her chest. "He should have been home with me, telling me how much he loved me." The intensity of her stare made my toes curl.

I felt like a butterfly pinned to a board. I had nowhere to move. "You must have been furious."

"You bet I was. I charged in here and started yelling at Carla. She told me I needed to calm down." Her eyes grew wide. "Calm down! Are you kidding me? So I hit her with the statue. That shut her up. The thing weighed a ton. The funny thing is, I gave her that statue as a housewarming present when she opened this place. The shop owner said that foo dogs bring good luck. Guess he was wrong."

"But she was still alive when you pushed her in the mud bath," I said. "Why did you have to kill her? You could have explained that you lost your temper and didn't mean to hit her."

Patricia tossed her head back and laughed. "Like anyone would believe that. I'd just discovered my husband was cheating with her. Everyone would say it was attempted murder. I shouldn't go to jail when I'm the one who's been wronged."

Well, she'd end up in jail if I had anything to say about it. I could only hope it wouldn't be for *my* murder. "Does Stan know you killed her?"

Patricia smirked. "I'm sure he suspects. I catch him watching me every now and again, like he wants to ask me about it. But he always chickens out, of course."

I'd run out of questions. I risked turning my head to peek at the desk. A smattering of papers and a small plastic container of paper clips sat in the far corner. Unless she had a paper-clip phobia, I wasn't getting any help there.

Patricia pulled out her phone. "Oops. I've got a book club meeting in a while. We'd better get this over with."

Fantastic. She was scheduling my death between cleaning out Carla's office and her book club meeting, as if getting rid of me was just another task on her to-do list.

She motioned with the gun toward the door. "Let's go."

My muscles tightened in protest. I didn't want to obey her, but if I wanted to have any chance of escape, I needed to get out of this room. Patricia went first, stepping out backward, keeping the gun trained on me.

I followed her through the doorway, and my eyes fell on the back door. The last time I tried to escape through there, the door had been locked. Was it still?

Patricia must have figured out what I was thinking. "Don't get any ideas. It's locked."

Disappointment and terror waged a war in my gut. I felt like every step closer to the mud room was one step closer to death. My palms were sweating, I was having trouble steadying my breathing, and still Patricia's resolve never seemed to waver. What was I going to do?

Patricia jerked her head toward the mud room, keeping a safe distance from me as we stood in the hall. "After you."

I swallowed hard and entered the darkened mud room. I sensed Patricia coming up behind me, and I tensed, but she was only turning on the lights. When I saw the long pits of mud, so much like graves, a sob threatened to burst out. I tamped it down. Now was not the time to cry. Now was the time to save myself.

"You're awfully quiet," Patricia said. She sounded almost gleeful.

I turned to face her. "Doesn't seem like there's anything left to say. You've made up your mind."

"Yes, I have. Now I need you to get in the mud so I can finish this."

My mouth dropped open. "That's your plan? I climb in and stick my head under the mud until I suffocate?" Saying the words sent a fresh spasm through my chest, but I kept my face neutral. I didn't want to give Patricia the satisfaction of seeing how terrified I was.

"I could shoot you first, but I don't think either one of us wants that."

Frankly, I didn't like either option, but I doubted Patricia cared.

She gave me a little shove, and I stumbled back toward the edge. "Now go," she said.

This was it, my last chance to escape. I turned and acted like I was contemplating my fate while I studied the room. This side was bare, save for a robe hanging on a nearby hook. A chair sat in the corner on the other side of the two baths, but I couldn't reach it. Everything else must have been packed up. I was on my own.

I made a show of inching to the edge of the first mud bath. I bent down toward the muck and slowly lowered a hand in, as if to test the temperature. The dense, ice-cold mud clung to my skin, and I shivered. Patricia followed behind me, close enough to shoot me if I tried anything, but still well out of arm's reach.

I tilted my head up toward her. "I wanted to ask one

last question. Do you think Carla was better in the sack than you are?"

Patricia reeled back. I scooped up a handful of mud and threw it in her face. It splattered in her eyes. Her free hand flew up to scrape at the mud, and she waved the gun wildly with the other.

What sounded like a sonic boom exploded in the tiled room. My entire body shuddered at the sound. A pungent smell burned my nostrils.

My God, Patricia had actually fired the gun! Ringing filled my ears as I tried to orient myself.

She fired another shot, and I threw myself to the floor. I scooped up more mud and haphazardly lobbed it at her. She wiped at her face and squinted through the goop that clung to her lashes. I couldn't stay on the floor all day. The second her vision cleared, I'd be the proverbial sitting duck. I shoved myself up and ran for the chair in the corner.

Patricia fired again. Tile chips flew off the wall near my head, her aim way too close for my liking. I glanced over my shoulder as I grabbed the back of the chair and prepared to throw it at her. She was running toward me, her face and chest covered in mud. As she raised the gun to fire again, I swung the chair up, hoping to block the shot. Patricia hit a patch of mud and started to slide.

Seeing my opening, I hit her with the chair. She let out a grunt and fell to the floor. I dropped the chair on top of her and darted for the door. I ran out of the room and pounded down the carpeted stretch of hall, aiming for the bright rectangle of light that marked the front door. As I ran, I expected to hear another boom, feel an agonizing pain in my back as a bullet struck, but no shot came.

I flew through the lobby and burst through the spa door, where I collided directly with Jason. He grabbed my arms.

"Hey, slow down! Were those gunshots I heard?"

Jesus. Patricia might be right behind me. Now she'd get me and Jason both. I wrenched out of his hold and tried to pull him by his shirt down the sidewalk. "Patricia has a gun! We have to get out of here!"

A woman walking toward us froze and clutched her purse tightly. "Who has a gun? Where?" The man with her stepped in front of her, as if to protect her.

Before I could warn them, Patricia burst out of the spa, the gun still in her hand. "I'm going to kill you!" she yelled when she saw me.

I snatched the purse from the woman and chucked it at Patricia's head. She put up her free hand to stop it. Beside me, Jason heaved himself forward, straight into Patricia. They both went down. Hard.

The gun flew from Patricia's grasp and skittered across the pavement. I chased after it as it slid under the bench. Dropping to my knees, I reached under the redwood slats and frantically felt along the ground until my fingers closed around the smooth metal. Gun at the ready, I whirled around to help Jason.

But Jason didn't need my help. Patricia lay flat on her back, with Jason sprawled on top of her. Each of his hands gripped one of her wrists, keeping them on the ground.

"Dana?" he called. "Are you all right?"

"I'm fine. And I've got the gun."

I kept it pointed down as he got his legs under him and crouched over Patricia, still holding her wrists. When she didn't seem to struggle, he let go of her. She immediately started to flail her arms, striking Jason in the face. I stiffened and brought the gun up, but Jason grabbed her arms and held them back down.

"Did she hurt you?" I asked.

"I'm okay."

"Let me call the police." I took one hand off the gun and started to reach in my pocket when I remembered my phone was in the car. I looked over at the couple, who stood to one side, both staring at Patricia on the ground. "Either of you have a phone?"

The woman snapped out of her trance and bent down to retrieve her purse where it lay on the sidewalk. She pulled out her phone and dialed.

When Patricia heard the woman talking to the 911 operator, she started to cry. "It wasn't supposed to be like this. It's not fair."

Jason continued to hold Patricia, but she didn't bother to fight him. Still, I moved a little closer just in case.

In less than a minute the first strains of sirens reached my ears, and I breathed a sigh of relief. My nightmare was over.

Chapter 33

Two days later Ashlee and I were back at the bowling alley, this time with Jason. As I sat down at a table in the snack area with my cardboard tray of nachos, I marveled yet again at how I'd almost been drowned in a mud bath.

I grabbed a cheese-covered chip and took a bite. "Mmm, this is so good," I said, my words muffled by the food.

Ashlee scrunched up her nose. "Do you know how much fat is in that? And it's not even real cheese. Don't you ever wonder what it's made of?"

I shook my head. "Nope. I file it under mystery foods I can't live without, like hot dogs."

She shoved the nachos closer to me and sipped her diet soda, as if her drink was any more natural than my nacho cheese. She leaned toward Jason. "What's the latest, newsman?"

Jason lifted his beer bottle and took a swig. "The DA has already filed murder charges against Patricia."

I poked through the nachos, in search of a chip that

wasn't too soggy, but ended up only with gooey cheese sauce all over my fingers. "Even after Patricia tried to kill me, I'm still not convinced she meant to murder Carla. At least not at first."

"Really?" Ashlee said. "As type A as she is, I figured she had the whole thing planned out on PowerPoint slides."

"It's that need for control that makes me believe her when she said she went to the Pampered Life strictly to talk to Carla," I explained. "She probably thought she could order Carla to stop seeing Stan. Then she'd spend the rest of her marriage constantly reminding him of his unfaithfulness. I bet when she saw Stan leaving the spa, she lost her mind and had no idea what she was doing."

Ashlee was texting on her phone, giving me only part of her attention. "I'm confused. I thought Gretchen overheard Stan and Patricia in the spa that night, but if Stan was leaving when Patricia got there, then it couldn't have been those two."

I tried to wipe the liquid cheese off my fingers, but the flimsy napkin tore and stuck to my skin. I scraped the paper remnants off. "She must have heard Carla and Stan. He probably drove straight over to warn Carla that Patricia knew about the affair. Gretchen overheard the guy say that everyone would know, so Stan must have been worried that Patricia would tell all her friends. That shows you how little he truly knows Patricia. She would never admit to being cheated on. Rather than run off to his girlfriend, he should have stayed home and tried to fix things with his wife."

Jason turned the beer bottle around and around in his hands. "You have to wonder how things might have turned out if he had."

"Guys can be so dumb sometimes," Ashlee said. She checked her phone again and scowled. "Fifteen minutes late? If Ryan thinks I'm sitting around the bowling alley all night, looking this good, he'd better think again, real fast. Five more minutes and I'm out of here." She glared at us as if we were somehow responsible for her date being late.

I gave up trying to clean my fingers and took another chip. "Do the police have enough to lock up Patricia?" I asked Jason. "Even with the way she confessed to me, they might need more."

"And they've got it," Jason said. "Like Stan, she had no alibi for the night of the murder. She can't prove she was home by herself, which is what she told the police. Let's not forget she also tried to kill you, so that alone will get her a long prison sentence."

"I know, but I'd like to see her convicted for Carla's murder, too. It wouldn't be fair if she got away with it."

Jason smoothed down the label on his bottle. "I wouldn't worry about that. The police found the statue. It had traces of Carla's blood on it. Rather than throw it in a Dumpster, Patricia stuck it in the back of her closet, in case the police started suspecting her. She planned to frame Stan with it."

"That reminds me," I said. "Was this mystery witness who saw Stan at the spa for real, or was that somehow Patricia's doing?"

"The witness was telling the truth about seeing Stan

that night, but the police initially focused on asking questions about Gretchen being there, and the witness forgot about Stan until later. When they came forward with this new information, Patricia saw it as another opportunity to deflect any attention from her. Since she'd also seen Stan at Carla's spa, she knew Stan's assistant had lied to the police about the two working nonstop together that night, and she manipulated the poor kid into coming clean."

My throat felt dry, and I took a sip of lemonade. "She probably decided that sending her husband to jail was only fair after he'd cheated." I unearthed a single crunchy chip from the pile of sodden ones and pulled it out. "Did you ever find out why Miguel lied about his alibi?"

Jason had been swallowing some beer and almost choked at the question. He brought the bottle back down. "Get this. He's a member of a swingers' club. Goes down there about once a week to meet people. He was worried his job would be in jeopardy if his employer found out, so he lied about attending the work meeting."

Ashlee giggled. "Oh my God, wait until I tell Brittany. She is gonna bust a gut." Her thumbs flew over her phone's keyboard.

"I knew he was a charmer, but a swinger?" I said. "I wonder if Carla was into that scene, too."

Movement over by the counter caught my eye. Ricky had just come on shift. He noticed me looking and waved hello. I waved back.

"Erin came to see me at work today," I told them.

"What for?" Jason asked.

"She claimed she wanted to apologize for threatening me, but I think she wanted to gloat a little about Patricia being the killer. She also told me that she's moving in with Ricky and his mom, after all, at least until she finishes her last semester at nursing school."

"What about Ricky?"

"Since Erin's almost done with her degree, he's talking about returning to school himself once he saves some money with his job here. Erin confirmed that Ricky's the one who refused Carla's loan. Carla was convinced he did so because he was too lazy to study and go to class. That's why she disapproved of him and kept arguing with Erin to dump him. Carla felt he was going nowhere in life."

"Looks like she was wrong," Jason said. "I hope things work out for them."

"Me too. They've had some tough breaks."

"Sounds like Gretchen has too," Jason said. "She must be relieved that she can put this mess behind her now."

"It's nice to see her excited about her job again," I said. "In fact, Esther was so pleased with how well her composting class turned out that she's already thinking up a whole list of additional topics to offer, and she asked Gretchen if she'd like to teach classes at the spa. They both seemed happy with the idea."

Ashlee stood and pulled her lavender T-shirt down over the top of her black tights. "Speaking of happiness, Ryan's on his own. I'm off to find me a new man. Wish me luck."

I eyed her long legs and trim figure. "Trust me. You don't need it."

She flipped her hair back. "So true." She grabbed her small purse off the seat and inspected the contents. "Oh, good. I've got my key. I'm guessing I'll get home pretty late, so I'll be sure not to wake you."

Wow. My sister was being a courteous roommate. Yesterday she'd even bought milk. Our new living arrangement might work out okay, after all.

She flounced out of the snack bar, and I smiled after her. "See you at home, sis," I called. I turned to Jason. "Looks like it's just you and me."

"I couldn't ask for anything better." Jason took my hand and squeezed it.

I squeezed back. "We do make a pretty good team, don't we?"

"The best." He leaned across the table until his lips were inches from mine. "And I plan to keep it that way," he whispered.

I gazed into his warm green eyes. "I'm not going anywhere."

Recipes and Tips
from the O'Connell Farm and Spa

I know one of these days Esther and I will see you out here at the farm. For now, here are some helpful recipes and tips to enjoy.

Whipping Up a Tangy Mustard Sauce

Zennia's tangy mustard sauce was so delicious that I begged her to give me the recipe. I tried it at my apartment, and it's a snap to make.

To make the mustard sauce, start by heating one teaspoon of olive oil in a small saucepan over medium-high heat. Add two minced garlic cloves to the saucepan and cook them for thirty seconds, stirring constantly. Whisk in a quarter cup *each* of white wine and chicken broth, two tablespoons of pure maple syrup, and two tablespoons of Dijon mustard. Bring the mixture to a boil and cook it until it reduces by half. This should take about five minutes. Remove the saucepan from the heat, stir in a teaspoon of minced rosemary, and serve. This sauce is a tasty topping for either fish, such as tilapia, or chicken. The recipe makes two servings, but if you like sauce as much as I do, you may want to double the recipe.

Cooking a Tater Tot Casserole

I thought I'd share my Tater Tot casserole recipe, but please don't tell Zennia that I passed it along. She won't be happy that I'm helping people make a casserole topped with gooey cheese and delicious Tater Tots.

To make the casserole, start by preheating the oven to 375°F. Next, chop up half a medium-size yellow onion. Brown the onions with one pound of ground beef in a medium skillet over medium heat, stirring frequently, until the beef is no longer pink. Stir in a ten-ounce can of cream of mushroom soup and one cup of thawed corn kernels. Season the meat mixture with salt and pepper to taste before pouring it into a 9 x 13-inch baking dish. Cover the meat mixture with a single layer of frozen Tater Tots from a sixteen-ounce package. Sprinkle two cups of grated sharp cheddar cheese over the Tater Tots. Bake, uncovered, for forty minutes, or until the cheese has melted and the mixture is bubbly. If you prefer, you can swap out the corn for an equal amount of green beans or peas.

Making Your Own Air Freshener Gels

While Esther prefers the smell of fresh flowers and the great outdoors, sometimes the weather isn't pleasant enough to open the windows. That's when she relies on homemade air freshener gels.

To make your own, you'll need two cups of water, two tablespoons of salt, about fifteen drops of an essential oil that you love the smell of, four small packets of unflavored gelatin, and three or four small glass jars to store your finished gels in. Mix the water, salt, and essential oil in a small saucepan. Bring the ingredients to a boil over medium heat and add the gelatin packets. Stir until the gelatin powder has dissolved. Remove the mixture from the heat, pour an equal amount into each of the jars, and let it cool completely to set. For an extra-cute look, you can toss in little leaves or peels that match the scent, such as lemon peels for a lemon-scented gel or mint leaves for a peppermint gel.

Creating a Simple Scrub

One of the best ways to brighten your skin is through exfoliation. Here's a super-simple recipe for a scrub that involves only oil and salt, although you can add some essential oils for a pleasant scent.

To make the scrub, pour a quarter cup of regular table salt in a small bowl and add two tablespoons of olive oil. (Canola oil or vegetable oil also works if you don't have olive oil.) Mix the salt and oil together with a spoon to create a thick paste, and then stir in a few drops of essential oil if you'd like. You can apply the scrub with your bare hands or with an exfoliating glove. Rub in the scrub in a circular motion, spending extra time on places like elbows and knees. When you're finished, thoroughly rinse off the scrub and pat yourself dry with a soft towel.

Getting Started with Composting

Starting a compost pile is easy. You can use the compost to fertilize the plants and flowers in your yard.

To get started, find a corner of your yard that gets partial sun and isn't too close to any trees. You can start the pile directly on the ground, or you can buy or build a compost bin. A good size for a compost pile is generally 4 feet x 4 feet x 4 feet. When you create your compost pile, you'll want a mix of wet material, such as grass clippings and food scraps, and dry material, such as small branches and dry leaves. As you add new items to your compost, turn the pile over occasionally.

If you notice your compost pile is starting to smell quite a bit, it may have too much moisture. You can turn it over more often to expose all parts of the compost to the air, or you can add more dry material to absorb the extra moisture. Also, during the cold winter months, the compost pile will decompose much more slowly or will even stop decomposing altogether. Either you can cover the pile to keep it warm and encourage decomposition, or you can leave it uncovered and simply not compost during the colder months.

Please turn the page for an exciting sneak peek of
the next Blossom Valley mystery
coming soon from Kensington Publishing!

Chapter 1

I pointed to a round, bumpy vegetable on a folding table at the Blossom Valley farmers' market and turned to Zennia, the health-minded and Zen-like cook at the O'Connell Organic Farm and Spa, the bed-and-breakfast where I worked. "What on earth is that thing?"

She gave me a patient smile. "Cauliflower, Dana."

"But it's orange."

"Some varieties are."

None that I'd ever seen. Then again, Zennia could identify more vegetables than anyone I knew. I surveyed the rest of the produce that was laid out on the table. "You must be in heaven when you come here every week."

She picked up a clump of pea pods. "Based on the way you keep wrinkling your nose, I'm guessing you're not."

I reached up and touched my nose. "It's an automatic reflex. I don't think all vegetables are bad. Those peas you're holding would taste downright yummy if you drowned them in melted cheese and covered them with a buttery crumb topping."

"Good grief," Zennia muttered. "And spoil the sweet peas?"

It was a warm evening in late May, and I'd agreed to accompany Zennia to this week's farmers' market. The event was held at Blossom Valley's largest park, where a wide sidewalk lined an expansive square of lush green lawn. Two dozen vendors had set up a collection of tables and displays overflowing with ripe vegetables, sweet-scented fruits, and brightly-colored flowers on the sidewalk in hopes of attracting customers. One innovative farmer had chosen to back up his pickup truck to the sidewalk and lower his tailgate to display several types of lettuce, saving himself the time and trouble of unloading his crop.

On the grass, children played tag while a handful of people sunbathed on beach towels and others tossed Frisbees or balls to their dogs. In the summer months, the park would host outdoor concerts, eating competitions, and the Fourth of July fireworks show, but for now, fruits and vegetables were the main focus.

Even though my primary responsibility at the O'Connell farm was to provide marketing services, my official duties rarely took up the entire work day. I often helped Zennia prepare and serve meals for the guests, so I figured it couldn't hurt to stop by the market and expand my fruit and vegetable knowledge. Considering I couldn't recognize several types of produce for sale, I clearly needed to brush up.

"Next time I make my spring barley risotto, I'll be sure to have you help me," Zennia said, sorting through a pile of string beans. "One bite and you'll realize why I love vegetables so much."

I pointed to a nearby stall, where a variety of cheeses and several bottles of local olive oil weighed down a folding table. My mouth watered at the sight. "Right now, I'm going to check out what kind of Monterey Jack that guy is selling."

"Suit yourself." Zennia moved on to a booth where a woman was displaying asparagus while I homed in on the cheese guy, a tall, thin man with a pronounced Adam's apple that bobbed up and down as he told me about each and every cheese on his table.

"If you're looking for a good Jack cheese, try the dill. What you want to do is toast slices of ciabatta bread and spread on a little mayonnaise. Then add the dill Jack, a layer of tomato slices, and a sprinkle of salt, and you're all set." He kissed his fingertips. "Perfection. Put it under the broiler for a minute, and it's even better, if that's possible."

I selected a wedge and studied the other offerings. "What about the garlic Jack?"

The man rubbed his stomach, as if the mere mention made him ravenous. "All you need is a hunk of plain, old bread to go with that."

I picked up a wrapped piece of garlic Jack and paid the man for both cheeses before storing my purchases in the reusable tote Zennia had given me a few months back. With a nod of thanks, I walked over to the booth where I'd seen Zennia before we'd separated, only to find she was no longer there.

The crowd had picked up considerably while I'd

been shopping, but I managed to spot her bright yellow blouse across the lawn. A few feet away from the table where she stood, an older man sporting a short gray beard and wearing a henley shirt and cargo shorts was giving her the once-over. I smiled. I'd have to let Zennia know she had an admirer. With her long dark hair and tall, athletic figure, she probably had more than one.

As I headed in her direction, I stopped to buy a green plastic container of sweet-smelling strawberries. I'd noticed some pre-made sponge cake shells at the Meat and Potatoes grocery store when I'd shopped there last week. With a little whipped cream, I was looking at the makings of easy strawberry shortcake.

I gingerly placed my strawberries in my tote and looked across the grass toward Zennia again. My gaze drifted to the left, and I shivered. The man I'd noticed admiring her stood in the same spot, apparently transfixed. He watched as Zennia browsed among the tables and talked to the sellers. When she moved to the next table, he advanced a few steps in her direction, never letting his stare waver.

I started across the lawn to warn Zennia. Maybe that guy had a perfectly innocent reason to be so focused on her, but then again, maybe not. Either way, I didn't like the way he was acting. I picked up my pace.

Out of the corner of my eye, I saw something moving through the air and jerked my head around as a Frisbee streaked straight toward my face. I raised my arm to deflect it, and the plastic disc hit my forearm with a sharp sting before falling to the grass.

A boy of about ten ran over and picked it up. "Sorry about that," he mumbled to his feet.

"No problem," I said. "Those Frisbees have minds of their own." I watched him run back to his friends, and then I scanned the people before me and frowned. Zennia was still in sight, but the man in the cargo shorts had vanished. I checked the nearby tables and spotted him standing behind a trio of women who were huddled in a semi-circle. They seemed to be comparing the contents of their bags as if the items were rare jewels from the lost city of Atlantis. The man cast one last glance at Zennia before moving farther back into the crowd and disappearing from sight.

I chuckled to myself. I really needed to stop watching so many scary movies. Seeing masked men with machetes stalking young co-eds in skimpy clothes was making me paranoid.

Shaking my head at my own foolishness, I reached Zennia as she was paying the vendor.

She caught sight of me. "There you are. Find anything good?"

I hefted my bag. "Cheese and strawberries."

"Oh, that's a lovely combination. I found some baby artichokes."

I glanced behind me but didn't see the mystery man anywhere. "I don't think you noticed, but some guy was totally checking you out while you were shopping."

Zennia's cheeks instantly turned pink. "Oh, stop. I'm not some young girl. No one checks me out anymore."

"Give yourself more credit. Mid-forties is prime dating age nowadays. And obviously guys do still give you the eye. I saw it for myself. He was staring at you for so long that I almost felt the urge to call the cops."

Zennia waved her hand, like she was swiping the compliment away, but I could tell she was pleased. "Shall we keep shopping? I think I saw some sunflower bouquets when we first came in. Those would really brighten the farm's dining room."

We wandered around the square, stopping at the occasional table. By the time we made the circuit, my bag was noticeably heavier, though it paled in comparison to Zennia's two teeming totes.

"Do you need help carrying your bags to the car?" I asked as we stepped to the edge of the park and away from the vendors.

"I'll manage." We carried our purchases to the parking lot and stopped at Zennia's Prius.

I bent down and gently set my own bag on the pavement so I could help Zennia load her bags into the trunk. As I straightened up, I glanced across the lot and froze.

The man was back. The one who'd been watching Zennia.

This time, he stood next to the open passenger door of a nondescript white van, the kind that always made me think of stories I'd heard about Ted Bundy. Once more, he was staring at Zennia.

"Zennia," I said sharply.

She was in the middle of lifting one of the bags to place in the trunk, but when I said her name, she immediately turned to look at me. The movement sent her off balance, and the bag slipped from her grasp and hit the pavement. Two heads of broccoli and several small onions fell out the top and rolled under a nearby car.

"The broccoli is making a run for it," she joked as she bent down to retrieve the wayward vegetables.

I knelt down with her and helped gather the onions as quickly as I could. "Don't worry about that. I saw that guy again." From my crouched position, I couldn't see over the car, but I jerked my head in his general direction. "Do you know him?"

Zennia stood and scanned the lot. "What guy?"

I hastily tossed the last onion in the bag and rose. I looked toward the van where I'd seen him standing only moments ago and shook my head. "Never mind."

For the second time that day, the man had disappeared.